LET
LICO

Also by Amanda Flower

Assaulted Caramel

LETHAL LICORICE

Amanda Flower

KENSINGTON PUBLISHING CORP.

http://www.kensingtonbooks.com

KENSINGTON BOOKS are published by

Kensington Publishing Corp.
119 West 40th Street
New York, NY 10018

All Kensington Titles, Imprints, and Distributed Lines are available at special quantity discounts for bulk purchases for sales promotions, premiums, fund-raising, and educational or institutional use. Special book excerpts or customized printings can also be created to fit specific needs. For details, write or phone the office of the Kensington special sales manager: Kensington Publishing Corp., 119 West 40th Street, New York, NY 10018, attn: Special Sales Department, Phone: 1-800-221-2647.

Kensington and the K logo Reg. U.S. Pat & TM Off.

ISBN-13: 978-1-4967-0641-6
ISBN-10: 1-4967-0641-2
First Kensington Mass Market Edition: March 2018

eISBN-13: 978-1-4967-0642-3
eISBN-10: 1-4967-0642-0
First Kensington Electronic Edition: March 2018

10 9 8 7 6 5 4 3 2 1

Printed in the United States of America

For Charlotte Plank

Acknowledgments

Writing a series about an Amish candy shop is a sweet assignment, and I'm so grateful for the opportunity. I would not have had this chance if it were not for my editor, Alicia Condon, and everyone at Kensington. Thank you for making the Amish Candy Shop Mysteries a reality.

Thanks too to my super agent, Nicole Resciniti, for being a wonderful advocate and dear friend.

Additional thanks to my assistant, Molly Carroll, for reading an early version of this book, and to Suzy Schroeder, for her help with the candy making. Thanks as well to my dear friend Mariellyn Grace, who helped me plot this novel when I was stuck.

Very special thanks to Charlotte Plank, dear friend and church organist extraordinaire, who answered my dozens of organ questions and even lent me her name for a character in this book.

As always, thanks to my family—Andy, Nicole, Isabella, and Andrew—for their love and support, and to my Heavenly Father, who sustains me through every up and down in writing and in life.

Chapter 1

When the pig went missing, I knew there would be trouble.

"Bailey, honey?" Juliet Brody asked me in her sweet southern drawl. "Have you seen Jethro?"

I looked up from the snack-sized bags of home-made black licorice I was stacking in one corner of Swissmen Sweets' competition table. The licorice was my entry in the first round of the Amish Confectionery Competition, which was like the NBA playoffs, but with way more sugar. No modern cooking implements or methods that included electricity were allowed in the competition since some Amish districts didn't allow their use even for business.

Everything had to be done the Amish way, which meant slow and deliberate. I'd thought I was up for the challenge of making candy using the Amish methods, but I was learning that it was much more difficult than I'd realized. It couldn't be more different from how I'd learned to make chocolates and candies as Jean Pierre Ruge's protégé for six years at JP Chocolates, a high-end chocolate shop in Midtown Manhattan.

"Jethro?" I glanced up and down the row of competition tables. There were fifteen tables in all, with Amish candy makers from as far away was Wisconsin and Florida there to compete. Just like mine, every table was cafeteria length, and behind each was a cooking station with an oven and stove that ran on propane. A white awning covered each space.

At the table next to mine, an Amish woman removed the candy thermometer from the boiling pot on her stove top and poured the sugary liquid into waiting candy molds.

If Jethro had been there, I was sure I would have seen him. He tended to stand out. There was no sign of the black and white polka-dotted potbellied pig.

"No, I haven't seen him all morning." I tucked a lock of dark brown hair behind my ear. "Is he running loose at the competition? I doubt the judges would like that. I wouldn't let Margot know he's unattended on the square if I were you."

Margot Rawlings was the village chairwoman as well as the English judge for the contest, and she was determined to make sure everything went perfectly for the Amish Confectionery Competition, also known as the ACC. Every year, the competition was held in a different Amish town. The towns had to audition to snag the competition, and every Amish Country community wanted it because the event was a big tourist draw. It was quite an accomplishment for a village as tiny as Harvest to host the ACC, especially in Ohio's Amish Country, where there were so many better-known Amish communities like Charm, Berlin, and Sugarcreek. Margot had campaigned hard and won the hosting spot for Harvest almost single-handedly, from what I'd heard. She wouldn't let anything mess up Harvest's time in the spotlight as the ACC's host town. That included Jethro the pig.

Juliet wrung her small, pale hands together. "I just don't know where he could have run off to. It's so unlike him. He rarely leaves my side."

That was debatable. "How long has he been gone?" I dropped another bag of licorice on the pile on the table.

She swallowed. "I don't know exactly. I was helping some of the competitors set up their spots, and that took several hours. You would not believe the amount of stuff that some of these people have brought for the competition."

I glanced back at my stack of crates, filled to the brim with candy-making supplies, pots, pans, and utensils. "I can guess how much."

Juliet pursed her lips. "There was so much to do that I didn't notice Jethro was gone until we were done." She clasped her hands together more tightly. "I thought he was there the entire time while I was working. The last time I saw him, he was standing in the shade under one of the bushes in front of the church. When I was ready to leave and went to collect him, he was gone."

I glanced at the large white church on the other side of Church Street at the opposite end of the square. It was midday, and the October sun shone down on it like an orange pumpkin ripening on one of the many pumpkin patches scattered around the county.

"I'm sure he's here somewhere. Maybe the crowd

spooked him. None of us are used to having this many people in town," I said.

Because of the ACC, the village had had a rapid influx of people. There were fifteen Amish candy makers in the competition, and as a rule, the Amish didn't travel alone. Many of the competitors had brought their entire families to Harvest to watch them compete. In the Amish world, that could be as many as twenty additional people per competitor. Those numbers didn't even include all the spectators, both Amish and English, who'd come to Harvest to watch the two-day event. I guessed there were a couple thousand tourists.

"What if someone took him?" Juliet's voice caught, and her Carolina accent became more pronounced. "How will I ever know who did it in this crush of people?"

I stepped around the side of my table and gave her hug. "No one took Jethro. I'm sure he's just hiding somewhere to get away from all the commotion. Why don't we—"

"There she is!" A shrill voice shouted over the din created by all the visitors and candy makers packed onto the square. "I demand that you do something about this!"

I let go of Juliet to see a petite Amish woman in a plain navy dress, black apron, and white prayer cap stomping toward me. Her hair was parted in the middle and coiled into a bun at the nape of her neck in the Amish style. The woman was rail thin and couldn't have been more than five feet tall. Despite her small stature, the crowd parted to let her pass like storybook villagers would for a dragon on a raid. I wouldn't be the least bit surprised if she breathed fire just like a dragon. She would be the world's tiniest dragon, but that didn't lessen my chances of being burned, and I knew that was just what Josephine Weaver wanted to do. She wanted to burn me out of the competition.

Jeremiah Beiler, the Amish judge and organizer of the ACC, lumbered behind Josephine. He was a large round man who was three times the size of Josephine but not nearly as fierce, even though he sported a luxurious Amish beard. If I had to choose between Josephine and Jeremiah to contend with, the big teddy bear of a man would always win.

Margot Rawlings was a few steps behind Jeremiah. Her short curls bounced on the top of her head as she made her way across the village green in Josephine's wake. She looked just as irritated as the Amish woman, but I wasn't sure if it was with me, Josephine, or both of us. Knowing Margot, it was both, and probably every other person on planet earth. She wasn't picky when it came to be being annoyed with people.

When Josephine was within three feet of where I stood with Juliet, she pulled up short and pointed at me. "She should be disqualified. She's not Amish!"

I looked down at my outfit. Purple suede ankle boots, designer jeans from my life back in NYC, and a pink and purple flannel shirt under a white apron. To complete the outfit, I wore multicolored feather earrings that hung down an inch from the bottom of my earlobes. There was no one in the world who would believe I was Amish.

Jeremiah folded his arms across his ample stomach. "Now, Josephine, we have been over this already. Bailey can compete in the ACC in her late grandfather, Jebidiah King's, place. Jebidiah's candy shop was accepted into the contest months ago."

Josephine's lips curved into a sneer. "If a contestant dies, I see no reason to allow his relatives to compete, especially if those relatives have turned their backs on the Amish way and become *Englisch*."

I balled my hands at my sides. My grandfather had died a few short weeks ago, and the loss was still too raw for me to take such a comment lightly. "I haven't fallen away from the Amish. I've never been Amish." My words were sharper than I would have liked them to be, but I made no apology.

The tiny woman sniffed. "All the more reason to expel you from the competition. You cannot possibly understand our ways."

"Please, please," Margot said, looking around. "Keep your voices down. There is no reason to cause such an uproar. You will disturb the tourists."

"They should be disturbed. They came a long way to see the ACC, and there is an imposter in the competition," Josephine snapped.

"Josephine," Jeremiah said as he inched away from her. I wondered if he was moving out of smacking range. The Amish weren't prone to violence, but I wouldn't put it past Josephine to raise her fists. Jeremiah, now a good two feet away from the angry Amish woman, said, "The board has made its decision, and it's too late to change it now."

"How are we Amish to fairly compete if we have to deal with a cheating *Englischer*?" Josephine wanted to know.

"I'm not cheating. I'm making the candies using

the same equipment as the rest of you." Now, I was really becoming annoyed.

"Clara King should be the one taking her husband's place in this competition, not you." Josephine placed her hands on her narrow hips. "At least she is Amish!"

"Don't bring my grandmother into this," I snapped.

Maami was back at Swissmen Sweets, minding the shop. Business would be brisk with all the tourists in Harvest for the ACC, but it certainly would be much quieter than it was on the square. Quiet was what my grandmother craved. Right after my grandfather had died, she had been a pillar of strength, going about her life in the same orderly way she always had, but as the weeks after his death had gone by, she had became quieter, withdrawn, as if she finally realized that her husband was gone, never to return.

Clara and Jebidiah King had truly been lifelong companions. Although they didn't grow up in the same Amish district, she and my *daadi* had known each other since birth because their family farms had been on the same rural road. My grandfather said it was love at first sight. As a young child, I would argue that point with him. I told him that babies can't fall in love. He would say, "Sure they can. You fell in love with me when you were a baby." I would protest and tell him that was different because he was my *daadi*. Boy-girl love was different. He would shake his head and say, "The soul knows when it's found its match, no matter the age." I didn't buy that at eight. I wasn't sure if I bought it at twenty-seven either, especially considering my own romantic record; maybe my soul was just as confused as the rest of me.

Juliet, who had been silent up to this point, said, "Could it be, Josephine, that you want Swissmen Sweets to be removed from the competition because they just might beat you?" Her voice was as sweet as molasses.

I winced. Even I knew that was not the best counter-argument to use with Josephine Weaver.

Josephine dropped her hands from her tiny hips. "How can you say such a thing, Juliet Brody? I just want to have a fair and safe competition of *Amish* candy makers. My shop, Berlin Candies, has a rightful place in the competition because I am Amish, and everyone who works for me is Amish. We do everything the Amish way. Unlike Swissmen Sweets. There have been rumors about the worldly recipes that have been showing up at Swissmen Sweets."

Worldly recipes, really? I wanted to ask her what she meant by that exactly, but I thought better of it and held my tongue. It was true that since I took over Swissmen Sweets, I had added a few new flavors to some of the traditionally Amish candies and sweets that we sold. I'd added lavender blueberry fudge, chocolate cherry ganache truffles, and more. Even if I was going to live in Amish Country, I couldn't leave my life's work as a chocolatier behind. I had worked too hard for too long mastering my craft to let it wither and die.

Margot put a hand on Josephine's arm. "Let's go to the concessions and get you some tea, Josephine. I think it will calm you down nicely."

Across the square, there was an Amish-run concessions booth selling tea, coffee, and hot apple cider to tourists. With the chill in the October air, the line ran all the way to the gazebo in the middle of the square. Amish teenagers filled plain white paper cups with hot drinks as quickly as they could pour them.

Josephine wrenched her arm away from Margot. "I do not need to be calmed down."

"What we sell at Swissmen Sweets doesn't have anything to do with what I'm entering in the ACC," I said.

"Doesn't it?" Josephine's eyes narrowed. "Shouldn't this competition be for Amish confectioneries? If yours is no longer an Amish candy shop, that's more reason than ever to disqualify you, and I'm going to make it my mission to do just that."

"Is that a threat?" I asked.

She lifted her pointy chin. "The Amish don't make threats. We make promises."

Sounded like the same thing to me, I thought, as Josephine stomped away with Jeremiah and Margot in her wake.

Chapter 2

When Josephine Weaver said she would have me removed from the competition, I assumed she wasn't bluffing. Most of the Amish I knew were true to their word. I watched as she stomped around the large white gazebo in the middle of the square and disappeared from sight.

At the edge of the square, a teenage Amish girl with curly strawberry-blond hair that was barely contained under her white prayer cap, caught my eye. She stared at the spot from which Josephine had disappeared and wrapped her shawl more closely around her body as if she felt some sort of chill. Maybe a hot drink like Margot had suggested would do her good too. She then ducked her head and ran across the village square in the direction of First Church, the large white church that was on the opposite side of the square from Swissmen Sweets.

"What are we going to do about Jethro?" Juliet wrung her hands and pulled my attention away from the girl. "I hate to be a bother. I know you have so much to do for the competition."

"I'm in a good spot. The licorice for the first round is done, and the judging doesn't happen for another hour. Emily will be over in a few minutes to help me with the next round, which is taffy. It's always good to have a second person on hand when making taffy."

Emily Esh was the sister of Esther Esh, who owned Esh Family Pretzels, which was right next to Swissmen Sweets. Both shops sat on the other side of Main Street directly across from the square gazebo. They had the most sought-after locations in Harvest.

Since I had officially taken over Swissmen Sweets, I had hired Emily from time to time to help out in the shop. This weekend, I had asked her if she could be my assistant at the ACC, and she readily agreed. Emily was always looking for an excuse to escape the pretzel shop and her older sister's judgment.

Esther and their older brother, Abel, allowed Emily to help me to an extent. I knew the extra money helped the family of three young, unmarried siblings. However, I suspected Esther and maybe even Abel would like to limit Emily's time with me. Maybe they thought I would corrupt her with my big-city English ways.

"I just don't know what I'll do if something happens to Jethro." Juliet sounded as if she was on the verge of tears.

"I'll help you look for him," I said quickly before she could break down. "I'll start looking around the church. Meanwhile, why don't you take a lap around the square and ask people if they have seen him. He's pretty distinctive-looking; people would remember if they saw a polka-dotted pig. We'll meet in front of the church in fifteen minutes."

She clasped my hands in both of hers. "Oh, thank you, Bailey. Thank you so much. I'm so glad that you moved here, not just for my son, but for the entire community. You're such a blessing."

I internally groaned when Juliet mentioned her son. I had not moved to Harvest, Ohio, for her son. Somehow Juliet had gotten it into her mind that he and I were destined for each other. I won't lie and say that I *didn't* find her son, Aiden Brody, appealing. He was the very handsome sheriff's deputy and had close ties to my family. After Juliet and Aiden moved to Harvest when Aiden was just a child, my grandparents gave them a place to live until they were on their own two feet. The Brodys had remained friends with my grandparents ever since. Despite the family history and the fact that I found Aiden almost painfully attractive, we were just friends, regardless of the plans his mother and my grandmother might have for our future.

Before I left the booth, I tidied it the best I could so it would be ready for the licorice judging.

By the time I finished, Juliet was already speaking to the third candy maker in the row, asking him if he had seen Jethro.

"You're looking for a polka-dotted pig?" the man asked in a thick Pennsylvania Dutch accent.

Even though I had an hour before the licorice judging, I didn't wait to hear Juliet's reply to the man. I shoved my cell phone into the back pocket of my jeans and hurried through the crowd, past the gazebo, and across the street, aptly named Church Street, to the large white church. Even though I hadn't lived in Harvest long, I knew the church well. On my first full day in the village, I had used the kitchen to make wedding desserts.

Two autumnal wreaths adorned the church's main entrance. Instead of running up the stone steps to that entrance, I jogged around the side of the building to the back. A small parking lot sat behind the church, where the pastor, Reverend Brook, and the other church staff parked. Next to the parking lot, a cemetery encircled by a weathered wooden fence stretched away from the church.

Two men in white coveralls were whitewashing the fence and were about two-thirds done. I wondered why Juliet hadn't mentioned the painters when she told me that Jethro had gone missing. Then again, I couldn't be entirely sure she'd noticed them. Juliet seemed to be caught in a daydream most of the time.

I approached the two men. "Excuse me."

"We need to hang a 'wet paint' sign on here," the first painter said to the second.

"Right, boss," the second painter said.

"Excuse me," I said a little more loudly.

The two men turned and stared at me. "Are you lost?" one asked.

"Lost? No. I'd like to ask you if you saw a pig a little while back, sometime this morning. The last place he was seen was here, behind the church."

"A pig?" the other painter asked. "Is this a joke?"

I shook my head. "No. He's about the size of a

toaster and is black and white polka-dotted. He has a black dot around his right eye."

"A pig with polka dots." He snorted. "Now, I know you are pulling my leg."

"I'm not. He was here this morning when volunteers for the ACC were taking candy-making supplies from the church."

"I saw a lot of people coming in and out of the back of the church," the first painter said. "But no pig with or without polka dots."

My shoulders drooped. "All right. Thanks anyway."

"Cheer up, girl. Don't cry over a lost pig," he said in a mocking tone.

I frowned at him.

"If I were you, I'd stay away from bacon until he shows. You know, just to be on the safe side." He grinned.

His partner laughed, and I glared at them before walking away. At least Juliet hadn't been there to hear the two men make light of Jethro's disappearance.

I checked my cell phone for the time. Almost fifteen minutes had passed since Juliet and I had parted ways at my table. I walked around the side of the church. Juliet was at the church steps waiting for me.

Her blue eyes were wide. "Did you find anything?"

I shook my head. "There were two painters working on the fence around the cemetery."

She nodded. "Yes, Reverend Brook hired them to

paint the fence. It goes all the way around the graveyard. What did they say?"

I frowned. "They haven't seen Jethro."

Juliet removed her crumpled tissue from her pocket again and dabbed at the corner of her eye. "I called Aiden, and he said he would come as quickly as he could and help us look for Jethro. I know he has a lot to do with so many people in town. I shouldn't have worried him with my little troubles." She looked as if she was about to cry again.

"Jethro missing is not 'little troubles,'" I said. "And Aiden knows that. I'm sure he's as worried as you are."

She sniffled. "He's such a good son. He'll make a good husband someday."

That hint was as subtle as a brick in the face.

I balanced on the balls of my feet, ready to flee in case of more husband material talk. "I should return to my booth soon, but I have a little time. Where else should we look?"

She shook her head. "I don't know. We've looked everywhere."

"Not everywhere. Let's check inside the church. Jethro might have gone in there while you were moving supplies, and he does feel right at home in the church." I didn't add that the reason Jethro felt at home inside the church was that Juliet spent most her time there. Everyone in Harvest knew she was sweet on the awkward widower pastor, Reverend Brook. Everyone, that was, except for the befuddled reverend himself.

Juliet clapped her hands and then threw her

arms around me. "Bailey King, you are a genius! Why didn't I think of that? Of course, Jethro would run into the church. He is so fond of Reverend Brook. He would run to the reverend for comfort if he was scared by the crowd. Let's go there now."

I glanced at my cell phone and checked the time once more. The closer the candy judging came, the antsier I felt. I had participated in all sorts of competitions in New York against the best chocolatiers in the world. This felt different, as if there was more on the line for me personally. If I won this contest, it would prove to the world, or maybe just to myself, that I hadn't thrown my career away when I made the decision to move to Ohio to take over Swissmen Sweets.

Juliet climbed the steps to the church. The front door was open, and Juliet marched inside without hesitation. I entered a little more timidly. I hadn't been back in the church since the wedding in September, which hadn't ended well.

By the time I stepped across the threshold into the building, Juliet had her hand on the handle of the sanctuary door. I stepped forward and paused. There was a hushed feeling to the place. It was as if the building was holding its breath for Sunday, the next time it would be needed. Until then, it stood tensely at attention.

I hadn't been in many churches in my life. When my father had left the Amish way to marry my mother, who was English, he had not only left his Amish life behind but also his belief in God. I believed in God, at least I thought I did. I knew that my grandmother did. My grandfather had, too, and they were some of the most contented people I had ever known. However, now that my grandfather was gone, my grandmother seemed a little lost.

A terrible groaning sound came from the other side of the sanctuary doors, as if some type of animal was being strangled. Juliet threw the door open and ran inside, and I raced after her, catching the door before it closed.

The enormous organ was the centerpiece of the sanctuary. It started at the base of the narthex and went all the way up to the cathedral-high ceiling. There was a golden star at the top of it. Sunlight streamed in through the clear glass windows and reflected off the silver pipes that could be seen through the openings in the wooden façade.

The girl, the same strawberry-blond Amish girl I had seen on the square less than an hour ago, sat at the three-tiered keyboard and pressed a key, and that terrible strangled cat sound started again.

Juliet covered her ears. "I don't think it's supposed to sound like that," she whispered to me.

The door to the sanctuary slipped through my fingers and slammed closed behind me with a resounding boom. Juliet spun around, and the girl at the very front of the sanctuary jumped as if she had been shot.

"I'm so sorry," I stammered.

Juliet covered her mouth with her hand. "Charlotte, I'm so sorry to disturb you when you are practicing."

Charlotte's face cleared. "It's all right. I think Reverend Brook is in his office."

Juliet shook her head. "I'm not looking for

Reverend Brook. I'm looking for my pig. Have you seen Jethro? He's been missing since this morning. We've looked everywhere outside for him. Bailey"—she nodded at me—"suggested that we try the church because he might have felt safer inside the church with so many people in town."

Charlotte looked stricken. "I wish I could say that I have seen him. I only just began practicing. If he wandered in here this morning, it was before I arrived."

Juliet's shoulders sagged. "Will you keep an eye out for him?"

"I will. Maybe Jethro tried to tune the organ," she joked. "It sounds very odd today. I would hate for your regular organist to think I harmed it in some way. It's very nice of him to let me practice here." Charlotte got up from the organ. I noted that she was in her stocking feet, no shoes. I don't know why that detail stuck out, but it did. She tiptoed to the small door at the left side of the organ and opened it. Her screams reverberated off the flying buttresses above our heads.

Propelled by the sound, I ran forward. Charlotte stumbled back from the door with her hand over her mouth and nearly collided with me. I grabbed her before she could fall over the organ platform. Silent tears rolled down her flushed cheeks. Once she was leaning against the organ bench, I let her go. I went to the open door, pulled it open more widely, and stepped inside the cramped space.

I found myself in an area no more than the width of a coffin. I was surrounded on three sides by wood and metal—the working innards of the organ itself.

The comparison to a coffin couldn't have been more accurate because a limp white hand hung down from the platform above me.

Jethro was still missing, but I'd found Josephine Weaver. She was dead.

Chapter 3

I stumbled backward, and a sharp lever rammed into my spine. I didn't care. I wanted to get as far away from Josephine as I could in the cramped space.

Josephine's swollen tongue stuck out as if it was too large to fit inside her mouth. Her lips were red and blistered, and so were her cheeks. It looked like a case of hives. My first guess was an allergic reaction. Was she allergic to bees and had gotten stung? But it was October, and there weren't that many bees around this time of year; most had returned to their hives for the winter or died in the cold nights. If she *had* been stung by a bee, the blistering on her face led me to believe she'd been stung in the mouth. I shivered at that thought. It seemed just too gruesome. It seemed much more likely that she'd eaten something she was allergic to, such as peanuts or shellfish. Those were the first two possibilities that came to mind because they were the most common allergies. There wasn't much shellfish

to speak of in Amish Country, but there was plenty
of food made with peanuts or peanut butter.

At JP Chocolates back in New York, we always had
to be careful about where we prepared anything
with peanuts or any kind of nuts because peanut
and other nut allergies were so common. I suspected this type of allergy was the most likely culprit
in the candy maker's death.

But that didn't answer the question as to how
she'd gotten inside the organ or on the platform
five feet from the base of the door. Had she felt
unwell and decided to climb up there to hide? Perhaps she had become disoriented and wandered
into the organ and climbed the platform. That
seemed unlikely. As far as I knew, Josephine had
no reason to enter the church. She was Amish, and
although I knew Amish ladies were members of
Juliet's quilting circle, which met in the church's
fellowship hall, I had never seen Josephine there.
If I ruled out her walking into the organ under
her own steam, that left only two possibilities.
Either someone had forced her inside the space or
put her there after she was incapacitated or already
dead. I swallowed hard. That meant only one thing.
That meant it was murder.

"The police are on their way," I heard Juliet say
from the other side of the organ's tiny door. Her
voice echoed inside the organ. I looked up. The
pipes rose twenty feet in the air. It was an engineer-
ing marvel and a wondrous instrument that was now
tainted with the stain of death.

"I hear a siren," Juliet called.

I jumped. The siren was my cue to move. The last
thing I wanted was for the police to find me in the

tiny space with Josephine's body. My plan was to stay under the radar. What Charlotte had discovered had nothing to do with me.

I wriggled out of the tiny space to find Charlotte sitting on the steps leading to the stage. Juliet knelt next to her, rubbing her back.

Sheriff's Deputy Aiden Brody strode into the church with a sure and long stride. Aiden was tall, with a loose, lanky build, and with hair and eyes almost the same shade of chocolate brown. If I was casting "small town sheriff's deputy" in a movie, the actor would look just like Aiden, right down to the lopsided smile, the dimple in his right cheek that appeared only when he was amused, and that penetrating gaze.

Aiden removed his navy Sheriff's Department ball cap. Something about the small gesture of respect for the place of worship tugged at my heart, and I had to look away.

Aiden Brody couldn't have been more different from Eric Sharp, my ex-boyfriend and the bad boy of the New York celebrity pastry chef scene, if he tried. Yes, in New York there was such a thing as a bad boy pastry chef. You could find just about anything in the city.

For nearly a year, Eric and I had kept our relationship secret because he had been on the board's selection committee for Jean Pierre's replacement when my boss announced his retirement well after age eighty. As Jean Pierre's protégé, I had been favored to win the position. If the rest of the selection committee had found out Eric and I were together, I would have been disqualified, and everything I had worked for would have been lost.

Even knowing that, I had been unable to stay away from Eric. Being with him was like playing with fire. I never turned him away when he showed up at my apartment doorstep. It was behavior that I had trouble explaining, even to myself. Maybe I was attracted to Eric because seeing him was exciting, reckless, and sneaky. I would never have used any one of those words to describe myself before dating him. I worked at being the best chocolatier that I could be. I gave my all to my career, and I lived and breathed chocolate. Eric seemed like an escape from the life I'd boxed myself into.

Keeping a secret of that caliber for a whole year was impressive, but that secret, like all secrets, couldn't be maintained forever, and it blew up in my face, thanks to a New York City tabloid. The newspaper revealed that I wasn't the only woman in Eric's life. I should have known a playboy like Eric wouldn't be satisfied with one secret girlfriend when he could have two. Was it any wonder I'd sworn off men? That included sheriff's deputies, especially sheriff's deputies who had once considered me a murder suspect and would—I know—do so again in a heartbeat.

Aiden scanned the room with his milk chocolate eyes.

I listed the different kinds of chocolate in my head as I always did when I was stressed. It was a mantra I went back to again and again. *White chocolate, milk chocolate, dark chocolate, sweet chocolate, semi-sweet chocolate, bittersweet chocolate, cocoa, couverture, vermicelli . . .*

The chocolate litany didn't help. I swallowed as the image of Josephine's dead body came to the forefront of my mind again. I couldn't believe that the woman who had been yelling at me in the middle of the square just shy of two hours ago was now dead and crammed inside an organ. There had been no indication that she'd been sick when I'd last seen her. In fact, she'd been full of vim and vitriol. That just strengthened my belief that she was most likely murdered.

Juliet rushed to her son's side. "Oh, Aiden, it's just horrible." She threw her arms around her son, who was a good foot taller than she. He patted her back. In that moment, she was more like the child than the parent. Aiden looked over his mother's head and locked eyes with me.

I turned away and went to Charlotte, who was perched on the steps leading to the organ platform.

Charlotte buried her head in her knees. I sat next to her, and she leaned into me. "Shh." I rubbed her back. "I know that it was a scary discovery, but the police are here now and will take care of everything."

She lifted her face from her skirt, which was damp with her tears. Her oval face was pale, and her light hazel eyes were wide with sheer fear. I thought back to when I'd first seen her on the square this morning. She had spotted Josephine and had seemed terrified then too, maybe less so, but she was clearly scared and worried as she'd watched Josephine. Did that mean that she knew her? Most of the Amish in Harvest knew each other. That, however, did not explain the kind of fear I'd seen on the girl's face.

A second deputy entered the sanctuary. He was a young, short, compact man who looked like he was fresh from the police academy. His hair was perfectly parted down the side, and his uniform was ironed to within an inch of its life.

Aiden patted his mother's arm one final time and stepped away. "This is Deputy Little. He will be working the case with me today."

I studied the newcomer with even more interest. Aiden's old partner and I had not gotten along. In fact, it had gone so badly that he was no longer with the Sheriff's Department. I hoped for better things from Deputy Little.

The younger deputy stared at Aiden with an expression I could only describe as admiration. Yep, Little was going to be a lot different from Aiden's old partner, who could barely contain his contempt for Aiden. At least one thing in Harvest had improved in the last few weeks.

Aiden looked at his mother, Charlotte, and me in turn. "Can someone please tell me what is going on here? We got a call about a dead body."

His question set Charlotte off in tears again. Juliet removed a tissue from her dress pocket and patted her own eyes.

I cleared my throat. "Your mother and I came into the church looking for Jethro, and—"

"Yes!" Juliet cried. "Aiden, Jethro is still missing. We must do something to find him."

Aiden glanced at his mother. "We will, Mom. I know you're worried about him, but I need to ask about what happened here first."

She covered her mouth. "Oh, I know. I know I shouldn't be worried about poor Jethro at a time like this, but I can't help it. I'm afraid whoever did this might have hurt my little pig too."

Aiden shook his head. "It's very unlikely Jethro's

absence is related to what's happened here in the church today." He nodded encouragingly to me. "Bailey, you were saying . . ."

I swallowed and started again. "Your mother and I decided to search the church for Jethro. We'd just stepped into the building when we heard a god-awful noise."

"What was the noise?" Aiden asked.

"The organ," I said, "although it sounded closer to a strangled cat than any instrument I've ever heard."

Charlotte covered her face with her hands, and I wished I could take the strangled cat comment back. It was too late.

I took a breath. "We came into the sanctuary, and Charlotte was at the organ. It was clear there was something wrong with the instrument. Charlotte opened the door in the organ and"—I paused— "made the discovery."

Aiden glanced down at Charlotte.

"That's Charlotte," I said, answering his question even before he could ask.

Charlotte rubbed her eyes but remained silent. She made a point not to look at Aiden.

Juliet held up her hand. "What about Reverend Brook? I should go find Reverend Brook to tell him what has happened." She took a step toward a side door behind the pulpit. "That's what I should do. He needs to know what's going on. It's his church."

Aiden held up his hand, traffic cop style. "We'll make sure Reverend Brook knows what's happened, but you can't leave the scene just yet. We should question all three of you." Aiden turned back to me. "Do you recognize the person inside the organ?"

I nodded. "It's Josephine Weaver."

"Weaver is an Amish name."

"The woman was Amish," I said with a nod.

Aiden closed his eyes for a second. I wished I knew what he was thinking.

"Does it make a difference that the victim is Amish?" I asked.

He glanced in my direction. "Of course, it does. Everything just got a lot more complicated."

I wasn't sure what he meant by that. Would it have been better if it were a non-Amish person—or *Englischer,* as the Amish called us—who'd been killed? I bit the inside of my cheek. I mean, really, the tragic loss of *any* person was cause for upset.

"I'm not sure how she died, but I would say since she was inside the organ, her death was not natural."

Aiden scowled at me, and I remembered the deputy hadn't been keen on me poking my nose into the last murder investigation. I doubted his opinion had changed much in the last few weeks.

"You think someone killed her?" Juliet gasped.

"It looks that way. Yes," I said.

Aiden scowled, and his dimple was nowhere to be seen. "I'll be the judge of that. You all sit tight here with Deputy Little."

"I'd like to take a look too, Deputy Brody," Little piped up, sounding a little miffed to be stuck babysitting three women instead of getting a chance to peek inside the organ.

Aiden glanced over his shoulder. "You'll get your chance. Stay here for now with them."

Little nodded and stood a little straighter.

Aiden walked up to the organ as if steeling himself

for what he might find inside. He disappeared
through the small doorway. I followed him.

"You should stay here," Little said to my back.

I glanced over my shoulder just as Aiden had.
"That is probably true." And kept going.

Chapter 4

I peered through the open door into the organ to find Aiden staring at Josephine's limp hand, just as I had a few moments ago. I averted my eyes. One inspection of the Amish woman's still form was enough for me. I still couldn't believe that she had been so alive just a short time ago. I hadn't known Josephine long, and what I knew of her was unpleasant, but at the same time she was still a person who would be missed by someone. If she wasn't, that would be terribly sad. She was also a candy maker, like me, and one of the best or she would not have earned a spot in the ACC. I had to respect her talent for the craft of candy making. A talent that was now lost. What could have possibly happened between the time she yelled at me on the square about not being Amish and when Charlotte began playing the organ?

"Just do me a favor," Aiden said without looking at me. "Don't touch anything, and don't cross the threshold. I would like to keep the scene as secure as possible."

"Okay," I said and remained in the doorway. At least Aiden hadn't shooed me away completely.

Aiden took a step closer to the platform where the body lay. He got much closer to it than I had.

"What do you think happened?" I asked.

He didn't turn around, just kept studying the body and the platform.

"Do you think she was murdered?" I asked.

He glanced back at me. "Why would you ask that?"

I shrugged. "She's in an organ. It seems suspicious to me."

"Me too." His shoulders drooped. "I can't say anything official just yet, but yes, it's possible. It's hard to believe that she would climb inside the organ and onto this platform to die by her own choice."

"And she died from an allergic reaction, right?"

He did turn and look at me then.

"I saw her lips and tongue. I know what hives look like. Cass is allergic to horseradish. She can't touch the stuff. I've only see her after she accidentally ate it once, and she was covered in hives." My eyes fell on Josephine's hand again. I had to look away. "But her reaction wasn't as severe as what happened to Josephine."

"I'm sure Cass wasn't happy when she got that bite of horseradish." Aiden had met my best friend, Cass, when she came to Harvest just before my grandfather passed away.

Despite the tension in the small space, I couldn't help but smile. "No, she wasn't happy, but the Benadryl she had to guzzle knocked her right out."

"Deputy Brody!" Little called from behind me. "The EMTs and crime scene techs are here."

I turned and saw a dozen official-looking men and women marching down the center aisle of the church. I turned back to the innards of the organ and found Aiden just inches from my nose. I drew in a sharp breath.

He didn't move. "Can you go sit with my mother and Charlotte while we get a handle on things? Little or I will be talking with you shortly."

I swallowed. "Sure," I squeaked, and retreated.

I joined Juliet and Charlotte on the steps. Juliet had her arm wrapped around the Amish girl's shoulders. I wondered if Juliet knew Charlotte well or if it was just her maternal instinct kicking in.

Charlotte was pale to begin with, but her face had blanched to the color of printer paper.

Juliet looked up at me. "What about Jethro? Should we keep looking for him?"

"We can," I said. "But for now, we should wait here. I don't think Aiden and the other officers would like it if we started traipsing all over the church. I imagine they plan to search the whole building for any evidence of the crime. If Jethro is inside the church, someone will find him."

By the organ's door, Aiden and Little spoke with the crime scene techs.

"It's going to be a trick to remove the body without knocking it all over the place. Whoever put her in there must have been crazy strong and flexible," a crime scene tech said.

"So we're looking for a gymnast," another tech joked.

"Wait until the coroner arrives," Aiden said. "He's removed bodies from trickier spots. He'll have some ideas about how to do it and still preserve the scene. Do what you can taking photos and gathering evidence until he gets here." Then Aiden walked over to Juliet, Charlotte, and me.

The deputy squatted in front of the young Amish woman. "Can you tell me what you saw?"

Little stood behind him with notebook in hand, taking copious notes. He should have been a court reporter instead of a cop, I thought.

Charlotte blinked at him with her round hazel eyes. She looked so confused, I felt an overwhelming urge to shield her. It appeared by the way Aiden's face softened that he felt the same way. "How did you find her?"

"I—I opened the door to the organ chamber, and I saw—I saw her hand. I screamed, and then Bailey came rushing in behind me."

Juliet squeezed the girl's shoulder.

Aiden shot me a look, and I met his gaze with an even, unapologetic stare.

"Why did you open the organ door?" he asked the girl, turning back to Charlotte.

She rubbed her cheeks with the palms of her hands until the skin was pink. "The organ sounded off. The keys were making the wrong sounds. That can happen every so often when one of the keys is bumped. The slightest adjustment inside the instrument can change the tone completely," she said, sounding a little more confident when speaking about the organ. "The organist has taught me how to care for the organ as well as play it. He says it's important to know what's wrong with the organ and identify the problems in the instrument."

"Do they have organs in Amish churches?" I asked.

Aiden shot me a look but didn't say anything to squelch my question.

Charlotte licked her bloodless lips, which were the same pale color as her cheeks. "No, no, they do not."

"But you are Amish and playing the organ," Aiden said.

"I am," was her simple answer.

Aiden seemed to consider this but made no further comment. I knew what he was thinking. He was thinking that this detail was important. I was thinking that too. Why it was important was still unknown.

"So the body bumped the pipes and caused their tone to change," Aiden said.

She shook her head. "I think it was leaning against the pipes and against the trackers. I noticed many of them were broken."

"Trackers. What are those?" Aiden asked.

"They are narrow strips of wood that open and close the pipes. Depending on the tracker, you can change the sound a certain pipe can make." Charlotte seemed to become more relaxed as she spoke about the organ itself. It was evident that she had a deep affection for the powerful instrument. "I hope the church will be able to have them repaired. It's a beautiful instrument. The best organ in the area. That's why I come here to practice."

Aiden rocked back on his heels. "And did you recognize the woman inside the organ?"

I opened my mouth to tell him that I had already identified the body as Josephine Weaver, but before

I could, the color drained from Charlotte's face again. "Of course, I recognized her. She's my aunt, and she's dead because of me."

"Your aunt?" Aiden asked the question that was on the tip of my tongue. "The woman in the organ is your aunt?"

She nodded and stared down at the hands folded in her lap. "She's my Aunt Josephine, my uncle's wife."

Her aunt. Josephine Weaver was Charlotte's aunt? No wonder the girl was so shaken by finding the body. It must have been doubly shocking to discover that her aunt was dead. I frowned. Why hadn't she said that when we first found the body? I know that we were all in shock—we were *still* in shock—but it seemed to me that this was an important detail she would normally have mentioned in the moment.

"Why do you think she is dead because of you?" Aiden asked in a deceptively calm and even tone.

She licked her lips. "Because I am here. She did not approve of me playing the organ. She made her opinion very clear on that."

"But did you put her in the organ?" Even as I asked this, I knew it was impossible. Josephine was small, but Charlotte was just as slight. I couldn't imagine the girl lifting Josephine's dead weight above her ankles, let alone above her head.

Aiden shot me a look, and Little's pencil was suspended in the air as his brow wrinkled, making him look more like a middle school student than a police officer.

One of the crime scene techs popped his head

out of the organ. "Brody, you might want to come and look at this. We found something."

Aiden pressed his lips together. "Little and I will check the scene. Wait here, please," he said to the three of us.

Aiden and Little walked back to the organ, and I was about follow when the church door opened again, and the county coroner marched into the church. All those years in Manhattan and I had had only one uncomfortable interaction with the police. Here, in what was supposed to be serene Amish Country, where conversation should be about quilts and cheese making, too many of my conversations had been about murder.

Juliet stood up. "I know Aiden won't like this, but I'm going to go find Reverend Brook. This is his church." She patted Charlotte on the shoulder. "You stay here with Bailey. She'll take good care of you."

Before I could protest, Juliet walked down the side aisle of the church and through a doorway that I assumed led to a set of stairs. The church was a huge maze of a building, and I wouldn't be able to tell Aiden where his mother had gone if he asked me.

"We didn't really formerly meet. I'm Bailey King," I said to Charlotte.

"I know. You're Cousin Clara's granddaughter."

I blinked at her. "Cousin Clara?"

"Your grandmother is my cousin." She gave me a wobbly smile. "You're my cousin too."

My grandmother had never mentioned any cousins to me in all my life. I wanted to ask Charlotte more about this, but she took in a sharp breath. "It's my fault." Her breathing grew shallow.

I studied her. "Are you all right?"

"I'm a little dizzy, and I'm hot," she whispered. "Is it hot in here?"

I shook my head. In fact, there was a chill in the wide and cavernous sanctuary that came in every time someone opened the doors.

"I think I might pass out," she whispered.

I touched her arm. "Why don't we step outside for a moment? It looks like you could use a break from all of this." I figured if Aiden's own mother could disobey his orders and leave the sanctuary, I could too.

Charlotte nodded, and I helped her to her feet. She stood on shaky legs. I started to lead her down the side aisle where Aiden's mother had gone.

"Wait."

I spun around to find Aiden coming down the aisle behind us.

"Where are you going?" he asked.

I frowned at him. "I'm just going to take Charlotte outside for some air. She doesn't need to be here for the removal of Josephine's body. She doesn't need that image in her memory."

Charlotte clung to my arm as if it was the only thing that was holding her up. I suspected it was.

He sighed. "Fine, but stay in front of the church." He stared at me. "Please don't go any further than that."

I nodded agreement and turned Charlotte back toward the door.

When we walked outside the church, I had a clear view of the activity on the square. The three judges were moving from table to table, tasting the licorice samples. The ACC judging was going on as if nothing had happened, but a handful of tourists pointed at the ambulances and police cars parked in front of First Church. It wouldn't be long before the word was out about Josephine Weaver's death.

There was a tug on my arm as Charlotte lowered herself to the second-to-last church step, taking me with her. She took a deep breath and seemed to regain some composure.

As I sat beside her, I wanted to ask about her aunt's death, but I didn't want to intrude on her grief. My own grief over the death of my grandfather was still near the surface of my emotions, and we might both end up crying.

We sat quietly for a full minute until Charlotte said, "I—I can't believe this happened. I didn't mean—" She stopped in mid-speech when a buggy pulled into the church parking lot. She jumped to her feet.

The buggy was one of the most lavish I'd ever seen. The battery-powered headlights were polished, and the sides of the buggy gleamed as if the exterior had just been waxed.

"Oh no," Charlotte said in a low voice. "Oh no."

"What's wrong?" I asked.

"Whoa," said a voice from the buggy.

An Amish man who was close to my own age, maybe a little bit older, jumped from the driver's seat and tethered his horse to the hitching post in one fluid movement. He was muscular and compact and wore a plain blue shirt under his suspenders. No coat despite the October chill. The sun reflected off his chestnut-colored hair.

A second man also exited the buggy at a much slower pace. I would guess he was twenty years older than the first man and had a grizzled red beard. However, he too moved with the ease of someone who had labored most of his life.

"Oh no," Charlotte whispered, staring at the two men.

"What is it? Do you know them?" I asked.

She swallowed. "It's the district's deacon and my father." Her voice held so much despair that I wanted to tell her to go hide in the church until they left, but it was too late. They had already seen her and were headed our way.

Chapter 5

The younger of the two Amish men, the deacon, strode toward us. The second man followed at a more sedate pace, allowing the deacon to take the lead. I'd lived in Ohio for only a few weeks now, but when I was young, I spent my summers here with my grandparents. The man walking in my direction was by far the youngest deacon I'd ever seen.

"He's your deacon?" I whispered to Charlotte as I helped her to her feet. I thought it would be better for Charlotte if she met the two men with the stern expressions standing up.

"*Ya*," she whispered. "It's Deacon Clapp."

The name tickled the back of my memory. Clapp wasn't the deacon in my grandmother's district. That was elderly Deacon Yoder. However, I remembered the name because Ruth Yoder, Deacon Yoder's wife, had just been in Swissmen Sweets complaining about the new "upstart" deacon in Harvest. Ruth had nothing kind to say about the man. But then again, Ruth didn't have anything kind to say about anyone, as far as I could tell.

Charlotte's father stepped in front of the deacon. "Charlotte, we've come to take you home. It's time for you to give up this foolishness and take your place in the community."

Charlotte gripped my arm and didn't reply. I looked down at the girl and saw that her pink mouth was set in a line. I wouldn't describe her expression as scared. No, her face appeared resigned, as if she had been expecting this moment for some time.

When it was clear Charlotte wasn't going to speak, I said, "Maybe I can help."

The deacon focused on me with blue eyes. "Who are you?"

His question was blunt. It was not an uncommon characteristic of the Amish to get right to the point of a conversation. Many didn't bother with small talk or pleasantries because they viewed those things as a waste of time. Their time could be much better spent working. Working, being productive, was the number one priority of the Amish. Since I also had a strong work ethic, which I must have inherited from my Amish grandparents, I could appreciate that. However, a simple "Hello, my name is . . ." would have been nice.

"I'm Bailey King." I held out my hand. Neither man made a move to shake it, so I let my arm fall to my side.

Clapp pressed his eyebrows together in a dark line. "You're Jebidiah King's granddaughter. The one who is working in the candy shop now. The one from New York City."

"I am," I said, meeting his eyes.

"I'm Charlotte's deacon, and this is her father,

Sol. We're here to take her home." He turned to Charlotte, and I had the very odd sensation of being slighted by the deacon. It wasn't that I wanted his approval, but it was almost as if confirming my identity was all he needed to dismiss me. An *Englischer* from New York was of no consequence to the people of Harvest or Holmes County. I wasn't part of their community. I wasn't Amish. That's what it all boiled down to.

"Charlotte," Sol said, "it is time to leave."

The girl took a step back, and I couldn't help but wonder what it was about home that she was so reluctant to return to it.

She shook her head. "I'm not going with you, *Daed*."

Her father scowled at her. "You're leaving with us now. The deacon has been kind enough to come with me to collect you. You won't insult him or shame me by refusing to join us."

"Why didn't you bring your own buggy? There are plenty of buggies."

I found this statement as odd. Why would Charlotte fixate on buggies?

"Charlotte," the deacon said in a cool voice, "it is my duty to support my flock, and that includes you. You are one of my lost sheep."

I made a face. I couldn't help it.

Charlotte let go of my arm and balled her hands at her sides. A little part of me wanted to cheer. I was glad she was angered by his patronizing tone.

"I cannot leave." Her voice was even.

"You choose to stay and indulge in *Englisch* music?" The deacon narrowed his eyes. "Your family and I are very distressed that you continue with the

Englisch music. It is time for you to come home and take your place in the community."

I almost laughed. He acted like Charlotte had fled the Amish community to join a rock band, not walked into a church to play the organ. I couldn't think of a less controversial instrument.

"You have brought shame on your community and your family," Deacon Clapp said.

Charlotte lifted her chin. "It's nonsense. Doesn't the Bible say that people should make a joyful noise? That's what I'm doing. It is how I choose to praise *Gott*. You are telling me there is a right and a wrong way to honor *Gott*. I don't believe that."

Her father took a quick intake of breath at his daughter's words.

The deacon narrowed his eyes. "It is not your place to choose how *Gott* should be praised. It is my job to tell you the right and wrong thing to do, and what you are doing is wrong. It is my duty to tell you this. You are going against our ways, and I am here to take you home. Put these ideas behind you. You are old enough now to make your choice. It is time that you decide to be baptized in the church."

Charlotte's father winced, and he said something in Pennsylvania Dutch that I didn't understand. Whatever it was, I know that it must have been addressed to Charlotte. She stared at her father with so much naked hurt that it made my heart ache.

The deacon reached out and grabbed Charlotte by the arm. She tried to pull away from him, but his grip tightened. She struggled against his grasp.

I grabbed his hand. "Let her go."

He glared at me. "Do not touch me, *Englischer*."

"Let go of her arm," I said in measured tones.

"This is none of your concern," he snapped.

"I'm making it my concern. Let her go."

Charlotte wrenched her arm away from him. She stepped slightly behind me. I dropped my hand from his hand like I had been burnt.

The deacon narrowed his eyes. "You do not know what trouble you are causing this girl, *Englischer*. You're only making it more difficult for her, and you are corrupting her with your ways."

Charlotte and I had just met less than an hour ago. I didn't know how I could already be corrupting her.

"I'm not going with you," Charlotte said, and then looked at her father. "I am sorry, *Daed,* but I'm not going with either of you."

The deacon glared at the girl. "*Gott* does not look kindly on those who disobey."

"I may not be following your wishes, but I am following *Gotte's*." She lifted her chin.

"My wishes and *Gotte's* wishes are the same. He chose me as the deacon. Did he not?"

I folded my arms. "That is quite a strong statement—to say that your wishes are equal to God's."

Clapp glared at me again. "This is none of your concern, *Englischer*."

"Yes, it is. Even if Charlotte wanted to go with you, which she clearly doesn't, she can't leave."

"And why not?" her father asked.

"Because . . ." I trailed off, unsure how to tell these men that a member of their district had been found dead, shoved into the church organ, the same organ that they believed it was a sin for Charlotte to play. And how could I tell Charlotte's father that the victim was his sister-in-law? This all felt a little bit above my pay grade.

"Bailey is right; she can't leave," a strong male voice said from behind us on the church steps.

I turned. Aiden stood in the church doorway. Standing there, looking down at us, he sort of resembled Moses standing on Mount Sinai. However, he was wearing a blue sheriff's deputy's uniform instead of biblical robes.

Briefly Aiden met my eyes, but I couldn't read his expression. I wished I had the same talent of hiding my own feelings so easily, but they were always clearly written on my face. No one ever had to wonder how I felt about something. My *daadi* used to say this openness was a gift from God. Because of it, I would have an easier time connecting with others. I wasn't so sure of that. I thought it was something that put me at a disadvantage because others could see where I stood on something even before I knew myself.

"Why are the police here?" the deacon snapped. He looked behind him and seemed to see the ambulance, Sheriff's Department vehicles, and coroner's car for the first time. "What's going on?"

Sol's face turned very pale.

Charlotte covered her mouth as if to hold back a sob.

Little appeared in the doorway behind Aiden. He poked his head over Aiden's shoulder like a groundhog peeking out of his burrow. Aiden jerked away from him and stepped out of the doorway.

"Deputy Little," Aiden said, "take Miss Weaver inside and begin the questioning. I'll fill in Deacon Clapp and Mr. Weaver."

Charlotte shot her father a pleading look. He stared back at her as if his face was made from polished stone. There was no expression. I bit the inside of my lip. My father and I didn't always get along, that was for certain, but he had never looked at me with so much unconcern. If he ever had, it would have broken my heart. From the look on Charlotte's face, it broke hers.

Chapter 6

Charlotte and Deputy Little disappeared back inside the church, and I found myself studying Deacon Clapp and Sol Weaver. The deacon looked defiantly at Aiden while Sol fidgeted with the brim of his felt hat in his calloused hands. What had caused these men to be so harsh? There had to be a reason.

"You owe me an explanation, Deputy," Clapp said. "You have no power over that girl. Her father and I are the ones who should be directing her where to go and what to do."

His statement immediately put my teeth on edge, and I was grateful for the hundredth time since I'd moved to Holmes County that I wasn't Amish. As much as I loved and respected my grandmother and the peace that her community gave her, I could never live under so much restriction. I would have felt strangled. I had a feeling that was how Charlotte felt right now.

Aiden glanced at me. "Bailey, we need some privacy."

I blinked. "Oh, of course. I'm sorry."

He nodded and turned to the two men. "Let's talk by your buggy, where we won't be overheard."

Without a backward glance at me, the three men walked to the far side of the polished black buggy out of my line of sight.

A horn honked and shook me out of my daze. I turned and found the front end of a hearse just a few feet away from me. I stumbled out of the way in the direction of the buggy. Beside the hearse, an ambulance pulled up in front of the church, forcing me closer to the buggy. Three EMTs hopped out of the ambulance and jogged up the church steps into the building with military precision.

A third vehicle came, and this was another Sheriff's Department car. SHERIFF was emblazoned on the side of the vehicle. Without a thought in my head, I ran around the side of the buggy. The last person on earth that I wanted to see again was Sheriff Jack Marshall. He and I had not gotten off on the right foot when I'd met him in September.

The sheriff climbed out of his SUV and readjusted his belt as he surveyed the parking lot.

I ducked behind the buggy to avoid being seen.

"What is this all about?" Clapp was asking in a sharp voice on the other side of the buggy.

I peeked around the side and spied Aiden, the deacon, and Charlotte's father standing in a tight circle at the edge of the parking lot about twelve feet from where I was hiding from the sheriff. I grimaced. I knew that I should not be overhearing this conversation. I looked over my shoulder. Sheriff Marshall was still standing by his SUV. I was stuck unless I wanted to reveal my location to one of them, which I did not.

Aiden looked from the deacon to Sol and back again. "I'm sorry to tell you, but the body of an Amish woman was discovered in the church earlier today."

"Someone has died?" Sol asked.

Aiden nodded. "I'm afraid so."

"Who?" Sol's voice was hoarse.

"It is your sister-in-law, Josephine Weaver," Aiden said. "I'm very sorry."

Sol's face grew even paler. I didn't know how that was possible. The man was already as white as bleached coral.

"Sol, are you all right?" Aiden asked, leaning toward the other man.

"How did she die?" Sol asked. "What happened?"

"We aren't certain yet. The coroner will have to make that determination," Aiden said and then turned to the deacon. "When was the last time you saw Josephine Weaver?"

The deacon scowled. "Why are you asking me this? What does it matter when the last time I saw her was?"

Aiden hooked one thumb over his duty belt, and the gun holstered there shifted ever so slightly. I don't know if he did that on purpose, but to me, it felt intentional.

Aiden nodded at Deacon Clapp. "You're the deacon of her district, are you not? Just as you like to know where Charlotte Weaver is, I assume that you keep tabs on her aunt and all the members of your church?"

The deacon straightened his shoulders. "I do, but I can't tell you the last time I saw Josephine. My best guess would be that I saw her two weeks ago at our last Sunday morning service. She is always there."

"Did you speak to her that day?" Aiden asked.

"*Nee*," Clapp said as if he was biting down on something hard.

Aiden turned to Sol. "And when was the last time you saw your sister-in-law?"

He frowned. "She stopped by the buggy shop yesterday afternoon."

Aiden's eyebrows went up. "The buggy shop?"

"Weaver Buggy Company. It is on State Route 39. It is my family business. Josephine stops in often to talk to me."

Aiden's eyebrows went even higher. "And why is that?"

Sol clenched his jaw. "Because I'm the head of the family, and if she has concerns, she must discuss them with me. That is our way."

"Did Josephine have concerns?" Aiden asked.

"Josephine always had concerns," Sol said. "She liked to have her hand in many things. Some of which had nothing to do with her."

"And did she express any concerns this last visit?"

Sol winced as if he regretted telling Aiden about the concerns part. He didn't answer.

Aiden shifted his hand on his belt again. "Sol, please answer my question."

Sol glanced at the deacon, and the deacon gave him a slight nod as if granting some type of permission. "She was concerned about Charlotte. She felt, as the rest of the family does, that Charlotte should not play the organ in the *Englisch* church."

"Did Josephine feel more strongly about this than the rest of you?"

"We have all been upset about it, but *ya*, my sister-in-law has been the most outspoken of all."

"And how did she seem yesterday afternoon?" Aiden asked.

"Seem? What do you mean?" Sol's red eyebrows came together.

"Was she upset?" Aiden rephrased his question.

Sol nodded. "She was upset. My sister-in-law was always upset. It was her way."

"Josephine Weaver is a busybody," Clapp interjected. "She always has been. She had no place addressing Charlotte's behavior. It's up to Sol and me to deal with Charlotte, not her aunt."

Aiden shifted his weight. "Can you give me another example of how she may have been a busybody? Was she upset by the behavior of others in your district besides Charlotte?"

"She wasn't happy that an *Englischer* was participating in the Amish Confectionery Competition," Sol said. "She also complained to me about that and said she planned to get the *Englischer* removed."

I winced. I knew that Josephine had been talking about me, and I was certain that Aiden knew it too. There went all my hopes of not being a suspect in this murder investigation.

Aiden turned to the deacon. "As her deacon,

did Josephine speak to you about Charlotte or anyone else?"

"*Nee.*" The deacon folded his arms. "I don't have anything else to say. Of course, I am sorry that Josephine is dead. We mourn when any person in our community passes. We mourn when any of *Gotte's* children are lost. The funeral will give use closure."

"I understand that, but I have an investigation to conduct." Aiden folded his arms.

"Why? What investigation?" the deacon snapped.

Aiden shaded his eyes from the sun, which was now high in the sky. "Deacon Clapp, Josephine's body was discovered inside the organ of this church. It is impossible for me to believe that she died inside the organ by her own choice."

Sol gasped, but the deacon gave no visible sign of surprise. He simply shook his head. "I never expected Charlotte to take her determination to play the organ so far."

It was my turn to gasp. I was surprised that the deacon was ready to name one of his own as a possible killer. He might as well have put her head on a silver platter for Aiden with a sign proclaiming her guilt.

"Deacon," Sol began, "I cannot believe that my daughter would do such a thing."

"Then who else would? Who else could have been in that church with her?" the deacon wanted to know.

Sol clamped his mouth shut, and despite the October chill in the air, beads of sweat popped up on his forehead.

Aiden cocked his head. "And how would a girl of Charlotte's size put her aunt inside the organ?"

Clapp pulled on his beard. "She had help then. It could have been from any number of the *Englischers* that she was fraternizing with here."

"You seem to be surprisingly eager to pin Josephine's death on a member of your own church district," Aiden said.

"Charlotte is barely a member of my district any longer. All signs point to her leaving the church. It is always easy to pick out those on *rumspringa* who are tempted by the world and cannot follow the Amish way. She has been one of those from the start."

"Deacon," Sol wiped at his sweaty face with a handkerchief, "I told you my daughter is confused, but I'm certain that she will make the right decision and stay with the Amish."

Clapp snorted. "She is rebellious. That is your fault, Sol."

The other man jerked back as if the deacon had slapped him.

Charlotte's sweet face came to mind. She didn't strike me as the rebellious type. Or the murdering type, for that matter.

Aiden opened his mouth as if he wanted to say something in return, but he was stopped when someone called out his name.

I spun around in my hiding spot. Deputy Little skipped down the church steps holding a small plastic bag in his hand. The sheriff was nowhere to be seen, but his SUV was still there.

"Deputy Brody! Deputy Brody!" He waved the bag over his head. There was something inside, but whatever it was, the object was far too small for me to identify from where I hid behind the buggy. I wanted to know what was in that baggie.

Aiden hurried over to the younger officer and gently reprimanded him. "Little, let's not wave the evidence out in the open for all to see, okay?'

The younger deputy's face fell. "I—I'm sorry. I thought you'd want to know right away."

Aiden patted him on the shoulder. "And I do, but I'm in the middle of an interview. Next time, call me on the radio to ask me to come inside to review the evidence."

Little looked from the deacon to Aiden and back again. "Oh, right. I'm sorry, sir." He fished a handkerchief out of his pocket and wiped his brow. I expected to see this gesture in Sol, an Amish man, but I was surprised to see Little use a handkerchief. It seemed like such an old-fashioned accessory for someone so young. He shoved the handkerchief back into the hip pocket of his uniform.

"Why would you be calling licorice evidence?" the deacon asked.

Licorice? My ears immediately perked up at the word.

"Little, take the evidence back inside the church," Aiden directed.

"There is no use hiding it now," the deacon huffed. "I saw the licorice in that bag as plain as day. Is that what killed Josephine?"

Aiden's head snapped around. "Why would you ask that?"

"Because everyone in the district knew that Josephine was allergic to licorice, more specifically anise. She made a point of letting everyone know, so that they wouldn't include anise in their baking recipes. She was very particular. At times, she refused to eat desserts that were offered because she was afraid they might include the smallest drop of anise. She offended many ladies in our church by refusing their desserts. There is no greater insult to an Amish woman than someone refusing to eat the food that she has prepared."

"Then how can she be in the competition?" Aiden asked, sounding as confused as I felt. "I thought licorice was one of the categories."

"You mean for the confectionery competition? Her shop assistant must have made the licorice; perhaps her assistant even made it at home. I don't think she would allow anise in her building. She was that allergic to it."

"And who is her shop assistant?" Aiden asked.

I was grateful that he was asking all the questions that were coming to my mind.

"Lindy Beiler," the deacon said. "She and Charlotte were friends, but she has already joined the church and married. She's followed the path that we like to see all our young members take."

"Where did you find that?" Clapp pointed at Little, who was still holding the bag of licorice out for all to see.

Little rocked back and forth on his heels and looked to Aiden for guidance.

Aiden sighed. "Where did you find the licorice, Deputy Little?"

He swallowed, and his Adam's apple bobbed up and down. "It was in her apron pocket, sir."

"That's impossible. She would never carry licorice in her pocket," Sol said. "She absolutely would never do that."

Clapp nodded. "As I just told you, she was deathly allergic to it."

Deathly allergic. Had the licorice killed Josephine, and if it did, was it possible that this wasn't a murder at all but a tragic and accidental allergic reaction? I suspected that was just wishful thinking on my part, especially when the image of Josephine lying on the platform inside the organ came to mind. I remembered how red, swollen, and cracked her lips were. They'd reminded me of the lips of someone with a serious fever.

Suddenly, the wheel of the buggy that I was hiding behind shifted. The horse pulled the buggy away from me. As my presence was revealed to everyone, I found Aiden staring at me with his hands on his hips but, if I wasn't completely mistaken, with a twinkle in his eye.

Chapter 7

"Well, well, Bailey King, what on earth are you doing right here?" Aiden asked. The dimple in his cheek appeared. The dimple didn't help me in the least.

"I—I—" No good answer came to mind. It was obvious that what I was doing was eavesdropping.

Clapp folded his arms over his chest. "What do you think you are doing, *Englischer*? You have no right to listen to our conversation."

I bristled at his tone. Yes, I knew that I shouldn't have been listening in on their conversation. That was wrong no matter how I rationalized it, but the tone of his voice was full of judgment, as if I had committed some sort of mortal sin and not just made a mistake. The mistake of getting caught. I knew I would do it again if the same circumstances arose.

"Deacon," Aiden said, "I'm sure Miss King just made an error in judgment."

The deacon snorted. "If you believe that, Deputy,

you are much more naïve than I thought. The King girl has a reputation."

"The King girl?" I asked.

Clapp narrowed his eyes. "I have heard the stories about how you tried to earn a promotion in New York by having *relations* with one of the board members. I would never have a woman like you in my community."

I felt sickened by his implication. I knew that was how my disastrous relationship with Eric Sharp had appeared to many in the New York culinary scene. They assumed the same as the deacon had. That was one of the reasons Eric and I had kept our relationship secret for so long. However, there was nothing tawdry about our relationship. I was a grown woman, and Eric was a grown man. We both knew what we were doing, and I had never asked for preferential treatment from him. "How dare you?" I took a step toward the deacon.

There must have been some type of warning on my face, because he took a small step back, but then held his ground. "How dare I? I'm not the one barging into a community that isn't mine and trying to corrupt its youth."

"Who am I corrupting?" I wanted to know.

"Charlotte Weaver, for a start," Clapp spat back at me.

I threw up my hands. "I only just met the girl. I know nothing about her or what she is thinking about the rest of her life."

The deacon looked as if he wanted to argue. I could tell that he didn't believe me. "Would you say the same about Josephine?"

"I must return to the shop," Sol called from the

buggy's driver's seat. "I have been away from it for far too long. There is no more that we can accomplish here. Charlotte will not come with us."

Clapp nodded. "Very well."

"Wait," I said. "What do I have to do with what's happened to Josephine?"

"I know that you're not Amish, but weaseled your way into the ACC. You learned your trickery in New York and have brought it into my community. I will not allow it." His eyes bored into me. There was so much anger there that it startled me, and despite myself, I took a small step away from him and his hatred.

I glanced at Aiden. He watched me with renewed interest, but it wasn't the kind of interest I wanted from him. I had seen that expression before. He looked at me the way he would at a suspect.

"We need to remain calm," Aiden said.

"I am calm," the deacon and I replied in unison; then we glared at each other.

"Jinx," Little piped up.

The deacon and I both must have given him an identical scowl, because he clutched the evidence bag of licorice to his chest. "Well, you both said the same thing at the same time, so jinx . . ."

"Uh-huh," Aiden said, ignoring the younger deputy's comment. "It looks like the two of you are calm."

"I don't have to stand here and listen to this," Clapp declared. He grabbed the handrail and climbed into the buggy next to Sol. "I trust that you will notify our district of your investigation, Deputy, as it goes on."

"I will," Aiden agreed.

"Let's go, Sol. We will deal with your daughter later."

Sol Weaver simply nodded and flicked the reins. The buggy rocked forward into motion. Aiden, Little, and I watched the dust settle back into the gravel parking lot.

Aiden finally spoke. "Do you know how dangerous it is to stand beside a buggy like that? If the horse had moved just a fraction, the buggy's wheels might have rolled over your foot—or worse. I can't tell you how many accident reports are filed that are related to buggy injury. And you shouldn't be eavesdropping."

I folded my arms. "I didn't mean to eavesdrop. I was—" I stopped myself. I couldn't very well tell him that I was hiding from the sheriff.

He removed his department-issued ball cap from the top of his head and folded the brim. "And I don't want you poking your nose into this investigation. Not again. I'm telling you this for your own safety."

I bristled. "If I remember correctly, the last time a person was murdered in Harvest, I *had* to get involved for my own safety."

Aiden sighed, because we both knew that this was true.

He turned to his deputy. "Little, please go back inside."

"Will do, Deputy Brody, but I also have to tell you that the sheriff is here."

Aiden grimaced. The expression lasted only half a second, but it was unmistakable.

"He wants to talk to you," Little said. As he spoke, the evidence bag swung from his hand. I caught sight of the piece of licorice inside. I could have been mistaken, but I believed that I spotted a double S inscribed in it. I prayed that I was imagining things, that I was confused by the stressful events of the last hour. It couldn't be what I thought it was. It just couldn't be.

"Can you go inside and tell him that I will be in as soon as possible?" Aiden asked.

Little nodded, wove around all the vehicles blocking the way to the church steps, and ran inside.

After his junior deputy was gone, Aiden sighed again. "Bailey, you have to trust me to protect you instead of doing things on your own."

"You will protect me from Sheriff Marshall? You will protect Charlotte from the sheriff? You know he will want to blame one of us for this murder because he hates me and she's Amish, and by accusing one of us, he can make this all go away faster. I'm sure that the last thing he wants is another murder to contend with going into his reelection, even if that election is uncontested."

Aiden continued to bend the brim of his hat. "Yes, I will protect you both, and anyone else who might be falsely accused. Bailey, I do wish you could trust me. Not all men are the same. I think you need to remember that."

I blinked. How had this conversation shifted from the sheriff to all men? How had this conversation shifted from the sheriff *to Eric?* I knew that was the point he was trying to make. Not all men cheated like Eric. Not all men made their girlfriends feel inferior like Eric. I swallowed, unable to speak.

"And what is your relationship with Charlotte Weaver?" Aiden asked.

I blinked at him, surprised by the way he could change the subject so easily from my personal life to murder. I cleared my throat. My mouth felt suddenly dry. "What I said to Deacon Clapp was true. I just met her today, but apparently she's my cousin."

Aiden raised his dark eyebrows into his hairline. "Your cousin?"

"She claimed to be my grandmother's cousin, so she must be mine as well." I wrinkled my nose. "I suppose that means I'm related to Sol Weaver too, and maybe even Josephine."

"I didn't know your grandmother had cousins."

I shrugged. "Neither did I."

Aiden's dark eyebrows disappeared into his hairline again. His hair hung low over his forehead. He could use a trim. But I would admit, although only to myself, that his unkempt hair was appealing. Most of the time his thick, dark hair was hidden away under his baseball cap, which was truly a shame. "You two looked like you knew each other well when you were standing on the church steps."

I shrugged. "I was comforting a girl who just found her dead aunt in an organ. I don't think a prior relationship is necessary for that. She needed a shoulder to cry on. Mine was available."

He nodded. "You get that compassionate heart from your grandparents."

I smiled, and not for the first time, I felt my heart softening toward Aiden. I just wasn't sure my heart was ready to soften quite yet. Time to change the subject. "Was she really killed with licorice?" I asked.

"How long did you look at the body?" he countered with a question.

"I just peeked. Your mother and I had no idea what Charlotte was screaming about, so I went into the organ to see if she was all right. I never expected to find a dead person on the other side of that door. Never."

He brushed back his hair from his face and replaced the ball cap on his head. "Of course, you didn't, and I am glad you and Mom were there to help Charlotte. However, this should be the end of it for you. You need to leave this alone. Can you do that for me?"

"Bailey! Bailey!" a voice called from behind me.

I spun around to see Emily Esh running toward me. The ribbons from her white prayer cap were flying behind her. "Bailey! You have to come. Now. They are one table away from yours in the licorice judging. If you're not there, the shop will be disqualified."

I hesitated and looked back at the church. "I—"

The deputy shook his head. "Go. I know where to find you."

I glanced back at the church again. "What about Charlotte . . ." I trailed off.

"I'll take good care of Charlotte. I promise you." He sounded so sincere that I couldn't help but believe him. "If I know anything about you, I know we'll discuss this more soon."

"Bailey, you have to come!" Emily cried, becoming increasingly more frantic.

That got me moving. I cared about Juliet and wanted to know what had happened to her pig, and even though I had just met her, I was concerned about Charlotte and those harsh men who'd tried to fetch her from the church. It didn't seem that she had the support at home that she would need to deal with the trauma of finding a dead body. And not just any dead body, but the body of her aunt. What was worse, she—if Clapp had anything to say about it—would be blamed for her aunt's death.

"I'll see you later, Aiden."

The dimple flashed again. "I'm counting on it, Bailey."

I spun away to contemplate what that might mean. Emily waved at me, and I ran to her, refusing to look back at Aiden as I went, no matter how much I was tempted to. As I ran away, I felt his dark eyes, the color of milk chocolate, boring into my back.

Chapter 8

As Emily had said, Margot Rawlings and the two Amish judges were just one table away from mine when I reached my spot on the square. Emily and I jumped behind the table together. The pretty Amish girl's cheeks were flushed pink after her sprint from the church, and a single blond-white lock fell from the knot at the base of her neck and curled over her flawless brow. She grabbed the wild strands and then expertly twisted them back into her bun.

At twenty years old, Emily Esh even made running across the square look graceful. She mesmerized the young men, both English and Amish, who wandered the square sampling the candies.

I, on the other hand, was panting from the run. I told myself it was because I was still in shock over the discovery of Josephine Weaver's body, not because I was terribly out of shape. I had run after taxis and for the subway enough times during my life in New York that a simple jog across the village square shouldn't have winded me.

Standing at the table next to ours, a round Amish woman wearing glasses held a piece of licorice out in front of her and stared at it as if the candy held the answers to the universe. "There's something not quite right about this piece of licorice."

"I agree, Beatrice," Jeremiah said. "There's a grainy quality to it, as if all the sugar hasn't mingled with the other ingredients as it should."

Haddie Smucker, the maker of the offending licorice, looked as if she might faint. Her Lakeside Amish Treats up in Geauga County was a candy shop I'd heard of even before I moved to Ohio. She had placed ads in national candy magazines, advertising it as the best place to purchase Amish candy and sweets. When I saw the ad, I cut it from the magazine and mailed it to my grandfather with a note, urging him to also place ads like hers. The letter he sent back to me was typical Jebidiah King. He said God didn't teach him to beg others to buy his candies, just to make the best sweets he could.

I stared down at the plate of licorice I had set aside for the judges to sample. Because I'd gone on the wild pig chase and then found a dead body, I hadn't had time to taste it before the judging. What if my licorice was grainy? Licorice was one of the most challenging candies to make, because the consistency needed to be both gummy and smooth in texture.

"Your licorice is not grainy," Emily whispered into my ear as if she'd read my mind.

I shot her a sideways look. "*Danki*," I said, using the Amish word for "thank you."

She smiled. "I swiped a piece while you were off searching for Juliet's pig."

"How did you know that was where I was?" I whispered. "I didn't get a chance to tell you, and I never expected to be gone so long."

"Abel told me."

I tried to keep a neutral expression. Abel was Emily's older brother and a few years older than I was. When we were children, he'd tried to kiss me once. I managed to dodge his attempt, but it seemed that he'd never forgiven me for the slight, even though seventeen years had passed. I hadn't known that Abel was on the square that morning or keeping tabs on me. That didn't sit well with me. "What's Abel doing at the ACC?"

She glanced at me. "Margot hired him to set up the tables and do general maintenance."

This surprised me. I wasn't exactly sure what Abel did for his family. Esther worked day and night at the pretzel shop, and so did Emily. As far as I could tell, Abel floated in and out of the shop at his leisure. It was always possible he had another business, but I knew they didn't have a working farm. The family raised just enough produce to feed themselves.

"I swiped three pieces of your licorice while I was waiting for you. When I'm nervous, I get hungry. Your licorice is the best I ever tasted. I would have eaten even more, but I had to leave some for the judges and visitors."

"You were doing quality control?" I grinned at her.

"Quality control?" she asked.

I chuckled. "Don't worry about it. I'm glad you did." I felt my body relax. At least grainy licorice was one thing I didn't have to worry about. That was lucky since I was already dealing with a missing pig and poor Josephine. I frowned as the dead woman came to mind again.

"Did you ever find Jethro?" Emily whispered. "Were all those police outside the church helping you look for him?"

I simply shook my head. The judges were headed our way, and there was no time to talk. I stood up straighter and plastered a friendly smile on my face. Out of the corner of my eye, I saw that Emily did the same. Her mimicking my pose brought a genuine smile to my face.

Beatrice addressed Emily, "Please tell us about your licorice."

Emily took a step back. "It's not mine. I'm just helping."

Beatrice squinted at her. "What do you mean it's not yours? Isn't this your booth? Whose is it?"

Emily pointed at me. "Bailey's. This is Bailey's booth."

Beatrice stared at me openmouthed. "But—but," she stammered, "you're not Amish!"

I looked down at my outfit again. Nope, still not Amish, not even close. "Swissmen Sweets, which belongs to my family, is an Amish candy shop." I pointed across the street. "It's right over there, if you want to verify."

She flipped through her clipboard. "I see Swissmen Sweets listed here, but Jebidiah King is the person who should be here."

"I'm Bailey King. Jebidiah King was my grandfather. He passed away recently, and I took his spot."

"You're runaway Amish then." Beatrice frowned.

Jeremiah cleared his throat. "Beatrice, I'm sorry. It seems that Margot has neglected to tell you about the exception we made." He shot a glance at Margot, who shrugged.

"I see." Beatrice pressed her lips together. I had a sneaking suspicion that she would not be a fan of my licorice.

"I agree," Haddie of the grainy licorice agreed. "This should be an Amish-only competition."

"You sound like Josephine," Margot said.

I swallowed. That was the moment I realized that none of them knew. Not a single person there knew that Josephine Weaver lay dead in the church just across the street from the square.

"Haddie, please," Jeremiah said. "This doesn't concern you."

The Amish woman scowled and started packing up what was left of her licorice. Apparently, after the judges had said that it was grainy, she wasn't planning on leaving the remainder out for the tourists to sample.

Margot waved her hand. "We have already been over this once today. There is no reason to beat a dead horse."

I winced at her turn of phrase.

Margot sniffed. "Bailey's participation in the competition was approved well over a week ago. Beatrice, I told you that one of the contestants had passed and that his granddaughter would be taking his place."

Beatrice shook her finger at Margot. "But you never said the replacement was *Englisch*. How can we call ourselves an *Amish* Confectionery Competition when not everyone in the competition is Amish?"

I looked heavenward. Here we go again.

"The candy shops are all Amish," Margot said smoothly. "And Bailey knows how to make all the candies in the Amish tradition. That's what is important. We all want to do the same thing here. We want to showcase Amish confectionaries, and Swissmen Sweets is one of the most popular Amish confectionaries in all of Holmes County, if not in the entire country."

Beatrice folded her arms around her clipboard and hugged it to her chest. "That's the real reason she's here, isn't it? You let her into the competition because her shop is in Harvest."

Margot pursed her lips but didn't outright deny the accusation.

"I see." Beatrice narrowed her eyes.

Jeremiah shifted his ample weight from foot to foot. "Beatrice, what's done is done. We can't go back on the promise we made to Swissmen Sweets about competing, not now."

Beatrice peered at me over her clipboard. "No, I suppose we cannot, but I am not surprised by the fact that Josephine and the other candy makers are upset by the exception you made, Margot—a very self-serving exception, I might add. You know Josephine Weaver would rather die than lose to an *Englischer*. She won't let this go."

I grimaced. Truer words had never been spoken, but Beatrice didn't know that. I fought the urge to tell them everything that had happened. I knew Aiden would not want me to. He would want to be the one to tell them all about Josephine's death, so that he could witness their reactions to his announcement. It took a little bit of effort, but I held my tongue.

"I don't expect Josephine to let it go," Margot said. "But it will not do to disqualify a candy shop because of a family emergency. That doesn't seem like a very *Amish* gesture to me."

Beatrice pursed her lips. "Very well." She shot a glance at Margot, then turned to me. "I'm Beatrice Mueller, and like Jeremiah, I'm an ACC judge. Since it seems you have already been accepted into the competition, we have no choice but to honor that decision."

"As an important figure in the hosting village of the Amish Confectionery Competition," Margot said, "I'm also a judge."

"We're aware of that." Beatrice sniffed before turning to me again. "Please know we will give you no special treatment because you are *Englisch*. You will be judged as strictly as all the Amish contestants."

I folded my hands in front of me, doing my best to look demure. It wasn't a look I came by naturally, nor did it go with my feather earrings. "I wouldn't expect anything else. In fact, I wouldn't want the competition to be anything but a fair and honest contest that showcases the very best in Amish candy making. That's what my grandfather would have wanted as well."

Beside me, Emily shifted from foot to foot. I knew she was just as anxious as I was to get on with the judging. I couldn't help but glance at the church again. Everything at the ACC was going on, business as usual, but a woman was dead. I wondered how long the usual activity would continue before that death disturbed it.

"We are very happy to hear that." Beatrice pointed

to the small plate of licorice squares on my table. Each square was stamped with a double S, the logo of Swissmen Sweets. The two cursive capital S's overlapped each other. I had created the logo years ago for my grandfather when I was taking a graphic design class. I thought it would be helpful to understand some elements of design for the times I was required to create intricate chocolate sculptures for JP Chocolates. My grandfather had never used the logo. Branding wasn't his priority. However, slowly, as I had been adding new candies to the shop, I had begun using the logo. My grandmother was resistant at first, but I told her that brand recognition was important, even Amish brand recognition.

"Is that the sample for the judging?" Beatrice asked.

I nodded. "It is. Please enjoy."

Beatrice held one thumb-size piece an inch from her nose and examined it as if it was a bug under a microscope. "How did you make these letters on the candies? In this competition, we accept only Amish candy-making techniques. We know the *Englisch* have many machines and electronic gadgets to do the hard work of candy making. We do not allow shortcuts in this competition."

"It's a metal hand stamp," I said. "It cuts the logo into the candy."

She nodded. Apparently, that answer was acceptable.

"It adds a nice touch to the presentation," Margot said.

Jeremiah put a piece of my licorice in his mouth and savored it. He rolled it around on his tongue as if he was testing it. I suppressed a shudder as my mind traveled back to the sight of Josephine's body inside the organ. Was that what it had been like for Josephine? Had she voluntarily put a piece of licorice in her mouth? Why would she do that when she knew what it would do to her?

"It's not grainy," Beatrice said with an air of disappointment.

"No," Jeremiah agreed. "The texture is quite pleasant."

Despite myself, I glanced over at Haddie, who had received the "grainy" criticism. She glared back at me. I was earning a good number of glares today, I thought.

Margot also tasted the licorice. "Licorice is not my favorite, but you make it almost palatable." She picked up a second piece. "I might even have another piece."

Despite myself, I raised my eyebrows, surprised by the compliment. "Thank you."

The three judges made notes on their clipboards, and I couldn't help but notice that Beatrice also grabbed a second piece of my licorice before she moved on to the next table.

When they were out of earshot, I said to Emily, "Beatrice isn't going to be eager to crown a non-Amish winner."

"She can't withhold her vote for that reason," she whispered back. "Swissmen Sweets has the very best candy, and you are doing everything by the rules. You're bound to win. The judges will be fair and make the decisions about who wins each round and the overall competition based on the best candy. That's all they will consider."

She was so naïve, but I thought it was better that

I not burst her bubble. Emily had not had an easy life, but somehow, she still was able to keep a cheerful and optimistic outlook. I wasn't going to be the one to spoil that for her.

But I was far more cynical. Emily hadn't lived in New York for the last six years and witnessed every kind of swindle that could be attempted against a person trying to run a business. The Upper East Side mothers were the worst.

I glanced over at the church. The parking lot was on the far side of the building, so the police cruisers and hearse were hidden from view. I was itching to get back over there to see what was going on.

"Bailey, should we start on the taffy while we wait for the results?" Emily asked.

The taffy. I'd forgotten. No matter what had happened at the church, I was still in the middle of a candy-making contest. I was torn, and then there was also the fact that Jethro was still MIA.

Before I could decide what to do, Margot floated back to my table, clipboard in hand. "That was a close call, Bailey. You almost got yourself booted out of the competition."

I pointed at myself. "I almost got myself booted out? I didn't realize so many would be so upset that I wasn't Amish. You might have warned me that my non-Amishness might be an issue with the other judges and competitors."

"You should have known it would be an issue. This is the *Amish* Confectionery Competition. The Amish are proud people."

I stopped just short of rolling my eyes. "I know that, but you could have warned me about people's reactions. I didn't know they would be so strong."

She laughed. "Welcome to Holmes County. Everyone has a strong opinion here, especially the Amish. You should have recognized that and been more prepared."

"Prepared for what? And how?" I asked.

She folded her arms across her chest. "Would it kill you to wear a plain dress during the competition? Throw on one of your grandmother's dresses and a prayer cap. No one would know the difference."

Beside me I felt Emily stiffen. The movement was slight, but I felt it.

I scowled at Margot. It was hard to believe that this woman had lived in Holmes County for so long and still had no respect for the Amish who lived there. To her, they just brought in the tourists. "I won't masquerade as an Amish person. I could never do that."

She sniffed. "Then you have no hope of winning this candy-making contest. Beatrice may not kick you out of the competition, but there is no way she will hand the victory to an *Englischer*." She sighed. "I suppose it wouldn't do you much good to throw on an Amish dress now. You've already blown it. For heaven's sake, feather earrings! Why don't you just wear a sign that says you're a hippy."

"I don't think feather earrings are limited to hippies," I commented. "If I win, I want to win because Swissmen Sweets has the best Amish candy, not because of my standing in the Amish community. I don't see why there has to be any kind of distinction."

Margot gave a laugh that was just short of bitter-sounding. "You really don't know where you live, do you? There's always a distinction here in Holmes County between the Amish and the non-Amish. You may think you've crossed that line and are accepted in both communities because of your grandmother, but not every Amish person in this county will accept you—or your family, for that matter—because you are not Amish."

I opened my mouth to protest again, and she held up her hand to stop me. "Believe me, Bailey, I would like you to win much more than you could ever wish to win yourself. If Swissmen Sweets brought home the Amish Confectionery Competition, it could put Harvest on the map as a top Amish Country destination. Tourists would come by the busloads."

"But tourists already come here," I protested.

"Of course they do, but it's not near the hordes that go to Berlin or Sugarcreek, and don't even get me started on Lancaster County. That place has it made. We have no hope of ever getting that big. Our Amish communities aren't as large, but we can do better with what we have. That's where Swissmen Sweets comes in."

"You hosted the competition here purely to increase tourism?" I asked.

She sniffed. "Yes, that's my job as the village chairwoman. What other reason would I have? There must be viable financial gain. I would think a sophisticated woman from New York City, such as yourself, would understand that."

I did understand the desire to get ahead all too well, and from painful personal experience. I had hoped that it would be different in Amish Country, but apparently, the need to be number one wasn't any different in Harvest, Ohio, than it was in Manhattan.

However, over Margot's shoulder, I saw something much more troublesome than her ambitions for the village. Deputy Aiden Brody and a crime scene tech strode across the square in the direction of the candy-making competition. I knew from the many times that Aiden had popped into Swissmen Sweets since I'd moved to the town that he had a terrible sweet tooth. As of yet, I hadn't been able to find a candy he didn't like. But I knew his approach had nothing to do with candy. Aiden and the tech walked with purpose and were headed straight for my table.

Across the square, Aiden locked eyes with me for the briefest of seconds before moving his gaze to zero in on Margot's back.

With a knot in my stomach, I remembered the piece of licorice with the double S inscribed on it sitting at the bottom of the evidence bag that Deputy Little had handed to Aiden outside the church less than an hour ago. I prayed that I had imagined that double S, that my mind had been playing some kind of trick on me due to the stress of the day. The problem was that my mind didn't play those kinds of tricks.

Margot wrinkled her nose. "What could Aiden Brody possibly want now?"

I opened my mouth to answer but shut it. It was best if Margot heard about the body in the organ directly from the police.

Aiden was only a few feet from us now. "Margot, I would like a moment of your time."

"Deputy Brody," she said, "I'm in the middle of

judging a candy-making competition. Whatever you have to say to me will have to wait until the licorice round is over."

Aiden's brow shot up when she said "licorice." I was tempted to hide my plate of licorice pieces under my competition table.

"All of the competitors have licorice?" he asked, and his chocolate-colored eyes scanned up and down the line of candy makers. I took a step back, but I knew it was pointless. Aiden already knew I was there.

Margot threw up her hands. "Of course, they do. That's the first round of the competition. All fifteen contestants have to make a licorice candy."

Aiden blew out a breath as he removed his Sheriff's Department ball cap. As he did, his eyes fell on my table behind Margot and focused on the plate of licorice pieces sitting there. His eyes narrowed.

I had a sneaking suspicion I had in fact seen a double S on the piece of licorice discovered in Josephine's apron pocket. I hadn't imagined it at all.

Chapter 9

I inwardly groaned. I knew I should have hidden the candies or at least thrown a napkin over the plate. Aiden would have discovered the candy was mine eventually, but I would have been much better off if I'd had more time to figure out how one of my candies ended up in Josephine's apron pocket.

Aiden locked eyes with me, but his expression was unreadable. He replaced his hat on his head and turned back to Margot. "I'm sorry, Margot, but it looks like we should stop the judging for a moment."

The town chairwoman jabbed her fists into her hips. "Aiden Brody, will I have to call the sheriff on you?"

Aiden grimaced, and I found myself wincing. Being reported to the sheriff was the last thing Aiden would want to happen.

Aiden cleared his throat. "There has been an incident at the church."

"The church?" Margot cried. "Then it would have

nothing to do with the ACC. Go tell Reverend Brook about it and leave us alone."

"We have spoken to the reverend, but we also need to speak with everyone who was on the square during the morning. That includes the people in your contest."

"What has happened that is important enough to interrupt the judging? You must give me a much better reason than saying there's an 'incident.' Is this about your mother's pig? I heard about the creature running off."

"This doesn't have anything to do with my mother," Aiden said calmly.

By this point, their conversation had garnered the attention of the two Amish judges and most of the contestants, who were inching forward as if to overhear what Aiden and Margot were discussing.

If I had thought that the Amish weren't interested in gossip, seeing them close in on Margot and Aiden like a pack of hungry wolves would have changed my mind in an instant.

Aiden noticed the crowd gathering too. "Margot, let's talk over here in private." He nodded to the gazebo.

She scowled and stood there for a moment as if she was considering his suggestion. Finally, after what seemed like a purposely long beat, she followed him to the other side of the gazebo.

The two Amish judges and the contestants went back to their tables with an air of disappointment. I wasn't so easily discouraged. I slid around the side of my table to follow them.

"Bailey, what about the taffy?" Emily asked.

I held up my finger to her, indicating that I

needed just one minute. The crime scene tech didn't seem to notice when I strolled by him on my way to the gazebo. He was too busy fidgeting with the radio attached to his belt.

I wove through a group of tourists who were walking around with plates of licorice samples. Several of them had samples from my table, and I realized that Josephine could have gotten a piece of my licorice from just about anyone on the square that day. I didn't know if I found that discouraging or comforting.

The crowd thinned as I drew closer to the large white gazebo. I circled the structure and stopped when I spotted Margot and Aiden facing off just a few feet away from me. Aiden's back was to me. For that, I was grateful. I didn't want him to know I was there. He would only assume I was meddling in his investigation again. That wasn't what I was doing, at least not yet, but if my licorice was somehow connected to Josephine's death, I wanted to know about it. I realized that just an hour ago, I had accidently eavesdropped on Aiden's conversation. Now I was doing it intentionally. I doubted he would see the difference between the two instances if he found out.

"Josephine Weaver is dead!" Margot cried loud enough for everyone on the square to hear.

Behind me there was an audible gasp from the Amish candy makers as they heard her outburst. Although Josephine wasn't well liked—or at least she didn't appear to be liked among the other candy makers—she was still respected as having one of the most successful Amish candy shops in the country. The news of her death sent a ripple effect through the crowd. Even at the distance I stood away from them, I heard the whispers traveling through the group.

I looked behind me and scanned the faces of the candy makers, looking for anyone who didn't have the expected shocked reaction, anyone who had known that Josephine was dead before Margot's outburst. I didn't see any telltale signs. All the faces appeared equally shocked and alarmed at the news, or perhaps I had been too late in looking and had missed the telltale expression.

"How did she die?" Margot asked at a more normal volume.

"We believe it was related to her allergy to licorice," Aiden said.

"Licorice?" Margot gasped. "You think someone in the ACC had something to do with her death? You think one of us killed her?"

He ignored her question and asked, "Did you know of her anise allergy?"

Margot frowned. "Yes, I knew. She made a big stink about licorice being part of the competition. She thought it should be removed because of her allergy. However, the other judges and I agreed that it should stay in. Black licorice is a traditional Amish candy and had to be represented. We didn't remove peanut brittle from the competition for those who might have a nut allergy, which is far more common."

"And she made licorice to participate?" he asked.

She shook her head. "No, her assistant made the licorice and was there for the judging. That was the one exception we made for Josephine. We didn't require her to even be at her table when her shop's licorice was judged. Her assistant took her place for the licorice round."

I felt my eyebrows go up. This made sense to me. I had wondered why no one had asked where Josephine was during the judging when Emily had practically panicked because I'd almost missed the licorice judging myself.

"Lindy Beiler?" Aiden asked.

Margot nodded.

"What was Josephine's relationship with Lindy like?"

"Well, I—I don't know," Margot stammered.

"What was your relationship with Josephine like?" Aiden asked.

Margot shook her index finger at him. "What are trying to say, Deputy? That I might know something about what happened to Josephine? Is that what you are trying to get at?"

Aiden held up his hands in a sign of surrender. "I'm only trying to understand Josephine's place in the ACC. That's all." He paused and then asked, "Would there be anyone here at the competition who might have had a problem with her?"

Margot lowered her hand. "You mean enough of a problem to kill her? That's what you are really asking me, Deputy, is it not? Do you think one of my competitors was murdered with licorice?" She couldn't have asked the question any louder unless she'd shouted it.

"I think it might be better if you and I went to my cruiser to discuss this," Aiden said.

"Your cruiser? Are you arresting me? I am not getting into your car."

"I'm not arresting you," he said evenly. "But it

would be much better to have some privacy while we discuss what might have happened to Josephine. We could go to my car or speak in the church."

"I'm not going anywhere. I'm in the middle of judging, and I can't leave." She leaned toward him and pointed. From where I stood, it appeared that her index finger was just inches from his face.

"What's going on here?" a deep voice boomed across the square.

I turned to see Sheriff Jack Marshall lumbering across the grass. He was a large man; if he didn't tip the scale at three hundred pounds, it was close. His belly hung over his duty belt, and he had a rolling, bowlegged way of walking. Unlike Aiden, he didn't wear a departmental hat as part of his uniform. His hair was closely cropped to his head, military style.

Aiden turned around and saw the small crowd that had gathered behind him while he and Margot had been talking. I was certain he had taken in everyone who was there, but his eyes focused on me before he moved his gaze to the sheriff. He didn't look any more pleased to see his boss than I was.

"Brody, what's going on here?" Sheriff Marshall hooked his thumbs through the loops in his duty belt.

"Sheriff," Aiden began.

Before he could explain, Margot jumped in. "Your deputy is trying to shut down the Amish Confectionery Competition. He doesn't understand how important this competition is to the village and the entire county."

"I never said that," Aiden protested. "We do need to interrupt the competition for a few minutes to speak to potential witnesses."

Margot waggled her index finger at him. Her index finger was certainly getting a workout. "Don't try to change your tune now. I know what you're getting at, and I won't allow it. This competition is too important."

Marshall cocked one eyebrow. "I agree. The county wants to see this event be successful."

Aiden grimaced at the sheriff's statement, and I wondered if there was something more to it. Did he not agree with the sheriff's statement? I knew the Amish Confectionery Competition was important to Harvest and Holmes County. It was bringing in a flood of tourists, and tourism was how both jurisdictions made their money. It was how Swissmen Sweets made money too.

"I understand that," Aiden said. "However, a crime has been committed, and I believe there is a connection to this competition."

Margot put her hands on her hips. "Just because busybody Josephine Weaver went and got herself killed, it doesn't mean we should ruin a good thing for the rest of the county."

"I agree," Marshall said.

Aiden opened his mouth as if to protest, but Marshall was faster. "Here's what we do, because Brody is right. We have to investigate the Amish woman's death." He made this statement with an odd lilt of reluctance. "Margot, you continue on with your candy-making shindig, and Deputy Brody and my other deputies will quietly and discreetly talk to the people right here." He narrowed his eyes at Aiden. "And we will do our best not to disturb what the village and Margot have worked so hard to build up."

"I already told you, sir, that I had no plans to shut down the competition." Aiden's jaw twitched.

The sheriff nodded. "I'm glad you're willing to listen to reason, Deputy." He paused. "For once. It will be good for us all if you remember your place throughout this investigation."

Aiden made a face, and I was confused by the sheriff's comment. It was as if the two men were having a conversation about the Amish Confectionery Competition, but that wasn't all there was to it. There was a much less friendly debate going on just beneath the surface.

"But it is important that we talk to the contestants to find out if anyone saw anything that might tell us when Josephine was exposed to the licorice," Aiden added. "We will be discreet."

Margot threw up her hands. "There is licorice on every table. It could have happened at any time, and I already told you Josephine had voiced her concerns and would have known to stay away from it. I can't see her seeking it out."

"Perhaps it was an accident," the sheriff mused. "Maybe she ate something that contained anise without knowing it."

Even as he said this, I knew Aiden didn't believe it was an accident. That would be saying that Josephine had climbed into the organ of her own accord after eating licorice. Why would she do that? Why would anyone in their right mind do that? I had no reason to suspect that Josephine had been unstable. She had spoken very succinctly about wanting to boot me from the ACC just before she died.

And clearly, she knew about her licorice allergy since she hadn't been shy about telling others of it.

She wouldn't have hidden away after eating the candy. She would have asked for help. That would have been the logical thing to do, and my impression of Josephine was that she knew exactly what she was doing in all things.

"That seems unlikely, Sheriff," Aiden said in measured tones.

The sheriff rested his right hand on his belly as if it was a shelf put there purposely for that reason. "Don't be an alarmist, Brody. Margot, you know that we will do our best to get to the bottom of this, but like you, I see no need to halt the competition. Brody will take a few samples from each contestant's table and ask a question or two, but it won't be anything more than that."

Margot beamed at the sheriff. "I'm glad that we could come to some sort of agreement. Now, if you gentlemen will excuse me, I have more licorice to judge." She spun on her heel and returned to Beatrice and Jeremiah.

"What's the problem?" the sheriff asked Aiden in an affectedly jovial tone. "I came over because there's been another suspicious death in our sweet town. As sheriff, I'm doing my utmost to stop the crime that is pouring into Holmes County from more urban places, destroying the innocence of this county." He said this as if he were recording a sound bite.

Aiden's jaw twitched again. "I would like to discuss the case with you in a more private setting, sir. Maybe we should return to the crime scene to talk."

The sheriff shook his head. "It's your job to investigate, Brody. It is my job to keep the public calm and happy."

It sounded like a campaign slogan to me. Not for the first time, I wondered how much police work Sheriff Marshall actually did. It appeared to me that a lot of the weight of it fell on Aiden.

Marshall clapped his hand on Aiden's shoulder and lowered his voice. "Let's get this cleaned up quick, Brody. I have a reelection to worry about."

Chapter 10

I returned to my table with the sheriff's last words to Aiden playing repeatedly in my mind. *I have a reelection to worry about.* Did he? Did he really? As far as I knew, the sheriff ran uncontested and was sure to win. Had a new candidate thrown his hat into the ring? If he or even she had, I would be more than happy to hear it. When I got a chance, I would ask Aiden about this.

I glanced over at Aiden where he stood with two other deputies, one of whom was Deputy Little. The trio was deep in conversation. My question for Aiden would have to wait.

Behind my table, Emily wrung her hands.

"Emily, what's the matter?"

She blinked. "Beatrice just told me that we are moving on to the next round. Two contestants have been eliminated. Between you and me, I thought we were doomed, especially when the judges didn't care for the S's in the licorice." She held up her hands. "I'm not saying that the S's were a mistake at all. All the tourists coming by loved them and have been taking handfuls of samples. They do make your candies so pretty. I keep pointing people across to Swissmen Sweets and telling them that's where they could buy an entire box."

I laughed. "I'm glad we advanced to the next round. For a moment there, I wasn't sure it was going to happen either. Beatrice didn't seem to care for me."

Emily shrugged and returned to the sugar melting in a double boiler on the propane burner, just as I had taught her to do. In the weeks after my grandfather's death, Emily had become a fixture at Swissmen Sweets. She often came to the shop in the early morning before it opened, when *Maami* and I were making the candies to be sold in the shop that day. She was curious and eager to learn about candy making, and the lessons that *Maami* and I gave her momentarily distracted us from the grief of losing my grandfather. I knew, too, that she visited Swissmen Sweets to escape the watchful eye of her disagreeable sister.

"I started the taffy," Emily said. "I didn't know how long you would be."

I smiled. "I'm glad you did. The head start is appreciated."

"I'm so happy we are moving on," Emily said, but then lowered her voice. "But what is going on? Everyone is whispering about something that might have happened at the church. Is that why the police are here? Someone said that the competition might stop for the day."

I swallowed and whispered, "The competition will go on. The sheriff promised Margot that it would, but there has been an accident at the church."

She stared at me with round eyes.

"Josephine Weaver is dead. The police are trying to figure out what may have happened."

She gasped. "Josephine? What? How?"

I shook my head. "I will have to tell you later, or Aiden will. He's going to speak to all of the candy makers. I assume that includes both of us."

She wrung her hands again. "I don't want to speak to the police."

"It's just Aiden," I reassured her.

She bit her lip and nodded. She would be able to speak to Aiden. The sheriff was a different story. I didn't want to speak to the sheriff either.

"Let's work on this taffy while we wait," I said gently.

She nodded and stirred the sugar on the burner. Like many Amish, she seemed calmer when she was working.

I started gathering the other taffy ingredients from our supply crates. We had decided to make two kinds of taffy, sour apple and peppermint, for the next round of the competition. "Do we know who was cut from the competition?" I asked.

Emily nodded her head toward the next table, where Haddie smacked her wooden crate of supplies onto the middle of the table and began packing.

"She didn't make it," Emily whispered.

"I can see that," I whispered back. Because of the success of her shop, I was surprised Haddie hadn't been chosen to move forward. Yes, the judges thought her licorice was on the grainy side, but I wasn't naïve. I knew how most competitions worked. I thought the judges would have kept her in because of the star power—if there was such a thing in Amish candy making—she brought into the competition. Perhaps I had unfairly judged the ACC judges.

"What do the candy makers do when the competition is over for them?" Emily whispered.

"I'm sure they could stay and see how the competition turned out, but I suppose a lot of them will go home right away." I added four drops of sour apple extract to the mixture in the double boiler.

"That's what I would do," she said.

I nodded agreement.

Haddie lifted her crate and stomped away from her table. She marched past us without even a backward glance. Instead, she walked up to another Amish candy maker's table. The woman was stirring her own taffy mixture when Haddie said something to her in Pennsylvania Dutch. I couldn't understand a word of it, but if the icy tone was any indication, Haddie wasn't wishing the other Amish woman well.

Emily took a sharp breath at our single burner. She had heard the exchange, and unlike me, she had understood it.

I put the cap back on the tiny bottle of extract and set it in our own crate of supplies. "What did she say? Who is she talking to?"

Emily ducked her head and mumbled, "That's Lindy Beiler."

I looked at the dark-haired Amish woman with wire-rimmed glasses. Her face was bright red. I suspected her flushed skin was more a result of Haddie's passing comment than the boiling pot on her stove top. "Lindy? Do you mean Josephine's assistant Lindy?"

Emily nodded. "That's Berlin Candies' table. Berlin Candies won the licorice round with the highest points."

I frowned. "How bittersweet now that Josephine is gone."

Emily nodded.

I lowered my voice. "What did Haddie say to her?"

"I don't know if I should repeat it."

I gave Emily a look, and she leaned in. "She said she's glad that Josephine is dead because Josephine stole her licorice recipe, and she deserved whatever happened to her."

"Yikes." I blinked and stared at Haddie's receding back. Now *there* was a murder suspect if I ever saw one. This was good. I needed to get the heat off myself and Charlotte. I had taken a liking to the sweet Amish girl. I had also taken a disliking to her father and the district deacon. I still needed to ask my grandmother how we were related, and why I was just learning today that I had other Amish relatives.

"Did you notice if Haddie left her table today?" I asked.

Emily wrinkled her smooth brow. "I can't say I noticed, but it's been such a crazy day with the missing pig, the contest, and all the police around. And there was a short time when neither of us were at our table because you were off looking for Jethro and I was still at the pretzel shop."

I sighed. "You're right. I'd forgotten about that." Every cell in my body wanted to chase after

Haddie and find out what she might know about Josephine's death, but the taffy round would be held in just an hour and a half.

"Should we finish the taffy?" Emily asked.

I blinked at her. "Yes. Sorry. I'm just preoccupied."

"That's understandable. Why didn't you tell me about Josephine's death before the police arrived?" Emily asked, sounding hurt. "You had to have known. You were at the church."

"I didn't have a chance before the judging began." I held out my wooden spoon to her. "Do you mind stirring for a little while?"

Emily took the spoon from my hand and my place at the stove top.

Even with the taffy round looming, I started to leave the table, and Emily noticed. "Where are you going now?"

I waved at her. "Just keep stirring, I'll be back in a second to help you pull the taffy."

Emily sighed, and I walked down the line to what was once Josephine Weaver's booth.

When I reached Lindy, I asked her, "Are you all right?"

She blinked at me over the pot she was stirring on her burner. "I'm fine. *Danki*." Her wire-rimmed glasses were slightly fogged from leaning over the boiling pot of sugar.

She didn't look fine to me. "Congratulations on winning the last round. I know that Josephine would have been very happy about that."

She covered her face with her hands.

"Are you all right?"

She shook her head. "*Nee.*"

I wanted to pat her arm to comfort her, but instead, I folded my arms in front of me. "I'm so very sorry about Josephine."

She touched the corner of her eye with a paper towel.

"I'm sure she'd appreciate that you're going on with the competition," I said.

She lowered the paper towel from her face and shook her head. "That's where you are wrong. Josephine Weaver didn't appreciate anything I or anyone else did. She was one of the most difficult people to please."

"Oh?" I asked, trying to downplay my interest in this news.

She licked her lips. "I know that seems unkind to say because of—because of—" Her voice caught.

"Do you plan to go on with the competition?" I asked.

She met my eyes. "I have to go on. It's what Josephine would have wanted, even if she'd certainly find something wrong with the way I am doing it. Her business was so very important to her. It might have been the most important thing. She was widowed and without children. She poured her all into her shop. She would want me to continue for her."

"And the shop?" I asked. "Does the same go for the shop? What will happen to it now?"

"I—I don't know," she stammered. "I haven't thought about that yet."

I frowned at the way she stammered out the answer. I wondered if she did in fact know who would inherit the shop and was lying to me. If so, the question was why.

"I'll take it from here, Bailey, thank you," a male voice said behind me.

I didn't have to turn around to know that Aiden was standing there. I stepped back from the table. "Hello, Deputy Brody."

He frowned at me. There was no sign of the dimple now. When I didn't make a move to leave, he said, "Please return to your table. I need to speak with Lindy. Alone."

I nodded my head as if my hesitance was just an oversight. "Yes, of course." I backed away. "Lindy, if you need anything, just let me know how Swissmen Sweets or I can help you."

She met my gaze. "*Danki.* That is very kind of you. I don't believe what everyone is saying about you."

I stopped. "Saying about me?"

She blushed. "That you tricked the judges to let you into the competition."

I bit the inside of my cheek to stop the sharp retort that threatened to come out. "I did no such thing."

Her face turned even redder.

"Bailey, please return to your table," Aiden said.

I gave him a look, and Aiden folded his arms. It was clear he wanted me to leave right that second. I gave Lindy what I hoped was one last sympathetic smile and returned to my own table.

Emily waited for me there. She had the molten taffy poured out on waxed paper in the middle of the table. It was still too hot to pull, but it wouldn't be long now. The taffy was bright green. In a nod to Harvest's booming apple season, I had decided to make green apple taffy. It was a bit of a gamble because there was always a chance that the taffy would be too sour. However, if I pulled it off, I could win the round.

Emily waved a tea towel over the taffy as if it would cool more quickly with a little help.

Before I took the towel from her, I cleaned my hands with hand sanitizer from under my table. "It will cool off when it's ready. How do you think Lindy will do in this round without Josephine's help?"

"I think very well. From what I have heard from the other candy makers, Lindy does most of the work in the shop. Josephine just takes the credit."

I glanced down the rows of tables at the mousy woman who was speaking with Aiden. Could she have a motive to kill her boss because she did all the work? It was possible. I would have to tell Aiden this little bit of Amish gossip. I wasn't sure any of the Amish would say it to him. They weren't that forthcoming where the police were concerned. Considering the years they had had to put up with Sheriff Marshall, who made no secret of having little concern for the Amish in the county, they had good reason.

Across the street in front of Swissmen Sweets, I saw an old Amish woman with a hunched back and cane hobble down Main Street. Despite all the noise and commotion coming from the square, she shuffled forward without glancing in the direction of the candy competition.

"Emily, do you know who that woman is?" I asked.

"Which woman?" she asked, looking over my shoulder. "I don't see anyone."

When I looked back at the street where I had seen the old woman, she was gone. I looked up and down the street, but there was no sign of her. Had she disappeared into thin air? It was as if she'd evaporated. "She was just there. Where could she have gone? She disappeared."

"Maybe she went into one of the shops," Emily offered.

"Maybe."

"It was probably just a tourist."

I shook my head. "She was definitely not a tourist. She was elderly, Amish, and had a hunched back and cane."

Emily smiled sweetly. "You just described half of the Amish grandmothers in Harvest. Not yours, of course. Clara is still very spry."

I shook my head. "I'll tell her you said that. I don't know. There was something about that woman that stuck out to me. I feel like I have seen her before." I was still looking for the woman. I couldn't help it. There was something about her that I couldn't ignore.

"Bailey?" Emily asked. "We need to start working on the taffy. We only have ninety minutes. I think it's cool enough now to pull."

I nodded, knowing she was right, and I didn't know why I was looking for that woman. I already had more than enough problems to occupy me, including what looked more and more like a murder.

Chapter 11

After being reprimanded by the judges for my licorice pieces being too fancy and not Amish plain, I decided to take their advice and keep it simple for the taffy round. I wasn't going to imprint the pieces with the double S. It was time to play it safe so I could move on in the competition.

Emily wiped her hands on a cloth. "The green apple is done. Now on to peppermint. That's my favorite. Although I guess green apple is better for you."

I cocked an eyebrow at her. "How do you figure that?"

"An apple a day keeps the doctor away. One of my *Englisch* friends said that to me once."

I laughed because I was guilty of this sort of logic too when it came to eating sweets of any kind. Even though I worked in a candy shop, I still loved sugar in any form I could get it. I was grateful that diabetes didn't run in my family, or we'd all be in trouble.

"We had originally planned to make cotton candy

flavor as the second taffy," Emily said as she rifled through our box of supplies. "Why did you change your mind and make it peppermint?"

"Because," I said with a chuckle, "mint is an herb, which makes it healthy."

She laughed. "It seems that we were thinking the same thing when it came to healthy candy."

I grinned. "I knew you were the right person to help me out during the ACC."

She beamed at me and searched through the box of supplies. "Bailey, we have a little problem."

I looked up from the green apple taffy, which I was examining for bubbles. "Problem? What kind of problem?"

"I can't find the peppermint extract. It's not in the box."

"Oh," I said, feeling relieved. "That's all? There's more at the shop."

She straightened up. "I can run over and get it."

"No," I said. "I can run over and grab it. I want to check on my grandmother anyway. She has been in the shop alone for a while."

Emily nodded with a slight frown. I knew she was worried about *Maami* too. I wasn't the only one who had noticed that she had become quieter and more withdrawn with each passing day since my grandfather's funeral.

"Start cutting the green apple. I'll be here in time to help you finish," I said to Emily. "I won't be long." I hurried out of the booth and ran toward Main Street. All the while, I kept an eye out for the old Amish woman. She was nowhere to be seen.

When I stepped through the front door of Swissmen Sweets, the cowbell on the inner door handle jangled, and my orange kitten, Nutmeg, met me. He looked up at me and meowed with annoyance. The kitten was used to my being in the shop most of the day. It seemed he didn't like my absence.

I scooped up the kitten and nuzzled him under my chin. There was nothing quite as comforting as fluffy kitten fur, and I needed some comforting as the image of Josephine's hand hanging from the organ platform entered my mind yet again. And then there was the image of my licorice in the evidence bag. That was enough to give me nightmares. Aiden hadn't spoken to me about the licorice yet, but I knew he would. I was certain he had noticed the double S imprinted on my licorice pieces for the judging and for tourists to sample.

Nutmeg purred, and I set him back down on the floor. He meowed in protest and wove around my ankles.

My grandmother stood behind the domed glass counter, which was the centerpiece of Swissmen Sweets. It was where we displayed all our delicious treats. Chocolates, truffles, fudge, and caramels sat on silver trays in the display case. A small English girl in pigtails had her nose pressed up against the glass. The glass would need to be cleaned again. It was a constant battle to keep the counter clean— people, and not just kids, had a powerful urge to touch the tasty treats.

My eyes moved from the counter to my grandmother. Her typically rosy complexion was pale, and her face looked drawn. She smiled at the English woman, who I assumed was the girl's mother. She looked like she was buying every flavor of fudge the shop had to offer, including a couple of the newer options I had introduced to the shop: lavender blueberry and salted cappuccino. They had been a hit at JP Chocolates in New York, and I wasn't the least bit surprised that they were a hit here as well.

I waved to my grandmother, who gave me a slight smile as I stepped around the counter, and I slipped through the swinging door back into the kitchen, where I grabbed the peppermint extract from the shelf over the industrial mixer. The mixer was large enough that I could sit in it, not that I had ever tried. Well, that wasn't completely true. I had tried it once as a child.

Like all extract bottles, the peppermint was a small brown glass vial. We had more extract in storage, but we continually filled the vials instead of pouring from the larger containers. This was an old habit of my grandfather's, who was the master candy maker in the family and the reason that I had studied to be a chocolatier. He claimed there was too great a risk of adding too much flavor when pouring from one of the extract jugs that we used to refill the vials.

In my mind's eye, I could see him sitting on one of the wooden backless stools, refilling bottle after bottle with a steady wrinkled hand. I bit the inside of my cheek to hold back the tears. It was still too hard to think of him without crying.

My childhood summers were spent on my grand-father's knee learning how to make candies and chocolates. I had fallen in love with candy making. It had never occurred to me to do anything else. What I hadn't expected was that I would be making candies in this very shop. I had assumed by this point in my life, I would be a head chocolatier at some fancy chocolate shop in a cosmopolitan city. That had almost happened. But, surprisingly, I didn't feel any sort of loss at not achieving that dream. Plans and priorities change, and I was starting to learn that.

But living and working in Harvest was an adjustment all the same. I didn't feel at home here, not yet. It was too new and so different from what I was used to. However, after a bit of time, I sensed that I could feel at home in this place that was so different from where I had come from.

As I plucked the brown bottle of peppermint extract from the shelf, my eyes scanned over the other bottles. There was an empty spot on the shelf. I frowned, as my grandmother and I were obsessive about keeping the kitchen clean and organized. Everything had a place, and everything was in its place. I studied the bottles. Vanilla, maple, cinnamon, banana, rum, lemon. I swallowed, realizing which extract was missing. Licorice. The small brown bottle of licorice extract was missing. There should be two on the shelf. One sat in the supply crate at my ACC table. The other was missing.

When I had gotten up that morning, there had been two bottles on the shelf. I took one for the licorice contest, but only one. The other bottle was now gone. My brows knit together. Maybe I had imagined there had been two bottles? We make so much licorice in the shop that we usually had two bottles of it on the shelf. We also had two bottles of vanilla always ready to go, as vanilla was the most popular extract of all. No, I knew there had been two bottles of licorice there this morning. I had seen both bottles.

My hand shook as the gravity of the situation sank in. Josephine had been killed by an allergic reaction to the anise found in licorice. One of my licorice pieces was found in her apron pocket, and now my candy shop's extra bottle of licorice extract was missing. It didn't take Sherlock Holmes to tell me I was in deep trouble or to tell me that someone was making a determined effort to frame me.

I closed my hand around the tiny bottle of peppermint extract and stepped back through the swinging door to the main part of the shop. I was happy to see that the lone customer and her little girl were gone. On the other side of the counter, Nutmeg patrolled the perimeter of the shop like a royal guard around a queen. It seemed, in recent months, that the young cat had taken it upon himself to be the head of security detail. Nothing got past Nutmeg. I always knew when a customer was about to step through the door because he would stop whatever he was doing and go into high alert.

My grandmother sprayed vinegar water on the front of the domed counter, wiping away the smear marks that the little girl had left there.

"*Maami,*" I said, clutching the vial of peppermint extract in my hand, "did you see the second bottle of licorice extract on the shelf in the kitchen? I can't seem to find it." I concentrated on keeping my voice even. I debated telling her about Josephine's death for the briefest of moments, then discarded the idea. I didn't want to say or do anything that would upset my grandmother. She already was upset enough. I refused to add to her distress.

She shook her head. "*Nee.* I thought you needed

it for the contest this morning. Wasn't the first round licorice?"

"It was," I said.

"Maybe Emily took the second bottle to be safe," she suggested. "Maybe she was afraid you might need a little extra."

As she said this, my worry began to fade. Yes, of course that must be it. There was no other answer. Emily must have taken the other bottle as a precaution. It was very sweet of her to be so thoughtful.

I smiled. "That must be it." I needed to hurry back to the contest so I could ask Emily about the licorice extract, but I hesitated before I left. "How are things here?" What I was really asking was how she was holding up that day, and we both knew it.

She set the bottle of vinegar water on the counter. "Do not worry about me, Bailey dear. You need to return to the competition."

I frowned. I wanted to ask her how she felt, but I knew the Amish didn't talk about their emotions as much as English people did. My father, who had been raised Amish, had trouble talking about how he felt too, and it had been a source of many arguments between him and my mother. My mother was the type of person who tells everyone how she feels, whether they want to hear about it or not. I fell somewhere in the middle of those two, and unlike my mother, I could recognize when someone else didn't want to talk about his or her emotions.

I changed the subject to avoid leaving my grandmother on an awkward note. "We made it to the second round of the competition," I said, forcing brightness into my voice.

She smiled. "I knew you would. Jebidiah would be

so very proud of you." Her face crumpled. For a moment, I thought she would cry, but she kept it together by grabbing the spray bottle of vinegar water and a cloth again. "You should go. You don't want to miss anything. What brought you to the shop in the first place?"

"I came over to get the peppermint extract." I held it up as if it were evidence.

"Then why were you asking about the licorice extract?"

"I happened to notice it was gone when I grabbed the peppermint," I said.

She waved at me with the cloth. "I'm sure it will turn up." She gave me a small smile that was half the wattage of the one I remembered. It hurt my heart to see her trying so hard to be happy when it had come so effortlessly to her before my grandfather's death.

I knew I had to get back to the competition, but I said, "I met someone new at the ACC today."

She looked up from the counter. "Oh, who was that?"

"Charlotte Weaver," I said, watching her closely for a reaction.

"Charlotte is a sweet girl." *Maami* wiped away an imaginary streak on the glass countertop.

"She said that she is your cousin."

My grandmother's face was pinched. "That is true to some extent."

I frowned. "To some extent. Aren't you either someone's cousin or not?"

"Yes, I suppose by blood, this is true, but an Amish person's district is a stronger bond than even blood."

eturn to body.

"You and Charlotte aren't in the same district," I said. I already knew this, of course, because I knew the two women had different deacons, but I wanted to hear her explanation.

"No, we're not in the same Amish district," she said.

"What happened?" I asked.

She shook her head and suddenly looked every bit her seventy-some years. "You had better return to the ACC. I don't want you to lose your place. Your *daadi* would be so proud of you for taking his spot in the competition." Her voice caught.

"But . . ."

"I will tell you another time," she said quietly.

I didn't press the subject. "Are you sure you are all right?" I couldn't stop myself from asking. Maybe I was more like my mother than I thought.

Maami flapped her cloth in my direction. "This is your last candy for the day. We can talk when you return home."

I wanted to argue and tell her that it couldn't wait, but maybe, just maybe, if I won the Amish Confectionery Competition in my grandfather's name, it would assuage some of her grief. I knew nothing could take away her pain. The loss of a love like my grandparents' had to be grieved to the full extent. Selfishly, I wanted that kind of love too, but I didn't know if it was something I could handle. It would be much easier not to love at all and to avoid the pain that I saw my grandmother suffer day after day.

Seeing her like this made me realize that I had never loved Eric Sharp. I swallowed. It was a horrible realization that I had stayed with the man for over a year, but I had been more in love with the idea of our secret relationship and the excitement surrounding him than the man himself. Knowing that, more than losing Eric, made me terribly, terribly sad.

I wanted to stay and ask her to tell me the story about Charlotte now, but I knew my grandmother was right. I didn't want to disappoint her or dishonor my grandfather's memory by missing part of the competition. I rushed over and gave her a hug. "I'll be back just as soon as the competition is over for the day. I promise."

She nodded. "I know, dear." She turned back to cleaning the counter. Her back was to me when I went back through the front door. She didn't even turn when the cowbell rang, signifying my exit.

Chapter 12

I returned to my competition table with peppermint vial in hand. Emily already had the taffy mixture well underway on the stove top.

"You're just in time," she said. "I was about to run over to Swissmen Sweets and grab the peppermint myself."

I opened the peppermint vial and inhaled. The scent seemed to calm me. I let three drops fall from the tip of the bottle into the melting sugar. That's all it would take to flavor our taffy. If it had been licorice extract, that was all it would have taken to kill Josephine Weaver.

She continued to stir after I added the extract. "What took you so long?"

"I stopped and spoke with my grandmother for a bit," I said, leaving it at that. I lowered my voice. "Did you bring a bottle of licorice extract over from the shop?

She pointed to the small brown bottle in the supply crate. "Sure. We needed it for the first round of judging. We were making licorice." She gave me a strange look.

I shook my head. "I know about that bottle. I mean the second one. There was a spare bottle in the shop kitchen, and I didn't see it when I picked up the peppermint extract."

She frowned. "I didn't even know there were two bottles. I suppose the second one could be in there by mistake."

I searched the crates. There was only one bottle. I told myself not to worry. I told myself that this didn't mean anything, but I knew I was lying to myself. It might just mean everything.

Emily studied my expression. "Is everything okay, Bailey? Your face is really white."

I forced a smile. "Everything is fine. I hate when I misplace something. That's all." I widened my smile. "There's nothing to be concerned about. Trust me."

She continued to stir the sugar and looked as if she didn't believe me. I couldn't blame her. I wouldn't have believed me in those circumstances either.

I considered telling Emily my real suspicions, but just as I wanted to spare my grandmother from worry, I also wanted to spare Emily. I cleared my throat. "I see you finished cutting the green apple taffy. It looks great."

She beamed at the six-foot-long, inch-thick line of bright green taffy that ran the length of our table on a sheet of waxed paper.

"Why don't you keep stirring up the peppermint, and I'll wrap these?"

She nodded and returned her attention to the stove.

I wrapped each piece in a two-inch by two-inch scrap of waxed paper; Emily and I had precut a supply of these in the shop earlier that week in preparation for this round of judging. I had to admit that it felt odd to be standing there making candies. Had a woman really passed away only hours ago? There were police around, but everyone was acting as if it was business as usual. Even me, and I knew better. The problem was, I didn't know what else I should be doing. Aiden certainly didn't want me asking questions. I knew that. I shook my head and continued working.

I had just wrapped my thirtieth piece of green apple taffy when Aiden walked up to the table. His movements were more confident and relaxed than they had been the last time I'd seen him, when he had been arguing with the sheriff or when he had been about to question Lindy.

Aiden nodded at Emily and then focused on me. "Bailey, can I have a moment of your time?"

I was relieved he'd asked. Acting as if nothing had happened in the church just a few hundred yards away was starting to grate on me. At the same time, I didn't want to talk to him. I needed time to figure out what had become of the second bottle of licorice extract before Aiden learned that it was missing.

"Shaking the cobwebs out?" Aiden asked.

I stared at him. "What?"

"I asked you if you were shaking the cobwebs out when you shook your head like that. Seems to me that you are trying to remember or forget something. Care to share?" He cocked his head.

"No," I said, hoping the deputy would leave it at that.

His smile dissolved. "I still need to talk to you."

"Can it wait until after the taffy judging is over?" I asked.

He shook his head. "No."

It seemed to me that both of us were digging in our heels.

"Go ahead, Bailey," Emily said. "This will take a few minutes to set, and then we can pull it together."

I gestured to the deputy to lead the way. Instead of walking to the edge of the square, as I expected he would, Aiden led me in the direction of the church.

I followed him as a feeling of dread came over me.

The coroner's car—and, I assumed, Josephine's body along with it—was long gone. It had been three hours since Aiden's mother and I had entered the church in search of Jethro. It was maddening to know that the pig was still missing too. Poor Juliet. I was sure if she'd found him she would have told me.

"What happened to Charlotte?" I asked.

"We questioned her and told her to go home," he said.

I grimaced, wondering what kind of reception she would receive when she got home. "Is she a suspect?"

He sighed. "You know I can't tell you that."

I folded my arms.

Aiden sighed and looked skyward. "Bailey, I

didn't pull you away from your table to talk about Charlotte."

"Oh," I said, playing dumb.

"We need to talk about this." He held up the baggie with my piece of licorice in it. Now that I could see the candy clearly, there was no mistaking it was mine. The double S was stamped right in the middle.

I grimaced. I had been right that Aiden had noticed that my candies matched the one found in Josephine's apron pocket. There was no point in playing dumb any longer. "That's one of my licorice candies."

"It is. Do you know where we found it?" he asked, sounding surprised that I came right out and admitted the piece of candy was mine.

"Deputy Little found it in Josephine's apron pocket," I said. I tucked a lock of hair behind my ear, and my feathered earring swayed back and forth.

The deputy seemed to be staring at the earring for a moment too long.

I cleared my throat.

He frowned. "Yes. Did you recognize it as one of your candies when Little came out of the church?" His voice was a tad too sharp for my taste.

"No," I said. I didn't consider it lying since I hadn't gotten a good look at the piece of licorice. I had only *thought* it was mine. I hadn't *known* it was until I saw Aiden's face when he spotted the licorice on my table. "He was waving it around too much for me to get a good look at it, but I can see plainly now that is one of my pieces."

"Any idea how your candy would have gotten inside Josephine's apron pocket? Did you give Josephine any licorice this morning?"

I shook my head. "No, I didn't give it to her, and I have no idea how it got there. She didn't take any candy from my table, as far as I know, but then again, we had samples sitting out all morning. Maybe someone else took it and gave it to her or slipped it into her apron. There were so many people who stopped by the tables to taste the licorice that it's really impossible to know."

He pursed his lips together as he removed a small notebook and a pen from his uniform pocket and made a note. "Did you know about Josephine's allergy to licorice?"

I scowled. "No. Not until after Charlotte found her in the organ and I overheard Deacon Clapp mention her allergy."

He pressed his lips together. "It appears her allergy was very well known among the Amish and many of the English too."

I shrugged. "I didn't know. I can't prove that I didn't know about her allergy, but you must remember that I haven't lived in Harvest very long, certainly not long enough to know what everyone is allergic to. I just met Josephine yesterday when we were setting up the tables."

"When she said you shouldn't be in the competition."

I shook my head. "That was this morning. I think it didn't occur to her yesterday that I was participating. She may have thought I was another volunteer helping to set up. A lot of the locals helped. As you know, the entire town has been involved in the ACC."

He made another note. "Okay, so let's go over the sequence of events. Tell me what happened from the moment Josephine approached you this morning."

I sighed. "This morning Josephine expressed to me and to the judges her feeling that I shouldn't be in the competition because I'm not Amish. You can ask Jeremiah or Margot about this. They were both there."

"I already have. Go on."

"And then I helped your mom look for Jethro, who is missing. We ended up in the church."

He nodded. "Just as Charlotte found the dead body."

I winced when he said "body." I swallowed. "Yes." I paused. "And I may not have known about Josephine's allergy, but if most of the Amish did, you should take a hard look at Haddie Smucker."

"Haddie? Why?" Aiden asked.

"She didn't make it to the second round of competition, and as she was leaving, she told Lindy Beiler—that's Josephine's shop assistant—that she was glad Josephine was dead because Josephine stole one of her candy recipes."

He frowned. "Lindy didn't tell me that when I interviewed her."

"She wouldn't. She doesn't know you, and she's Amish."

He nodded, accepting the realities of the county. "You overheard her say this?"

"I heard her say it, but it was in Pennsylvania Dutch. Emily heard too. She translated for me."

"I'll keep it in mind, but I will remind you, Bailey, that this is a Sheriff's Department investigation." He looked me straight in the eye. "I don't want you involved. This isn't like last time. You don't have any personal connection to Josephine. Don't get involved."

"So it was okay that I was involved last time?" It was my turn to cock my head.

He groaned. "I didn't say that. You just have less reason to meddle this time."

"It seems Charlotte is my cousin, so that would be enough of a reason to worry about the case."

"A cousin you didn't know about until today."

"She's still family, and I could tell *Maami* cares about her, and I have to worry about myself too. You're standing there in front of me holding evidence that implicates me in Josephine's death. After what happened just last month, you'll have to excuse me if I'm not one hundred percent confident in the Sheriff's Department."

Aiden scowled, and I realized a little too late how that must have sounded to him. I had practically said that I wasn't confident in him. I swallowed.

He ran his hand through his dark hair. "I can understand that. I can."

I raised my eyebrows. "You can?"

He nodded. "The sheriff didn't give you an easy time when Tyson Colton was killed. For that I'm sorry, but you have to understand why you can't get involved now."

"Do you consider me a suspect?"

He sighed again.

"It's a simple question with a yes or no answer."

"Yes."

I sucked in a breath. For some strange reason, I had expected him to say no, but I don't know why, with all the evidence against me. Of course Aiden considered me a suspect in Josephine's death. Any good cop would, and Aiden was a good cop. I could at least admit that, but I didn't want him to think I was capable of such a crime.

The way I felt about his reply must have shown on my face because he said, "Not a serious one, no. As you said, anyone could have taken that licorice piece from your table, even Josephine herself. Had you killed her, it would have been stupid to leave such incriminating evidence behind. You're smarter than that."

"Thanks, I guess," I said, no longer feeling as bad about what I had said.

He smiled.

"It seemed to me that the sheriff was giving you a hard time earlier when you were talking with Margot."

He shook his head. "Bailey, let's not make this conversation about me."

I folded my arms. "There's something going on there."

"It's not related to Josephine's murder, so it doesn't concern you."

I rocked back on my heels. "You just admitted that I should be concerned about Josephine's murder."

He groaned. "Somehow you always twist my words into whatever shape you want."

"It's a talent of mine."

"I noticed." He smiled, and the dimple in his right cheek appeared.

I bit down on my lip to stop myself from smiling too. I needed to focus on the murder, not on his distracting dimple. "Was it my piece of licorice that killed her?" My voice quavered. I hadn't known Josephine well at all and couldn't say that I liked what I did know about her, but I didn't want something that I'd made to be responsible for her death or anyone else's.

He shook his head. "The coroner doesn't think so. She died too quickly. He thinks the reaction happened in under five minutes. He will know for certain if she ate any licorice candy after he does the autopsy."

I grimaced. "If she didn't eat the licorice candy, how does the coroner think she got the licorice into her system that fast? What else could it be?"

"Licorice in liquid form. Margot informed me you can buy licorice extract. It might have been something like that. We'll know more when the coroner runs his toxicology reports."

I tried to keep my face calm and neutral. Aiden had just said I was off the hook for the murder. Well, that was basically what he'd said. If he knew I was missing a bottle of licorice extract, that might change.

"It'll be difficult to pin down where the licorice extract came from. It seems that all the contestants in the candy-making competition had some with them today."

I nodded. "Everyone in the competition would have used it in their licorice recipes."

He folded the brim of his department hat and put it back on his head. "When I find the source of the extract, I'll find my killer. I know that in my bones."

I swallowed hard and hoped that he hadn't noticed the nervous habit.

"I should get back to my other deputies and touch base with them." He looked me in the eye. "You will tell me if you run into anyone who might be low on licorice extract or perhaps is missing some of it, won't you?"

I nodded again. Unable to speak. I told myself that I wasn't lying by keeping quiet, that he'd asked me to tell him if I ran into anyone who might be missing the extract. He never asked if *I* was missing it. I knew full well that I was kidding myself.

He smiled at me, and the dimple reappeared, stabbing a nail into my chest. "Thank you, Bailey. Please don't worry about this. I'll take care of everything." He turned and walked away and seemed to be certain that what he said was the truth. I wasn't nearly as certain that he'd be able to take care of any of it, let alone everything.

Chapter 13

I returned to my table just in time to help Emily pull the peppermint taffy. The taffy itself looked like a smear of bubbly red slime across the waxed paper. The red looked like blood.

Emily stood beside me with her hands on her hips. "Rethinking the red?" She must have notice the similarities too.

I winced. "Maybe."

"Once it's pulled, cut into pieces, and wrapped in waxed paper, it will be just fine," she reassured me.

I eyed her. When I had met Emily a little over a month ago, she had been a scared girl, begging me to give her kitten, Nutmeg, a home because her brother, Abel, wouldn't let her keep him. Since Nutmeg was now a permanent fixture at Swissmen Sweets, you know how that story ended.

She handed me a tub of butter. "Butter up, *Englischer*."

I barked a laugh. After washing my hands with the hand sanitizer that I insisted we keep at the table and putting on plastic gloves, I dug three fingers of my right hand into the butter. As I rubbed the butter into my palms, Emily sanitized her hands, put on her own pair of gloves, and plunged her hands into the tub of butter, just like I had. We buttered our hands so that the taffy wouldn't stick to them during the hand-pulling process.

Emily picked up the metal spatula from the table and pushed the taffy across the waxed paper, pulling it away from the surface. As she did this, I put my hand under the sticky taffy and gathered it into my hands. It was a huge red glob.

With all the taffy off the waxed paper, Emily scraped the portion of the taffy that was on the spatula into her own hands. We connected our two pieces by pushing them together and then began the long process of pulling the taffy—stretching the ends of the glob away from each other, folding the taffy, and then repeating.

By pulling the taffy, we added air to it. As this happened, its consistency and color changed from a brightly colored sticky mess to a satiny light shade of pink. It wasn't the deep color of blood any longer.

"It does smell like peppermint," Emily said.

I grinned as we set the now pulled taffy down on a fresh piece of waxed paper. The judges couldn't find any fault with my techniques in this round. All by hand, all the *Amish* way.

I glanced over at what had been Josephine's booth. Lindy was there, pulling the taffy offerings for Berlin Candies on a metal hook that she had clamped to her table. She seemed to be having some trouble with it. Even from where I stood across the square, I could tell she was on the verge of tears. There was a group of English tourists standing in front of her, but none of them made any move to help her.

Emily and I removed our gloves.

"Em, you go ahead and start cutting the taffy. I think I will run over and give Lindy a hand."

Emily looked up from the long piece of taffy that ran the length of the table.

"And ask her a few questions while you're at it?"

"She looks upset." I wiped my hands on a cloth before walking around the side of our table. As the day had gone on, the number of guests at the ACC had increased. Both English and Amish onlookers watched in awe as fifteen of the best Amish candy makers pulled taffy in every color of the rainbow.

"Mommy, can we have some?" an English boy asked as he bounced in place. A few feet away, an Amish boy repeated the same question to his mother. The two boys must have realized they'd said the same thing at the same time and laughed together. Despite the sad events of the day, I found myself smiling. The boys' excitement over the taffy was what the Amish Confectionery Competition was all about, and the connection the two boys shared was the end result we all wanted for everyone who attended the event. I supposed "all" might have been an overstatement. I couldn't imagine Sheriff Marshall wanting the Amish and English to come together. It seemed to me that he had wanted from the beginning to keep them apart, so they would be separated into very divided camps. Not for the first time, I wished someone in the community would have the nerve to run against him in the upcoming election.

When I reached Lindy's booth, she was still struggling with her taffy hook. It toppled over, and she just caught her long band of pulled taffy before it hit the grass at her feet. She appeared to be on the verge of tears now.

"Do you need some help?" I asked.

She eyed me with suspicion. "*Nee*, I am fine." She gathered the taffy in her hands and set it on a large piece of waxed paper that lay across her table. The taffy was a light yellow color and smelled strongly of lemons. After she did that, she attempted to affix the pulling hook on her table again, only to watch helplessly as it tumbled into the grass.

We both stared at her feet.

"If you have any hope of pulling that taffy before it gets too stiff to manipulate, you will take me up on my offer," I suggested.

She stared down at the glob of yellow on the table, and her frown deepened. "Very well. *Ya*, I can use your help."

I washed my hands again, put on gloves, and stuck my hand into her tub of butter just as I had done at my own table. Grabbing one end of the taffy that Lindy had gathered into her hands, I began to pull.

I pulled the yellow taffy toward me and then folded it to meet Lindy's end of the taffy. "Haddie seemed upset when she learned that she was eliminated from the competition."

Lindy stepped away from me, pulling the taffy with her. "Anyone would be upset. If a candy shop wins the Amish Confectionery Competition, it could completely change the owner's business. Everyone in the Amish world and many candy makers in the *Englisch* world would know about the winning shop. People would come from all over just to taste candy that came from a shop that won the ACC." She folded the taffy toward me.

"I'm starting to realize that. When I lived in New York, I was in many candy competitions for my old employer. The competition was fierce. It took me off guard to learn that the competition in an Amish candy competition would be just as fierce."

Lindy smiled and visibly relaxed. "We Amish are people too. We have goals and dreams, and we can be competitive, just like anyone else."

I blushed. "I wasn't implying—I—" I stumbled over my words.

"It is fine. I know you didn't mean anything by it."

My face turned a deeper shade of red. "It came out horrible though. I know that. It's just, I guess, when I think of the Amish, I think of my grandparents. Neither of them had a competitive bone in their bodies."

She smiled again. "True. Your grandparents are the kindest people. How is your grandmother?" She folded the taffy toward me again. "I heard that she's been having a difficult time since your grandfather passed."

"It's been hard. Yes."

The taffy was beginning to take on a satin texture and lighten in color. It would be ready for cutting and wrapping in waxed paper with just a couple more pulls.

She frowned. "I'm sorry. I shouldn't have brought it up."

I shook my head. "It's all right. I think grief snuck

up on her." It was the most honest answer I had given about my grandmother's state of mind to anyone.

"Grief is the most terrible pain. It's a wild animal that you cannot control." She said this like someone who spoke from painful personal experience.

I started to ask her what she meant by her comment, but before I could she said, "I think we have pulled the taffy enough."

Together we set it on the piece of fresh waxed paper on her long table.

"*Danki* for your help," Lindy said. "It was very kind of you to come over. I'm sorry if I was rude at the start. It's just been very hard."

I stepped back from the table. "Because of Josephine?"

She nodded. "I'm carrying on and making candy for her sake and the sake of the shop, but I don't honestly know if that's what I should be doing. Maybe I should quit the competition. No one would blame me."

I shook my head. "No one would."

She licked her lips. "But I want to continue for Josephine's sake. Winning this competition meant a lot to her, and I know that is what she would have wanted me to do."

"Were you and Josephine close?"

"For the last five years, we worked side by side every day." She began rolling the taffy back and forth over the waxed paper to shape it into a one-inch-thick tube to be cut into bite-sized pieces.

That really didn't answer my question. I'd had coworkers I didn't care for. One of Jean Pierre's chocolatiers named Caden was the first to come to mind.

I decided to change tactics. It didn't seem to me that Lindy would speak outright against her deceased boss. I wasn't sure if her hesitation was out of respect for the dead or because of something else. "Haddie Smucker didn't seem to care much for Josephine. I noticed that she said something to you as she was leaving."

Lindy pressed her lips into a thin line. "Haddie Smucker has no right to be speaking to me about Josephine or anyone else. I'm glad the judges saw her for what she is, a mediocre candy maker, and removed her from the competition." She said this with so much venom that it took me off guard. Could this be the same woman who was speaking about grief just a few moments ago?

I decided to press, even though I knew it might destroy any camaraderie that had developed over pulling taffy together. "She claimed that Josephine stole her licorice recipe."

"That's a lie!" Lindy yelled.

Visitors to the ACC who were walking around the square stopped and stared at us openmouthed. It wasn't common to hear an Amish woman yell.

She looked down at her taffy. Her face was beet red. "I'm sorry. I shouldn't have burst out like that. It just makes me so angry that Haddie would make such a blatantly false claim."

"Josephine didn't steal her licorice recipe?"

"Of course she didn't. Josephine's licorice recipe was her great-grandmother's and was passed down through her family over the generations. Haddie is trying to sabotage Berlin Candies' chances."

That was interesting. I wondered why Haddie would lie about it. Was it just sour grapes over being removed from the ACC, a parting shot as she made her way to the door?

"Haddie isn't from Holmes County, is she?"

Lindy shook her head. "*Nee*, she's not. She's from Geauga County."

"Then how well do you know her?"

Lindy removed a knife from her supply box and began cutting the lemon-flavored taffy into one-inch pieces. "Even though she may not live close by, yes, I know her. All the Amish candy makers know or know of each other. Haddie has a reputation."

"Oh?" I said. I hoped that the "oh" was just non-committal enough to encourage Lindy to share more.

She sniffed. "Haddie Smucker gets what she wants. Her little shop in Geauga County wouldn't receive half the attention that it does if she wasn't so pushy. Mark my words, we haven't seen the last of her in this competition. If the judges think that Haddie will leave quietly, they know nothing about her."

"I don't see how she could return if she's been disqualified. She lost the round. The competition will move on without her."

Lindy just shook her head as if I couldn't possibly understand, but that was where she was wrong. I came to Harvest by way of New York City. Everyone has a little bit of a competitive edge to him or her in New York. It was just a matter of survival. It seemed to me that I needed to have a little chat with Haddie Smucker if she was still around. I hoped that Aiden had stopped her from leaving the county. He had to consider her, like all the candy makers, a suspect.

Lindy continued cutting the taffy. "She will do whatever it takes to win. Being removed from the competition won't stop her. I won't make the mistake of counting her out. I've made that mistake before. *Danki* again for all your help," she concluded in a way that made it very clear I was being dismissed.

"If you need any more help, Emily or I will be happy to pitch in. I know it can be hard to run the competition table on your own." I removed my gloves, tossed them in the trash, and washed the butter from my hands in a bowl of water at the end of her table.

She simply nodded and continued to cut her taffy into precise one-inch pieces.

I dried my hands on a plain white tea towel and suppressed a sigh. There was a sadness to Lindy Beiler that I couldn't quite pin down, though I wasn't convinced that it had anything to do with her employer's death.

I had started across the square back to my table again when a voice stopped me. "Bailey! Bailey!"

I turned to find Juliet running toward me. Her orange and white polka-dotted skirt flew behind her as she ran.

Chapter 14

"Oh, Bailey." Juliet waved to me from across the square. "Bailey." She came to an abrupt stop in front of me. Her usually perfect hair was disheveled and her eyes red-rimmed.

I placed a hand on her shoulder. "Juliet, are you all right?"

She grabbed my hand from her shoulder and clasped it in both of hers. Tears brimmed in her eyes. "I'm so sorry to have dragged you into this mess with Josephine! If I'd never asked you to help me find Jethro, you would have had nothing to do with this. I feel just horrible about it all. Now, you're a suspect in a murder again, and it's my fault."

A woman walking by us stopped and stared. I forced a smile. "We are practicing lines for a play."

She narrowed her eyes as if she didn't believe me.

I removed my hand from Juliet's tight grasp. It took some doing. "Juliet, you might not want to announce to the world I'm a murder suspect."

She clamped her hand over her mouth. "I'm

so sorry. What was I thinking?" Her words were muffled because her hand was still over her mouth.

"Don't worry," I said, keeping my voice low. "How did you find out I was a suspect?"

"Aiden," she said, barely above a whisper. "Of course, you know he doesn't talk to me about his cases, but when I said that he couldn't possibly suspect you of any wrongdoing, he got very quiet. That's how I knew." She shook her head. "That boy! He should know you well enough by now to know that you are incapable of such a terrible act."

"Aiden has known me for only a few weeks, really," I said, automatically coming to her son's defense. I didn't know why I was defending him when he considered me a murder suspect. I couldn't stop myself from doing it.

"But he's known your grandparents for most of his life. That should be enough for him." She placed a hand on my arm. "I hope this doesn't have any impact on your future together."

Future together? What future together? There wasn't one, as far as I knew. I thought it was best that I not ask Juliet those unspoken questions. "In any case, I don't think it's your fault I'm a suspect. Even if I had not been there when Charlotte found the body, I would still be a suspect. Because of how Josephine died, all the candy makers at the ACC are suspects."

She nodded. "Maybe this is true." Juliet pressed a tissue to the corner of her eye. "But I still can't believe he would think that about *you*. What happened to Josephine is just awful. She wasn't the kindest woman in the world, but to be shoved into the organ like that? It's just so awful."

A couple walked by and glanced at us in surprise. Clearly, the middle of the square was not the best place to have a conversation about murder. Time to change the subject. "Any news on Jethro?"

She shook her head. "No. He's still missing. It's almost been a full day. I'm just heartbroken over it." She removed a tissue from her purse, dropped the tissue in the grass, and clasped a hand over her mouth. "I can't believe I said that. You must think I'm a horrible person. Here I am crying over my pig being missing while Josephine . . ." She dissolved into tears again.

I patted her arm. "Jethro is important to you. A member of the family. There is no reason for you to feel bad about missing him."

She lifted her head and looked up at me with tears in her eyes. "Yes, that's exactly it, and he's never been away from me for so long. I rarely let him out of my sight. He must be terrified."

"What can I do to help?" I asked.

"I can't ask you to do anything else. Not after what happened this morning." She shook her head like a stubborn toddler who had made up her mind.

I laughed. "Sure, you can. If you can't ask your friends for help, who can you ask?"

She smiled, gripping my hands a second time much more tightly than the first. "You are my friend, aren't you, Bailey? I never had a daughter. I love my son, of course, but part of me always wanted to have a girl too. I think that's what most mothers want, whether they admit it or not. And now I have you. You will be like a daughter soon."

I opened my mouth to protest, but she was faster.

"I knew when you moved to Harvest that it would be good for Clara, but I've quickly learned that it's good for the whole town."

I felt myself blush.

"If you have the time, there is a way that you can help look for Jethro."

"Name it." I glanced over my shoulder at the table. I knew that I needed to get back to it. Emily would worry about me missing the judging again if I took too long. When I turned, I saw her brother Abel standing in front of our table. Abel was a large man. Like his sister, his hair was blond and almost as light as Emily's from countless hours in the sun.

"Reverend Brook is such a dear man," Juliet said. "Of course, the poor reverend is beside himself because Josephine's body was stuffed into his organ, but even with that extra stress, he's organized a search party for Jethro." As she spoke, her southern accent became thicker. I had noticed that tended to happen when she spoke of the good reverend.

"How very kind of him." I did my best to keep the smile out of my voice.

"He's so sweet to be concerned about my missing pig with all that is going on." She wiped a tear from her pale cheek.

Despite the seriousness of the situation, I found myself smiling. For some reason, Juliet and the reverend seemed to believe that their affection for each other was a big secret, but as far as I could tell, everyone in town knew that they cared about each other. Honestly, I didn't know what she saw in the ineffectual little man, but she was smitten. That was plain to see.

"The search party will go out this evening. As you can guess, Margot is being very unhelpful and won't let us search while all the tourists are around. We're all meeting at the gazebo right after the competition ends for the day. The church choir will be there and several other church members."

"That sounds like a great idea. We can cover more ground with more people. I'm happy to join in. I want to find Jethro too. I've grown to like the little guy even if he does bite me."

"Bailey, those are love nips. I told you that!"

I laughed. "I know. I shouldn't tease you when you are so worried about him. I'll help in any way that I can."

She clasped her hands again. "Oh, would you? We're looking for all the volunteers we can gather. But I don't want to put you out."

"You aren't putting me out," I reassured her. "I will feel better when Jethro is safe at home again."

She glanced at the silver watch on her wrist. "I must go. The reverend and I were going to make some calls to gather up more volunteers for the search." She gave me a final hug and jogged across the square with her skirt flowing behind her again.

I turned and headed to my own table, hoping that Abel had left in the meanwhile. No such luck.

Emily and Abel spoke softly together at the table in Pennsylvania Dutch. Even though I couldn't understand the words, Abel's tone was obviously disapproving.

"Hello, Abel," I said.

He turned and made a sound close to a grunt.

"Bailey," Emily said with obvious relief, "I'm so glad you're back." She had placed the newly wrapped taffy into a basket for display.

"This looks great, Emily. I can always count on you."

She blushed, and her brother glared at me. I suspected that Abel had been glaring at me ever since I was ten years old. I just didn't know it. Abel had a crush on me back then, but I was much more interested in climbing trees and learning to make my grandfather's famous fudge. After Abel tried to kiss me in the shadow of the gazebo and I jumped away, he never forgot it. I went back to Connecticut and my busy suburban life and never gave the Amish boy another thought until I met him again as an adult. As far as I could tell, he had never forgiven me for the rebuke, even though so much time had passed.

I cleared my throat as Abel continued to stare at me without speaking. "Emily told me that you are helping the ACC with setup and maintenance. That's nice of you."

"It's a job," he said.

"Umm, right." I glanced at his sister, and her eyes went wide. I just couldn't win as far as Abel was concerned. "I'm sure Margot and the other judges appreciate all your work."

He scowled.

"Abel, I will be home just as soon as the competition is over for the day," Emily interjected. "You can tell Esther that."

He nodded.

"Abel, before you go," I said. "Did you happen to

see anything odd outside of the church this morning when you were helping with the setup?"

"You mean the missing pig?" There was the smallest smile on his face when he said this, and his reaction caught me off guard. I don't think I had ever seen him smile before, not even when we were children.

"Well, yes, and I wondered if you happened to see Josephine around the time you arrived and were beginning to set up."

The tiny smile disappeared. "I didn't see the pig, but yes, I saw Josephine."

My pulse quickened. "Was she with anyone?"

He shook his head. "She was alone."

I felt my face fall. I should have expected this answer. It was very likely that Aiden had already asked Abel if he'd seen Josephine that morning outside the church.

"She was alone," Abel said. "But she seemed to be waiting for someone."

"For who?" I asked.

"I don't know. I know nothing about how she died," he said and scowled a little bit more. I wouldn't have thought that was possible. "This is what you want to know, is it not?"

"Well, maybe you saw something that will help the police."

"I didn't." His tone left no room for argument.

"Did you speak to her?"

"*Nee*, why would I speak to her? She is not a member of my district," he said as if that was reason enough not to speak to someone.

I gave him a half smile. "I'm not a member of your district either, but you are speaking to me."

"And I should not be." He turned and said something to his sister in their language and stomped away.

Chapter 15

Emily blushed as she watched her brother walk away. "I'm so sorry that Abel was rude to you."

I waved her concern away. "It's fine. There's nothing to worry about."

She scrunched up her face. Not for the first time, I wondered what living with her two unhappy siblings must be like for Emily.

"You really have done a great job on the taffy. Thank you," I said, feeling I needed to give her a compliment. Even though I couldn't understand their language, I doubted her brother had said a kind word to her before I'd arrived at the table.

The Amish girl blushed. "It was nothing."

I smiled. "I appreciate it all the same."

She smiled.

Down the line of tables, the judges had just begun judging the taffy. Two uniformed deputies followed a couple tables behind the judges, asking the contestants questions about Josephine Weaver and, I noticed, bagging samples of each table's offering of licorice from the previous round of judging.

I patted Emily's arm. "It's showtime."

She raised her white-blond eyebrows. "Showtime?"

I simply laughed at her confusion over the English expression.

"Oh, green apple," Jeremiah said when he reached my table. "How unique. Most of the other contestants went with more conventional flavors."

"I'm not conventional," I said.

Beatrice wrinkled her nose. "We noticed this."

I stopped short of rolling my eyes at her comment. "The green apple is a little nod to our town's apple harvest. Peppermint is my traditional offering." I smiled.

"That was a very sweet idea of yours," Margot said. "I like it that you thought of incorporating Harvest in your choice of flavors. That does speak well of you."

Beatrice gripped her clipboard a little more tightly. "Let's just see if the taffy is edible before we start patting her on the back."

Emily lifted a small plate with three pieces of green apple taffy on it. Each judge took a piece, unwrapped it, and tasted. Jeremiah put the entire piece in his mouth. Beatrice took a dainty bite, and Margot pulled at the taffy until it broke into two pieces and ate one half.

Jeremiah's eyes watered. "My, you really packed each piece with green apple flavor. Doing Harvest proud, I would say."

"The texture is perfect," Margot said.

"It is not terrible," Beatrice added. Considering the source, I took that as high praise indeed.

They all made notes on their clipboards.

"Now the peppermint," Margot said.

The three judges tasted my second taffy offering.

"This is just as good," Jeremiah said.

"We should move on to the next table." Beatrice folded the scrap of waxed paper her piece of peppermint taffy had been wrapped in.

"Yes, of course," Margot said. "We have to keep to our schedule. Thankfully, this is the last judging for the day. We can regroup this afternoon and evening and, hopefully, put all the unpleasantness of the day behind us."

I frowned. Was Josephine's death mere unpleasantness for the ACC judges?

Before following the two female judges to the next table, Jeremiah grabbed another piece of my green apple taffy and winked at me.

"I think you have a good chance of winning this round, Bailey," Emily said with a bright smile.

"Let's not get our hopes too high. They still have a lot of candy makers to judge," I said.

Emily started to package the taffy in small white boxes with SWISSMEN SWEETS embossed on the side, six pieces in each. She set them on the table for the tourists to grab. There was no candy for sale at the candy-making contest. All the candy made was given to the visitors for free. The visitors paid a small cover charge of five dollars each to attend the ACC. That didn't seem like a lot, but with over one thousand people expected through the weekend, it added up.

The town hosting the ACC could choose how to use the money raised. Harvest planned to use the money to update the playground next to Juliet's church. The playground equipment was the same as

I had played on as a little girl when I visited my grandparents in Harvest for the summer. Even back then it had been outdated.

The ACC would be open for another hour or so after the winner of the taffy round was announced. Even so, I began to tidy up the table in between speaking to visitors who stopped by and grabbed what was left of the licorice and taffy we'd made that day. I noted, as I spoke to a woman in a red coat, that the two deputies skipped our table. I knew that Aiden had already collected a sample of my licorice since it matched the piece found in Josephine's apron, but I was surprised that they didn't stop to ask me any questions as they had the other ACC contestants. Had Aiden instructed them not to? I didn't know if that was a good sign or a bad sign. My intuition was leaning toward bad.

Across the square, Lindy packed up her booth. She didn't have a single piece of taffy left on her table. There was no doubt in my mind that she was going to bolt the moment the judges announced the winner of the taffy round. I mulled over my conversation with her before the judging. I couldn't help but wonder what had happened to cause her to speak so personally of grief.

My table was in order, and Emily was chatting with friends on the other side of the square. I considered going over to Lindy's booth to see what else I could learn from her. Before I could even walk around the table, Margot pulled out a bullhorn and walked to the top step of the gazebo. Who thought it was a good idea to give that woman a bullhorn?

"Thank you again to everyone who came to the Amish Confectionary Competition," she shouted into the horn. "We are humbled and overjoyed by the turnout of candy makers and visitors to our little hometown of Harvest."

The crowd that had gathered around the gazebo clapped. Emily joined me at the foot of the gazebo and squeezed my hand. "You'll win this round."

I winked at her.

"We hope that you will all join us tomorrow," Margot went on, "for the last day of the competition, when we'll announce the overall winner of the ACC. Now, without further ado, it's my pleasure to announce the winner of this round. With the most points in taffy in the categories of taste, texture, and presentation . . ."

I felt my body tense.

". . . the winner is—" She paused dramatically. It was evident that Margot was enjoying keeping both the crowd and the candy makers in suspense. "Swissmen Sweets!"

Beside me, Emily gasped, even though she had predicted the win. I blinked in surprise. I had wanted to win, of course, but I had never expected to take a round of the competition. I was not Amish.

Emily hugged me, which shook me out of my stupor. "Congratulations, Bailey. The green apple taffy was a hit!"

I blinked. "I guess so. Or maybe it was the peppermint."

"It was both," she assured me.

While Emily was hugging me, I missed the name of the candy shop that was eliminated from the candy-making competition that round, but from the resigned expression on the face of the candy maker from Florida, I guessed it was he. Everyone else just appeared to be relieved that they hadn't been chopped. Who knew Amish candy making could be so cutthroat?

I grinned at Emily. "We live to make candy another day." I grimaced as I realized what I had just said. Josephine hadn't lived to make candy, literarily or figuratively, another day.

Emily smiled, clearly missing my faux pas. "We did!"

The visitors were starting to stream out of the square. Traffic on Main Street would be a mess for the next half hour. It was lucky that all I had to do was weave around the cars and buggies to cross the road between the square and Swissmen Sweets. As far as commutes went, it didn't get any better than that.

Margot came down the gazebo steps and made a beeline for me. "Congratulations, Bailey. You have done Harvest and your grandfather proud."

Tears sprang to my eyes at the mention of my grandfather. "Thank you."

She held her bullhorn at her side. "Now keep it up. We need you to win it all for the town." With that, she spun around and went to speak to the other judges.

I had to win it all for the town. No pressure, right? I sighed. I knew Margot's compliment came with a price. It seemed everything she did had an ulterior motive, and most of the time it was furthering the success of the village of Harvest.

As I made way back to my table, visitors and other candy makers stopped me to congratulate me on the win. I couldn't help but wonder if they had

had the same reaction to Lindy Beiler when she won the licorice round. There had been so much commotion over Josephine's death, it was lost in the shuffle.

Emily beat me back to the table. I smiled at her. "I'll finish cleaning up here. You should go back to your shop. I don't want to keep you too long. I know Esther must be wondering what is taking so long."

Emily scrunched up her nose. "Esther knows I'm helping you."

"All right," I said. "I will leave it to you to contend with your sister."

Emily laughed. "I've been doing it all my life, and I'm happy to help you, Bailey. Whatever gets me out of that hot pretzel shop works for me. It's nice to have a break and do something different. That's something that my sister will never understand. She has been doing the same things every day since our parents died. I don't think she knows how to do anything else, and she would be perfectly happy if I did the same." She said this last part with a slightly bitter tone that I had never heard in her young voice before.

Emily and I finished packing up my table for the evening. All the while, I couldn't help but keep a close eye on the church across the square. In the last few hours, there had been little or no activity around the church. I itched to sneak inside the large white building and take another look at the organ.

I was mystified as to how someone could have lifted Josephine onto the platform inside the organ. True, she was a tiny woman, and I could have picked her up if I was forced to. However, it would take someone with a good deal of strength and coordination to lift the woman's body over their head. But how else could she have wound up on that platform? I couldn't imagine that she went inside the organ of her own volition. But I could be wrong. What did I know about Josephine Weaver? Next to nothing. Most of what I had learned about her had been in my short conversation with her niece, Charlotte Weaver. I still had to find out how Charlotte was related to me. That would be the next item on my agenda as soon as I returned to Swissmen Sweets.

"Do you know Charlotte Weaver?" I asked Emily as I set my supply crate in the rolling cart from Swissmen Sweets.

She looked up from the basket that she was filling with supplies to be carted back over to the shop for the night. "Charlotte? *Ya*, I know her from town. We're from different districts, though, and she is a couple of years older than me."

Emily was twenty, so that would put Charlotte's age at twenty-two or twenty-three. For some reason, I'd thought she was still a teenager.

"Is there anything you can tell me about her?"

She shrugged. "She's quiet and likes to be off to herself. Maribel doesn't care much for her."

Maribel Klemp was Emily's best friend. She worked with her grandmother Birdie at the cheese shop next door to Swissmen Sweets, on the opposite side of the candy shop from Esh Family Pretzels. I wasn't too surprised to hear Maribel didn't care for Charlotte. As far as I could tell, the girl didn't care for many people other than Emily.

"Why doesn't Maribel like her?" I asked.

"I suppose she doesn't have anything against Charlotte personally. She just doesn't much care for the entire Weaver family."

"Why's that?" I leaned on the table in our booth.

Emily's smooth brow wrinkled as if she'd just realized that she might be revealing too much. She forced a laugh. "Oh, you know."

It was my turn to wrinkle my brow. "I know? I know what?"

"Nothing. I must have misspoken."

I didn't think she'd misspoken at all. I squinted at her for a beat. She looked away from me. Maybe I needed to have a chat with Maribel about the Weavers.

Emily's frown deepened. "I'm just surprised Charlotte hasn't left the Amish way yet."

"Why's that?" I asked again.

"You can always tell when someone is going to leave," she said, sounding much like her know-it-all sister. "There is a feeling about them. Like a nervousness. They are just itching to escape to something new. I always got that feeling from Charlotte. And then there is her love of music." She snapped the lid on the gallon container of white sugar.

"What's the issue with the music?" I asked. "Why can't she love music?"

"It's not that she can't love music. It's just that she wants more than we are supposed to have. My district lets us sing in church and even play a few simple instruments, but all music should be used to praise God in church. Charlotte's district allows some singing, but no instruments. Charlotte is disobeying her bishop by playing the organ, and I

heard that she's been listening to the radio too."
She added this last part in a whisper. She shook her
head. "I suppose technically she can do that since
she is still in *rumspringa*, but it is frowned upon."

"Why would there be a limit on music?" I asked,
still not understanding what the problem was.

"It's not our way. It can give us ideas if it's not
controlled. Some bishops, like mine, are more le-
nient. Charlotte's is not . . . ," she trailed off.

The light finally dawned inside my head. "Ideas
about leaving?"

She shrugged. I took that as a "yes."

Emily frowned. "Why do you want to know about
Charlotte? Does this have anything to do with her
aunt dying?"

"Maybe," I said.

"That's as good as a 'yes' coming from you, Bailey
King." She placed the sugar container in the basket.

I chuckled; maybe Emily knew me better than I
thought she did. "What about Deacon Clapp? What
do you think about him?"

She frowned and appeared much more reluctant
to answer than she had been about Charlotte.

"Does something bother you about him?" I asked.

"*Nee*, of course not. He is a deacon and should be
respected."

"Tell me about him."

She glanced down at her slim wrist even though
she wasn't wearing a watch there. "We should really
hurry up. I know my sister will start to wonder what's
become of me."

I smiled, knowing that Emily had not been in a
rush to return to the pretzel shop just a few minutes
ago. I decided to let her off the hook for now. It had

been a long day, and she'd been a huge help to me. I didn't want to make her think that I was ungrateful for everything she'd done by quizzing her about her community. "Thanks for your help, Emily." I hugged her.

"Any time, Bailey." She smiled. "You took in Nutmeg. There's nothing I wouldn't do for you."

"I should be the one thanking you for Nutmeg. Not to say that he doesn't get into his fair share of mischief, but I do like having him around. He's good company for *Maami* too, though I don't think we'd be able to get her to admit that."

She lowered her voice. "I'm glad. I want Clara to find peace."

"So do I," I whispered. "So do I."

Chapter 16

When I returned to Swissmen Sweets, the shop was hopping with customers. My grandmother was serving a line ten deep that ran all the way back to the door. I slipped through the front door with my cart and tucked it in a corner of the shop. I jumped behind the counter and started serving customers. *Maami* smiled at me, but there was no time to talk.

After the crowd died down, *Maami* took a breath. "Bailey, so many people have come over from the ACC wanting to buy taffy, we're just about out of it. Is it true that you won that round?"

I grinned. "Yep."

She smiled back. "*Gut.*"

I was relieved to see a little bit of sparkle back in her eye.

"Ahh, it is closing time," she said. "Lock the door before any more of the tourists can bombard us—not that I have much left to sell."

I laughed and went to the front door to lock it. As I did, Nutmeg appeared from under one of the candy shelves. He was a social cat, but he much preferred it when we closed shop for the day and he had *Maami* and me all to himself. He wove around my ankles.

Behind the glass-domed counter, *Maami* wiped her hands on a tea towel. "Many of the tourists were speaking about an accident at the church today. A woman was killed." She studied me.

I winced. I should have known that my grandmother would have heard about Josephine's death. I should have told her when I was at the shop earlier in the day, so she wouldn't be blindsided by the news.

"It was Josephine Weaver," I said.

She frowned and began stacking empty silver trays to be washed that night for tomorrow's candy display. "Was that why you were asking me about Charlotte earlier?"

I nodded. "Charlotte was the one who found Josephine. Juliet and I were inside the church at the time looking for Jethro."

She frowned. "Jethro is still missing?"

I nodded. "I'm afraid so. I'm going to help Juliet look some more this evening."

"*Gut.*" She rested her elbows on the counter and folded her hands into a prayer shape. "She needs your help. Jethro is important to her."

I nodded.

"And you should help Charlotte too. She needs all the help we can give her."

"Help we can give her?" I asked. "Are you encouraging me to investigate the murder?"

She pressed her lips together in a thin line. "You need to help Charlotte. She is family."

"How exactly are we related to Charlotte?"

"Her grandmother is—was—my cousin. Her grandmother has been gone many years now. We weren't close at the time of her death, but we were very close once upon a time." She said this with such sadness, I blinked.

"What happened?" I asked.

Maami grabbed a broom from where it rested on the back wall by the swinging door that led into the kitchen. She began to sweep.

I thought she wasn't going to answer me. "*Maami*? Will you tell me what happened between you and your cousin?"

"It wasn't just my cousin; it was my whole family. I had once been a member of that district, but when I decided to marry your grandfather, they turned away from me."

"But you're still Amish. What difference did it make?"

"Not all the Amish are the same. Some are stricter than others, and my father was very strict. He didn't want me to leave the district or marry your *daadi.*"

"But you knew *Daadi* your entire life," I protested, leaning on the counter.

"This is true, but it didn't matter, not to my family. They wanted me to stay in the district and marry a man from our community, but I knew in my heart that your *daadi* was the one for me. It was a difficult decision, but I never regretted my choice."

"Your family cut you off after you married *Daadi*? You never told me that before."

She smiled. "I don't remember you ever asking."

I felt myself blush. *Maami* was right. I had never asked her about her family. All she had ever told me was that her parents had died when my father was a child. I never asked for more information than that. Now, because of my lack of curiosity about her, I was just learning that I had cousins. I swallowed. "Did they shun you?"

She shook her head. "My parents didn't, although our relationship was never the same. They still communicated with me, but after they passed away, my relationship with my family fell away even though I tried to stay in touch. After a time, I'm ashamed to say that I stopped trying."

"This is why you let my father marry my mom."

She nodded and continued to sweep. "Jebidiah and I were disappointed. We wanted our son to remain Amish, but when it was clear his mind was made up, I knew it was his choice to make. It was harder for your *daadi*, but I reminded him of our marriage, and he couldn't argue." She took a deep breath. "I could never cut my child off. I wasn't much different from my son. I left my district for love. How could I deny my son the same chance?" She held onto the broom and turned to me. "And I cannot imagine not knowing you, my child. That's what would have happened. That is what happens when someone closes herself off to another person. So much is lost."

Tears sprang to my eyes. I couldn't imagine not knowing my grandmother either. It was my grandparents and their candy shop that had inspired me to become a chocolatier. I would have had a completely different life without them. I took a deep breath. "I'm glad that you and Dad still get along."

"Me too."

I nodded. I needed to change the subject before I started crying. "Charlotte is your cousin's granddaughter? Does that make her my second cousin? I never know how that works." Taking my lead from my grandmother, who was incapable of standing still, I started flipping the chairs over onto the table in the small eating area in the front of the shop, so we could sweep the floor more easily.

"A cousin is a cousin. It doesn't matter exactly how we are connected. We are family, even if most of my family no longer would make any claim to me."

"How did Charlotte know that you had once been a member of her district? You left long before she was born."

"Her grandmother told her. Charlotte said that she told her my story when she was a small child. Maybe my cousin could tell even then that Charlotte was likely to leave the district, and my cousin shared my story with her as a cautionary tale to scare Charlotte into staying in the district. It is very frightening to young people to be told that they will be cut off from all of their family if they leave. Many young Amish stay in the faith even though they might not want to because they don't want to lose their family. However, I think in the case of Charlotte, the threat of shunning backfired. Charlotte showed up in the shop a couple of years ago and wanted to talk to me about leaving the district. I told her that it was hard, but it was a choice that only she could make. She has visited me from time to time since then. She was here just this morning."

I froze, holding a chair in midair. "Charlotte was in Swissmen Sweets? Where was I? I'd never seen her before we met in the church."

She frowned.

I finished flipping the chair over onto the table.

"She was here while you were over at the square setting up for the day. It was early. Eight maybe."

I nodded, but a knot began to form in my stomach. I had packed my supplies for the ACC before I left the shop that morning, which meant that was last time I'd seen the two vials of licorice extract. "*Maami*, when was the last time you saw the licorice extract?"

She blinked at my abrupt change of subject. It might have made perfect sense to me, but it clearly did not to my grandmother. After a moment, she answered, "A week ago. That was the last time I filled the extract bottles."

I frowned. That was what I was afraid she would say.

"Charlotte is a sweet girl. I think she is close to making a choice. She won't be able to live in both worlds much longer. She must decide if she wants to be Amish or *Englisch*. Every Amish child must make this choice."

I frowned. "Why are they forcing her to choose? Why must she choose at such a young age? I didn't know what my life would look like at twenty-two."

"You're looking at it as an *Englischer*, not as an

Amish person. Charlotte may be struggling with her choice, but it's one that she has to make."

"It doesn't seem fair to me."

She lifted the block of wood that divided the main room from the area behind the counter and handed the broom to me. "It is fair."

"But—"

"No but," she interrupted me. "Every person has to make a decision about how she will live her life. That is no different in the Amish world or the *Englisch* world. It is the free will that *Gott* gave us. It is not only a choice, but a responsibility to choose."

I thought about this for a moment. I had thought that I had chosen my life, but maybe I had been wrong, because after six years pursuing the dream of being the head chocolatier at JP Chocolates, I had suddenly shifted my course.

"It is those who cannot choose," my grandmother went on, "those who cannot decide what their life will be, who are stuck. They remain broken. They don't trust themselves to decide. They don't trust *Gott* to guide them to the right choice. Charlotte is a *gut* girl. I don't want that painful uncertainty to be part of her life. *Gott* wants us to choose because it's better for us in the end. But Charlotte won't be able to make this decision with her aunt's death hanging over her head. That's why you have to help her."

"I—I—" I wasn't sure what to say. I had liked Charlotte, but I didn't know her. Before, I'd gotten involved in a murder investigation because my grandparents were suspects. Charlotte might be my second cousin, but I didn't know anything about her.

My grandmother stepped around the side of the counter and dropped the block of wood after her. She began to sweep the floor and was quiet for a while before she whispered, "Do it for me, Bailey."

When she said that, did I really have any choice?

Chapter 17

"Have you eaten today?" my grandmother asked.

I smiled at her. "Does candy count?"

She shook her head. "Your *grossdaadi* would say *ya*, but I say *nee*." She grinned.

I was happy to see that some of the tension caused by our conversation had left her face. "I'm not hungry."

She frowned. "Now I know that you are worried. You don't eat when you're anxious. You never have since you were a little girl. I will make you something to eat." She leaned her broom against the front of the domed counter.

"*Maami*, please, you've been in the shop all day by yourself dealing with all the customers while I've been busy at the ACC. I can get something when I'm ready. I can take care of myself."

Her face fell. "Let me, my dear."

At that moment, I realized that my grandmother's need to feed me was greater than my need to eat. "All right," I said, but she didn't hear me. She was already making her way up the stairs to her apartment before I could say a word.

After I had eaten, I told my grandmother I was going out again.

She sat on the small sofa in the sitting room of her apartment and knitted quietly. "Where are you off to now?"

"I'm going to help search for Jethro, and I think I promised you that I would help Charlotte."

"You are going to look for Charlotte?"

I shook my head. "Not yet. I need to talk to her again, but there are a few people I would like to track down first."

She nodded. "I have knitting to do. I know you will help Charlotte."

"You could come with me," I said. "The shop is closed for the night."

She simply shook her head and returned her concentration to the knitting in her lap. My heart hurt as I left the room. I had moved to Ohio to help my grandmother, but I didn't think that I was helping her at all. I grieved over the loss of my grandfather as well, but her grief ran so much deeper.

Maybe if I helped Charlotte, it would raise her spirits. I didn't tell my grandmother my other motivation because I didn't want to worry her, but I also had to investigate the crime because I was a prime suspect. I knew Sheriff Marshall would be perfectly happy if he could charge me with any crime. Murder would be his preference.

I stepped out of Swissmen Sweets onto the sidewalk and saw that the sun was making its downward trek as Amish men worked quickly to clean up the square. Abel Esh was among them. He was carrying a cafeteria-style table by himself as if it weighed no more than a paperback book. He caught me staring at him, and I looked away.

I shook off the eerie feeling that Abel always gave me and looked at the street. An Amish girl walked down the sidewalk and turned right on Apple Street, which ran perpendicular to Main. As she turned, I caught sight of the side of her face. It was Maribel Klemp.

I jogged to the corner and made it there just in time to see her start to untether her buggy horse from a hitching post.

"Maribel!" I called.

The Amish girl turned and frowned, but I was happy to see that she didn't jump into the buggy and gallop away. She held the reins lightly in her hand and waited for me.

I jogged up the street. When I came to an abrupt stop in front of her, my feather earrings brushed my shoulders.

"Do you need something?" she asked. "Did your friend need some more cheese?"

When I had first come to Harvest, my best friend from New York had visited and almost completely bought out the Cheese Haus. "No, I think Cass is well stocked for a long time to come."

Maribel put her foot on the step to climb into the buggy.

"I was wondering if you had heard about what happened at the church today?"

She paused with one foot on the step. "*Ya*, I

heard about Josephine. Emily told me. I am sorry for her family."

"Do you know her family well?" I asked.

"As well as I know anyone else.'" Her answers were short, as if she didn't want to answer me at all, but politeness forced her to speak.

"When I was talking with Emily, I got the feeling you might not care for them."

Maribel scowled. "I don't like or dislike them. I don't know them well enough to care."

"That's not the impression I got from Emily."

She sniffed. "Your impressions are of no matter. Was that all you wanted to ask me?"

It was, but I scrambled to think of something else because I doubted that Maribel would be willing to talk to me about the Weavers again. "What about Josephine? How well did you know her?"

"I already told you how well I know the family." She climbed into her buggy. "If that's all you have to say, I will leave now."

I stepped back as she pulled the buggy away from the curb. My shoulders sagged as I watched her buggy roll down the street and then around the corner. I should have known better than to take the direct route with Maribel. I shook my head. There was no way I could change the conversation now. It was time for me to meet Juliet and the rest of the Jethro search team on the square. I turned to go but caught a glimpse of the hunched-over Amish woman I had seen earlier in the day. She disappeared around the corner where Maribel had turned. I blinked. How could she have gotten there when I had been watching Maribel drive down the street? I know I would have noticed an older woman shuffling down Apple Street.

I ran to the corner to catch up with the woman and stumbled to a stop. Apple Street was a quiet residential street in Harvest. Most of the homes were English. However, a few were Amish. The easiest way to distinguish between the two was to check whether or not power lines went to the house or if there were plain clothes hanging outside to dry on the line. The Amish line-dried their clothes, even in October.

I looked up and down the street, but there was no sign of the woman. I supposed she could have gone inside one of the houses on the street.

"Thank you all for coming!" I heard a shout come from the square and knew that the search party for Jethro was about to start. I sighed. I would have to put the mystery of the old woman on hold for the moment.

I buttoned my coat as I stood around the gazebo with the church's choir members and other residents of Harvest. The group waited in the cold for an explanation as to how the search for Jethro would go. It was nearing six in the evening. We didn't have much light left. Sunset would arrive within an hour and a half whether or not Jethro was located. The temperature was already dropping.

Juliet stood on the gazebo's step next to Reverend Brook, wringing her hands. Her worry had only increased as the hours since Jethro's disappearance ticked by. Jethro was a pampered pet, not a sturdy farm animal like most swine in the county. He wouldn't do well in the wild overnight.

As much as I wanted to be optimistic that we would find the polka-dotted pig, I was doubtful. Jethro had been missing for nearly twelve hours, and we were out in the country. Anything could have gotten him. It made my stomach twist to think something might have snatched up the little animal. Yes, Jethro was a troublemaker, but he was also a charmer. I didn't want anything to happen to him.

I scanned the crowd. Harvest was a very small town. It had about the same number of residents as there had been on my block back in New York. Even though I didn't know everyone gathered around the gazebo that evening, I recognized their faces. Many of them had visited Swissmen Sweets at least once in the time I'd been working there. Most of them were English, but there were also some Amish in the crowd. Everyone in the village knew how important Jethro was to Juliet, and she was well liked by both the English and the Amish in the community.

Aiden was noticeably missing from the search. I should have expected that he wouldn't be there. He was in the middle of a murder investigation. I knew he wanted his mother's pig found just as much as she did. I told myself that I was disappointed for Juliet—not for me—that he wasn't there.

"Settle down, settle down," Reverend Brook said, breaking into the conversations whirling around the group like the leaves shaking in the breeze on the tree limbs above our heads.

Slowly, the crowd grew quiet.

The small man nodded. "Thank you. W-we are here to look for Jethro," the pastor stammered. "As you know, he is very important to Juliet."

"He's important to all of us. Jethro is important to the entire community," a voice called from behind me.

I turned back to see who this polka-dotted pig fan was but couldn't pick out who'd made the statement.

Tears welled in Juliet's eyes, and she gripped Reverend Brook's arm. "I just want to say how grateful I am to each and every one of you for being here this evening. It warms my heart to know so many of you care about Jethro."

"Don't worry, Juliet," someone else called from the crowd. "We'll find him."

She buried her face in Reverend Brook's shoulder and cried.

The reverend appeared stunned by her sudden display of emotion. If it had not been for the gravity of the situation, I would have chuckled at his semi-terrified expression. If I had been a betting woman, I would have said that the good reverend and the southern belle would be marching down the aisle in the big white church within a year.

"Here, here!" another voice called.

I was happy Juliet had so much support from the community.

Reverend Brook clumsily patted Juliet's back. "We don't have much light left today, so we should fan out. I hope you all brought flashlights for when the sun does set. The gas lampposts around the square won't give off nearly as much light as you'd think."

I patted my pocket. I didn't have a flashlight on me. I hadn't thought to bring one, but I had my cell phone and could use the flashlight app in a pinch.

Juliet lifted her mascara-streaked face from the reverend's now damp shoulder. "Remember to call out if you see any sign of Jethro."

Chapter 18

Slowly the group broke up, and searchers walked in every direction. Reverend Brook was left standing inside the gazebo with Juliet, and it was clear he didn't know what to do with her when she buried her face into his shoulder a second time.

As the search party fanned out, I felt like I was in the search-for-the-beast scene from *Beauty and the Beast*, minus the pitchforks and the heart-pumping musical score. Then I looked again and saw that the man in front of me *was* carrying a pitchfork, albeit a small one. I hoped he didn't plan to use it on Jethro or anyone else.

Two women stood to my right, and I recognized one of them as the church secretary. The other woman I had seen in town but couldn't place. The church secretary's name was Cate. Somehow, I had been able to pull that out of the back of my mind. I bet Juliet had been the one who'd told me the woman's name. She was my only real connection to the church and its congregation.

"A missing pig and a murder—who knew that Harvest would ever be this interesting?" Cate's friend shook her head.

"Joy, that is no way to talk," Cate reprimanded her searching companion. "But you know the murder happened in the church. The whole place should be doused with holy water to get the bad ju-ju out."

Joy rolled her eyes. "We aren't Catholic, Cate. We don't have holy water sitting around."

"We should, and Reverend Brook better get on that." The secretary wrinkled her long nose. "At the very least, he can sprinkle some on the organ. That's where she died, you know. Inside the organ. Who would bother killing someone inside an organ? That seems like very cramped quarters to me. I've only been in there once, and I was dying—excuse my poor choice of words—to get out."

"I don't think she was killed inside the organ," Joy replied. "Why would Josephine have gone in there with someone?"

"Why was Josephine inside the church at all? You know how she felt about us *Englischers*."

"That's easy. She was there to see Charlotte, her niece. It's as plain as the nose on your face."

Cate wrinkled that nose. "You know how much I hate that expression."

"It's just an expression," Joy argued.

"You wouldn't feel that way if you had a nose like mine." She touched the end of her long nose.

"There's nothing wrong with your nose. It's a perfectly good nose." Joy folded her arms. "Can we focus on the task at hand? We haven't even looked for the pig yet."

Cate looked around the square. "Maybe we shouldn't be out here. I like Juliet as much as anyone, but my husband wouldn't be pleased if I got killed searching for her pig when he thinks I'm at choir practice."

Joy snorted. "You're not going to get killed. We have the buddy system, and we'll be fine. Besides, I don't think we have anything to worry about. We aren't Amish."

I stepped closer to the women, cracking an unseen twig under my foot.

The two women screamed in unison and covered their chests as if to hold their beating hearts in place.

"I'm so sorry," I said, stepping on another twig. There were so many twigs and sticks in the grass; I wondered how long it took for the town lawn service to pick them up.

"You nearly gave us both a heart attack," Joy said. "You need to be more careful where you're going. You can't sneak up on people when there is a murderer loose in town. It's just not done." She shone the flashlight in my eyes.

"She's right," Cate agreed.

"I really am sorry. I'm just here like you are, to look for Juliet's pig." I held up my hand, blocking the flashlight's beam. "Can you put that out? It's not even dark yet."

"You're not a member of the church," Cate said in a less than friendly tone.

"No, I'm not. I'm a friend of Juliet's."

Joy clicked off the flashlight. "You're Bailey King. Clara and Jebidiah's granddaughter."

"God rest his soul," Cate said. "Jebidiah was the kindest of men. Always gave my kids extra free samples from his candy shop."

"Mine too." Joy smiled at me. All the suspicion that had been there a moment ago left her face. "Sorry to holler at you just now, but as you can see, everyone in town is on edge, what with the murder and the missing pig."

"Do you think they could be connected?" I asked, happy that they seemed willing to talk to me about the murder. Gathering information, at least from these two women, was going to be easier than I'd expected. "Maybe whoever killed Josephine did it to steal the pig," I suggested.

Cate shook her head. "Jethro went missing before Josephine died. I can't see how the two things could be related at all. Besides, Jethro and Josephine have nothing in common. The Amish don't have pigs for pets."

"But both incidents happened around the church," I said. "The square was the last place Juliet saw Jethro, right across from the church, and Josephine was found inside the church."

"Inside the organ," Joy clarified.

I nodded. "Right. Inside the organ."

"I still can't see how they could be connected." Joy shook her head. "I wonder if Aiden has given it any thought."

Cate eyed me. "Speaking of Aiden, aren't you and Juliet's son an item? Juliet talks about the two of you quite often. She's very happy about your relationship with her son."

"There is no relationship." A blush rushed to my cheeks. "We're not an item. Our families are friends. That's all."

Cate shook her head. "That's not how Juliet sees it. In her mind, the two of you are practically married."

"We aren't," I said in a tone that left no room for discussion.

Cate shrugged. "She thinks the same about her and Reverend Brook, for that matter, so it's possible she has it wrong, I suppose."

Joy frowned. "In any case, it's a shame. You can't do any better than Aiden Brody. Aiden is one of the nicest men in the county, even if he works for that tyrant of a sheriff. I wish someone in the county would work up the nerve to run against him.

"If Aiden ran, he'd be the next sheriff. Mark my words, and then he'll be a real catch." She winked at me. "If I had an unmarried daughter, I would be throwing her into his path every chance I got. Sadly, I do not. My daughter married a grocer in the next town over, a year ago. He's nice enough, but he's no Aiden Brody."

Cate nodded in agreement. "Take my advice, Bailey, and lock that boy down. If you have his mother on your side, you're set. Aiden has always doted on Juliet. He's at the age that he should be looking for a wife by now."

"I know young people seem to be getting married older and older nowadays," Joy said with a sigh. "My daughter was thirty-eight when she got married. Thirty-eight! Can you believe that? Now she's thirty-nine, and I have very slim hope of any grandchildren."

"A lot of women have children later in life now. I don't think it's all that uncommon," I said.

"Maybe less so where you are from," Cate said. "But in Holmes County, most people still get married at a proper age."

"And what's a proper age?" I asked, even though I suspected I'd find the answer annoying.

The church secretary placed a finger to her chin and thought for a moment. "I'd say between twenty-two and twenty-six. At twenty-seven, it might take longer to find someone, and each year it becomes harder and harder."

I was twenty-seven. Had I been a milk cow, Cate would have put me out to pasture.

"If you count the Amish in the county, it's even younger," Joy added.

"Many of the Amish still marry in their late teens or early twenties," Cate said.

Joy nodded. "I wanted my daughter to get married right out of college. Was that too much to ask? I even sent her to college so that she'd come back with a ring on her finger. No luck. Over ten years later, she showed up with a grocer on her arm. Heaven help me. I'm losing hope for grandbabies. My daughter told me to call her dog my granddog. Can you believe that?"

"Maybe she doesn't want children. Maybe they are happy with the dog," I suggested.

"Hold your tongue," Joy said. "Are you saying that I'm going to die without having the joy of grandchildren in my life? That's why I had children in the first place. Well, that and to have someone to take out the trash on garbage day. My children were never consistent with that, so I should at least be given grandchildren to make up for the disappointment."

It was time to steer this conversation back on track. "I happened to overhear the two of you talking about the murder. I'm sorry if it sounds like I was eavesdropping, but I couldn't help but pick up on your conversation. It's so horrible what's happened."

Cate nodded. "And during such an important weekend for the town too. Right in the middle of the ACC. We have never had an event in Harvest as important as the Amish Confectionary Competition."

"Did you know Josephine?" I asked.

"I did," Joy said, looking as if she had a sour taste in her mouth. "She was a prickly woman and not a kind neighbor."

"She was your neighbor?" I asked.

"Not my neighbor, but my brother's neighbor. Or at least Jeffrey's store is next to her candy shop in Berlin. And all she ever did to him was complain about the noise and traffic going into his shop. He told me she'd even called the sheriff's office once about it. Whoever heard of an Amish woman voluntarily calling the sheriff's office? I sure haven't."

"What happened when she reported him to the police?" I shoved my cold hands in my jacket pockets, wishing I had thought to bring gloves for the search.

"Not much," Joy said. "Aiden was the one who went out, and I think he was able to talk my brother down. Jeffrey was mighty worked up over it. In his forty years of running the hardware store, he'd never once had someone call the police on him."

I considered this new piece of information. If Aiden was the deputy who went out to talk to Jeffrey about the complaint, that meant he knew about it. It also meant that he might have Jeffrey on his suspect list. I needed to learn all I could about the hardware store owner.

Cate tapped her chin. "I still don't know why Josephine was inside the church. I've never seen Josephine Weaver there. She's very strict, you know. I think that was why I thought it was so odd when I saw her."

I froze. "You saw her? When?"

"This morning," Cate said. "She was outside the church."

I thought for a moment. "But can't that be easily explained? Except for myself, almost all the contestants are storing their ingredients and other supplies inside the church fellowship hall."

Cate nodded. "Yes, I remember that now, but she was there much earlier than any of the rest of them. Besides, Berlin is less than ten miles away. She really didn't have to store her things."

"What time was she there?" I asked.

"Maybe seven. I was at the church early. Reverend Brook always arrives at seven-thirty on Thursdays because that's the day he writes his sermons," Cate said confidently. "I arrive just before him to make sure he has everything he needs, including his Earl Grey tea. The reverend is very partial to Earl Grey tea."

Joy snorted. "He should make his own tea, if you ask me."

Cate shook her finger at her friend. "I'm not going to give him a hard time about it. He gives me four weeks' paid vacation plus personal days. I'm not going to put up a fuss about making tea."

Joy rolled her eyes.

"Was she with anyone?" I asked.

Cate blinked at me. "Who?"

I inwardly groaned. "Josephine. Was she with anyone when you saw her outside the church?"

"No, I don't think so, but she was pacing. I remember that for certain. It struck me as odd. It's not often that you see an Amish woman pace back and forth like that. Typically, they're better at hiding their emotions. If I was pressed to decipher what that meant, I'd say Josephine Weaver was nervous."

And a few short hours later, she was dead.

Chapter 19

As it turned out, the flashlight app on my cell phone might be decent for finding my keys at the bottom of my purse, but it wasn't great for searching for a missing pig in the brush. The tiny light illuminated only a few inches of space beyond my outstretched hand. Two hours had passed since the search for Jethro began, and the sun had set.

Because I wasn't doing much good searching for Jethro in the bushes dotting the square, I walked across the street that divided the church's property from the square. A half dozen strong beams of light moved back and forth around the church as the searchers canvased the area for the missing pig in a grid pattern. There were enough searchers moving about the grounds with adequate flashlights to help me see where I was going.

Flashlights moved across the parking lot's blacktop, and dozens of voices called Jethro's name. "Jethro?" I called, adding my voice to the mix.

"I should have expected to see you here searching for Juliet's pet," a man said behind me. I turned to see Jeremiah holding high a battery-operated lantern.

I raised my eyebrows. "You're looking for Jethro too?"

He nodded.

"I didn't see you around the gazebo," I said.

"I was a little late. I had to go home and feed the animals on my farm. I've been away so much, with the ACC being in town, that I haven't been able to give my farm much attention."

"Is it a large farm?" I asked.

"*Nee*, just enough to sustain me. I don't need much." He patted his ample stomach. "Although it may appear otherwise. All this candy tasting might make the problem worse. I have a sweet tooth, but I don't know when I've eaten so many sweets."

"You're not a candy maker?"

He laughed. "*Nee*. I'm only a candy eater."

"Then how . . ." I trailed off.

He smiled. "Then how did I end up one of the judges?"

"Well, yeah," I said.

He laughed. "Margot asked me to do it as a favor to her. She was having trouble finding a second Amish judge. Most Amish don't like to make judgments on each other."

"But you do?"

He shook his head. "I can when the need arises, and judging candy isn't that difficult. The ACC was supposed to be an easy assignment, and it was until . . ."

"Until Josephine died."

He nodded. "It is tragic what happened to Josephine. It's a great loss to the community."

While we spoke, I was aware of other searchers shaking the bushes around the church and calling Jethro's name.

"What time did you get to the ACC this morning?" I asked.

He frowned. "Maybe eight. Not too early."

Only an Amish person would think eight A.M. wasn't too early.

"Were you the one to open up the church to let the candy makers collect their supplies?"

He shook his head. "I left all that to Margot."

"When would she have done that?"

"She said she got to the church just before me, so I would say sometime between seven-thirty and seven forty-five."

"That's specific," I said.

"It is because the ACC judges met at eight-thirty sharp in the gazebo. I arrived at the gazebo first."

"Did you see Josephine before that meeting in the gazebo?"

"Josephine Weaver? No. Why on earth would she be there? She didn't store her supplies in the church the night before because we are so close to her shop in Berlin."

"Jeremiah!" an Amish woman called and waved from across the parking lot.

"That is my wife," he said. "I should go see what she wants. I do hope someone finds Jethro tonight, so we can put this all behind us."

I hoped so too.

After Jeremiah left to speak to his wife, I scanned the group of searchers milling around outside the church. I didn't see Cate or her friend Joy anywhere. Or Reverend Brook, for that matter, although I knew he would be there until the bitter end of the search because of Juliet.

As I walked around the building, keeping my eyes peeled for any sign of Jethro or Reverend Brook, my thoughts kept returning to what Cate said about seeing Josephine pacing outside the church. The only explanation was that she was waiting for someone. Was it Charlotte? According to the two women I'd just met, that was the only explanation that made sense. Things didn't look good for the young Amish organist.

I wanted to help Charlotte, and not just because my grandmother had asked me to. There was something about the vulnerable, confused Amish girl that made me want to protect her. Maybe it was because, in a way, we were in the same situation. After having a life planned for us for so long, we were changing our minds. My life plan was to be the head chocolatier of JP Chocolates in New York, to have wealth, prestige, and a relationship with one of the most eligible bachelors on the culinary scene. In one visit to Holmes County, I had abandoned the plan and chosen a new life, not just to help my grandmother, but also myself. I didn't like the person I had become in New York, but choosing a new path was much harder than I'd anticipated. I had naïvely thought that, by choosing a new and better way, the pieces of my life would fall into place like the gears of a clock. I had been wrong. If it wasn't for my grandmother and the work I loved at Swissmen Sweets, I might have given up by now and returned to my old life.

A shout came from behind the church, and it didn't sound like the victory cry of someone who'd found Jethro. It sounded like a cry for help. I ran around the side of the large white building and found myself in the back parking lot. A security light illuminated the rear entrance of the church; it flickered on and off above the stainless-steel door, which I knew led into a tiny utility room and then in turn to the church's kitchen.

"This will never come out," a large man in a wool peacoat exclaimed to two women. I recognized the trio from the gathering around the gazebo at the beginning of the search.

The man stood on the edge of the parking lot that butted up against the church graveyard. The stark white fence set off the cemetery. The fence posts were so white they reminded me of clean bones, which wasn't the most comforting of analogies considering where they were located.

"This paint will never come out." The man threw up his hands. "Where is the sign? Shouldn't there be a sign here that says 'wet paint'? I'll make sure that Reverend Brook hears about this." He stomped past me around the side of the church without giving me a second glance. The two women hurried after him.

I walked over to the fence. I could clearly see the place where the man had brushed up against the newly painted wood. I looked up and down the fence line, and just as the man had said, there was no sign that warned of the wet paint.

Normally, I would have thought nothing of it, but it did strike me as odd. Hadn't the two workmen mentioned hanging a sign or wanting to hang a sign? Where could it have gone?

A breeze picked up, and cold wind snaked down

the collar of my coat. I shivered, wishing that I had thought to grab one of my grandmother's hand-knitted scarves before leaving Swissmen Sweets for the pig search. Perhaps the wind had blown off the workmen's sign?

A shrill whistle broke into my thoughts. I followed the persistent and irritating sound of the whistle around the side of the church, across the street, and toward the gazebo. When I reached the gazebo where the rest of the search party were gathered around just like they had at the beginning of the search, I caught my breath.

"Reverend Brook, for goodness' sake, take that whistle out of your mouth before you wake all the dogs in the neighborhood!" a male voice called from the crowd.

As if on cue, a dog somewhere nearby began to howl.

Reverend Brook let the whistle fall from his mouth, and it dangled from a string around his neck.

"What about my coat?" the man I had seen behind the church cried. "Who is going to pay my dry-cleaning bill?"

"Yes, yes. Charlie, please send the church your cleaning bill for the coat," Reverend Brook said. He stood beside Juliet again at the top of the gazebo steps.

Juliet clutched the reverend's arm. "Thank you all so much for looking for Jethro. The reverend and I both agree it's far too dark to continue today. With his coloring, Jethro tends to blend in with shadows." She took a shaky breath. "I can't tell you how much it has meant to me that you are all here. If you could, say a little prayer for Jethro. I know there are much bigger problems in this world and much bigger problems in our town even. I think of what the Weaver family must be going through tonight, but a prayer for my little pig will help if you could just spare a minute. I—" She burst into tears and buried her face in the reverend's shoulder again.

Reverend Brook looked every bit as perplexed as he had when she'd done it the first time. He awkwardly patted her back and managed to say. "Thank you all for coming. Please keep your eye out for Jethro."

As the group broke up, I climbed the steps to the gazebo. Juliet released her death grip on the reverend's hand. I hadn't even reached the top step when Juliet threw her arms around me, nearly sending me flying back into the grass.

"Whoa!" I said, sounding like an Amish buggy driver pulling back on her horse's reins.

"Bailey," she moaned, "thank you so much for coming to help. If only Aiden had been here. I know that, between the two of you, you would have found Jethro. You make a good team."

"A team?" I tried to step away, but she held me fast.

"The two of you solved that murder weeks ago together."

I frowned and stopped myself from correcting Aiden's mother. Yes, a murder had been solved when I'd first arrived in Harvest weeks ago, but it had not been a team effort. I had solved that murder on my own. Aiden had arrested the wrong person. Despite the murder and her missing pig, Juliet always seemed to be able to steer the conversation back to Aiden and me. What she didn't understand was that we weren't a couple. Our families were friends. That was it.

It was time to direct the conversation away from Aiden. "Jethro will turn up," I said with more confidence than I felt as I finally pulled away from her.

"Did you see any sign of him?"

There was so much hope in her voice, I hated to squash it. I shook my head. "There was no sign of him."

She nodded. "We're calling off the search for the night. It's the right thing to do, but so hard."

Before I could say anything, the reverend jogged across the square to his church. He could move pretty fast for a stout man.

Juliet gave me a final squeeze and ran down the steps of the gazebo after him, waving her hand. "Simon! Simon!"

They disappeared across the street, leaving me on the top steps of the gazebo, shaking my head and wondering what had just happened.

I removed my phone from the back pocket of my jeans and checked the time. It was just after eight in the evening. My grandmother would be in bed by the time I returned to the candy shop. She and my grandfather had always been early to bed, early to rise folks, so that they could make their sweets and candies fresh every morning for their customers. However, since my grandfather's death, my grandmother had been going to bed earlier and earlier. It was as if she was happy to see the end of each day.

I didn't have to be a psychologist to recognize the signs of depression. If I had been back in New York and found my best friend, Cass, or another friend in such a state, I would have suggested she go to a therapist to work it out. I knew better than to make such a suggestion to my grandmother. The Amish weren't ones for counseling, and they would certainly not seek out professional help from an English person they didn't know.

I had thought that by staying in Harvest after my grandfather's death I could make my grandmother's life easier. I couldn't say definitively that I had. Yes, I had taken over most of the day-to-day work in the shop, but she seemed to move through her days in a cloud.

My grandmother had many trusted friends in her community, but she seemed to be pulling away from them now too. When I encouraged her to see her friends, her excuse was that she had too much work to do at the candy shop. I couldn't argue with her on that point. In the last week, *Maami* had been almost solely responsible for minding the shop as I prepared for the ACC. I promised myself that, after the competition ended, I would lighten my grandmother's workload if she would let me. I wasn't certain she would.

I left the gazebo and wondered if I should return to the church to double-check that the reverend had locked the storage unit but thought better of it. It had been an impossibly long day, and tomorrow promised to be just as long with the second and final day of the ACC.

As I walked away from the gazebo in the direction of Swissmen Sweets, I couldn't help but be disappointed that Jethro remained missing. In the short time I had known him, I had become attached to the little oinker. Even if he did have a tendency to bite me. Juliet insisted that the bites were love nips. I wasn't so sure. But as of yet, he had never bitten down hard enough to break the skin.

After such a difficult day, it would have been nice to have something go right.

I shook my head. It was still so hard for me to believe that Josephine Weaver was dead. She was very much alive when she had yelled at me in front of everyone at the ACC that morning. I knew I shouldn't concern myself with her death. Aiden would agree with that, but when it came down to it, I was just as much a suspect in her murder as anyone else. Maybe more so, since I had had access to the murder weapon, and I had a strong motive since Josephine had wanted me removed from the competition.

I stepped up to the locked door of Swissmen Sweets and removed my key from my coat pocket. I was just about to put it into the lock when someone said, "I need help."

And my keys flew into the air.

Chapter 20

I scooped my keys off the sidewalk and shoved them into my right fist with the pointed ends poking out of my knuckles, the way I had done when walking home from the subway at night. I scanned up and down the sidewalk. Nothing. The square was empty. When the choir members and others who had helped search for the pig decided to clear out, they didn't mess around. I was the only one on the street.

"Is someone there?" I asked.

"It's me." The whisper came from around the side of Swissmen Sweets in the narrow alley between the candy shop and the pretzel shop next door. "I need your help." The voice was high and young.

"My help?" I asked. "I can't help you if I don't know who you are."

A small figure inched out from around the side of the building. She had her head down, and a large black bonnet covered much of her face, but the light from the lamp over the door reflected off strawberry-blond hair. "Charlotte?"

"You said if I needed help, I should come find you. I do, so I did." Her body trembled beneath her black cloak.

I turned to unlock the door to Swissmen Sweets. "You had better come inside and tell me what's going on."

When we stepped into the shop, the sharp scent of vinegar filled my nose. Despite its harshness, I found the smell comforting. As always, *Maami* had cleaned all the counters and tables before going to bed. Even in the middle of her great grief, she completed all her self-appointed tasks.

Nothing conjured the image of my grandmother more than the smell of vinegar. When I had lived in New York, my best friend, Cass, had never understood why I loved the scent so much or insisted that we clean all the work stations at JP Chocolates with vinegar instead of chemical disinfectants. Until recently, Cass hadn't known about my connection to the Amish. I simply told her the vinegar was more ecofriendly, which was true.

Nutmeg wove in and out of my legs and meowed. He looked up at me with his big amber eyes. I shook my finger at him. "I know perfectly well *Maami* fed you dinner before going to bed. Don't give me those 'poor me' eyes."

Charlotte laughed. "You talk to your cat like he's a person."

"He's not a person?" I asked in a teasing tone. "Don't tell him that. It would break his kitty-cat heart."

She stared at the cat in alarm.

I chuckled. "I'm teasing. Even if you told Nutmeg he wasn't human, he wouldn't believe you."

"He is a sweet kitten." She knelt and held out her hand to the small orange-striped ball of fluff. As she moved, her cloak and long skirts hit the floor.

Nutmeg, never one to turn down the chance to make a new friend, toddled over to her. While the two got acquainted, I removed the chairs from the top of one of the café tables in the front room. "Why don't you have a seat while I grab us some fudge. Then you can tell me what you are doing here." I walked across the room to the sale counter and lifted the piece of wood that separated the front of the shop from the work area behind the counter and slipped through.

She perched on the edge of one of the chairs, and Nutmeg jumped onto her lap. The cat spun in a circle before settling into a tight ball.

Charlotte stroked the cat's back. "I don't want any fudge."

I set the knife on the cutting board. "You might not want any, but I think I'm going to need a substantial helping. My grandmother doesn't keep alcohol in the house, so this is the next best thing for a day like today."

I opened the back of the refrigerated, glass-domed counter and removed the tray with the chocolate peanut butter fudge on it. I knew I needed to pull out the big guns for this one, and in times of crisis, nothing worked better than my grandfather's chocolate peanut butter fudge . I sensed that Charlotte was in a time of crisis. I took two small white plates from the shelf behind me and set two healthy pieces of fudge on each.

"How does chocolate peanut butter sound?" I asked.

She smiled. "That's my favorite."

I grinned, holding the two plates up for her to see. "A girl after my own heart."

She looked at the ceiling. "I don't want to wake your grandmother."

I stepped back around the counter. "Don't worry about that. *Maami*'s bedroom is in the back of the building." I set the plates on the table and took the seat across from her.

She had removed her black bonnet, but she left the cloak on as if taking it off might signify that she planned to stay for a little while.

I glanced at the large plain clock that hung on the wall behind the counter. It reminded me of the clocks that had hung in every classroom of my high school back in Connecticut. It was close to nine. "Charlotte, does your family know where you are?"

She shook her head. "*Nee*, they do not."

"Oh-kay." I slid her piece of fudge in front of her and waited.

"They can't know that I came to talk to you. They would not like it. They believe I'm in my room at home."

"You snuck out of your house?" I broke off a small corner of the chocolate peanut butter fudge. It seemed to me that sneaking out of the house wasn't a very Amish thing do to. I started to stand. "I can give you a lift home, and you can tell me what's going on in the car. I don't want your family to worry."

She shook her head and placed her hand on the table. "Bailey, please. I can't go home right now."

"Won't your family worry if they discover you are gone?" I hesitated for a moment and sat back in my seat.

"When they realize I'm gone, they will. But that can't be helped. I can't go home. I can never go back home again."

"What happened? Did someone hurt you?" I leaned forward in my chair.

She shook her head. "*Nee*. At least not in the way that you mean. I am hurt because my family . . ." She trailed off.

"Your family what?" I prompted.

"My family doesn't believe in me, in who I am. If they cannot do that, I can't stay with them." She stared at me with her large blue eyes. "I was hoping I could stay here."

I shifted back in my chair away from her. "I . . ."

"It wouldn't be forever." She folded her small hands on the table. "It would just be until I figure out what I want to do or what I should do."

I broke off a big piece of fudge and shoved it into my mouth. It seemed like the best idea, and the moments it took for me to chew and swallow the ginormous piece gave me time to think. I swallowed finally, and my throat felt raw.

"I know it's a lot to ask of you. I know you are in the candy-making contest and . . ."

"There's nowhere else you can go?" I asked.

Her face fell.

I reached across the table and patted her hand. "I'm not saying no. I only wondered if there was someone else you could stay with whom you know better," I said quickly.

"I know Clara well."

I reached across the table and patted her folded hands. "I know. Of course, you can stay here. We are cousins, aren't we?"

Her face broke into a smile. "We are. *Danki*, Bailey. You won't even know I'm here."

"My grandmother will be pleased."

She frowned. "I don't want to cause Clara any trouble."

"I wouldn't worry about it. *Maami* wanted me to help you."

"She was from my district." She dropped her hands to her lap. "They will disapprove."

"I know; she told me that, but she hasn't been part of your district for a lifetime. I seriously doubt she cares what they think of her at this point."

Her face cleared, but just as quickly it clouded over again. "I wish I didn't care."

"Charlotte, do you say your family doesn't believe in you because of your aunt's death?"

"*Nee*. It has been like this for a long time. It just took what happened to my aunt today to show me that they will never change and to show me that I don't want to change either."

"Can you tell me what happened?" I asked.

She studied my face. "You were there."

"I was, but I want to hear your side of the story. You know something, don't you? That's why you are here, isn't it?"

"It is." She picked up her bonnet, stared at it for a moment, and placed it back on the table. "And you are right. I do know things."

I pulled my plate of fudge within easy reach. Something told me I was going to need it. I broke off a small piece.

She moved her black bonnet from the tabletop to the lap of her plain navy dress. "I don't even know where to begin. Everything has become so jumbled in my head. I have tried to pray for clarity. I have asked *Gott* to tell me what is the right path, what I should do, but I get only silence in return. Perhaps He has abandoned me."

I shook my head. "My grandparents taught me that their God will never abandon them."

"It is their *Gott*, not yours?"

The piece of fudge I was chewing seemed to become lodged in my throat. "I don't know yet." I swallowed again, forcing the fudge down. "Why don't you start by telling me why you left home?"

She looked up at me. "That might be the most complicated question of all. I've been planning on leaving for a long time, but I've been afraid. Have you ever been in a situation when you knew the right thing to do, but you've been too afraid to act?"

Several memories rushed into my mind. The most prominent was how long it had taken me to break up with Eric. That decision was still fresh and still held a sting. I had known for months that I needed to break up with him, but fear had stopped me. Fear of being alone. Fear of how he would react. I never feared that he would hurt me physically, but Eric had the power to ruin my chocolatier career in New York. He was that well connected. I hoped that he would be a grown-up and not be vindictive after the breakup, but I wasn't sure, which was just more proof that I needed to get out.

You should know how a person will react to something after being together for a year. Thankfully, a tabloid had saved me the trouble of making the decision. Bad press ended our relationship; there was nothing Eric hated more than bad press.

I smiled at her. "More than once."

She took a breath. "What happened today, what I found today, finally gave me the courage to do it. I know that must sound terrible because I'm telling you that another person's death, another person's murder, gave me the courage to leave the only life I have ever known, especially when . . ." Her voice caught.

"Because it was your aunt who died."

She nodded, and a large tear rolled down her round cheek. "Yes, because my family believes it is my fault she's dead. When they said that, I knew there was no way I could put off leaving any longer."

I stared at the piece of fudge I was about to pop into my mouth and dropped it on the plate. "They think you killed her?"

She shook her head. "You don't understand." She clenched the rim of her bonnet. "My family doesn't think I killed my aunt. They don't think I gave her the licorice to eat, but they do blame me for her death. My father said that my disobedience to *Gott* led to her death."

I blinked at her. "How is that even possible?"

"Because my aunt would never have been at the church if I hadn't been there playing. Don't you see? It comes back to being my fault. She was there to take me home."

I shook my head. "I would have thought she was there because of the ACC."

"I suppose that could be true, but my being there was what brought her into the church. She had no other reason to go inside."

"You can't know that," I said. "It's very possible no one will know why Josephine went inside the church this morning."

"What other reason could she have for being there?" she asked.

Nutmeg jumped onto my lap and curled up. I dug my fingers into his soft fur. "Do you think you were doing the wrong thing by playing the organ?" I asked. "Do you agree with your family?"

"My deacon believes that I was. My district and my family believe I was too."

"I'm not asking what your deacon believes or your district or your family. I'm asking you what you believe. Do you think that you did something wrong by playing music?"

She was quiet for a long moment. "How can music be against *Gott*? I have asked the deacon this so many times."

"What does he say?"

"That we should not use instruments to improve the sound of *Gotte's* world. That is the *Englisch* way to want to improve things, not the Amish way. We should be happy with the way *Gott* created things and not look for ways to improve something that is already perfect from the start."

"The Amish never improve anything?" I asked. "What about farming, building, and quilting?" I pointed at the piece of fudge on my plate. "What about making new recipes that are better than the last?"

"That's different," she said. "We don't spend time on anything that is impractical, and music, I suppose, is impractical. It brings joy but is not something that we must have to survive, like food or shelter."

I nodded at the fudge on the table. "My grandfather perfected his fudge recipe. Wouldn't you say that was impractical?"

"But it is food," she countered.

I shrugged. "Maybe. But it's unnecessary food. You can eat much healthier things than fudge, things like vegetables, bread, and fruit. Wouldn't his time have been better spent on more practical things?"

"But it was his livelihood. This candy shop supports your family. That makes it different."

"Doesn't music support some families?" I continued to play devil's advocate.

"I don't know. I suppose it does for some, but not for me." She placed her hand to her temple. "When I play, I feel happy, and I can share my happiness with those who hear me."

I pointed at the plate in front me. "My fudge gives happiness to the person who is eating it. It's really the same thing when you think about it."

She nodded. "Yes, I suppose this is true."

"Can't happiness be enough of a reason to create something?" I asked.

"I—I don't know. I've never given myself the chance to think about all these things. My church and family teach me what to think."

"That's the real reason you are here, isn't it?" I asked. "You need to think this all through for yourself."

She looked me in the eye for the first time and nodded.

Chapter 21

Early the next morning, I reached out for my phone where I always leave it on the nightstand, and my hand connected painfully with the hardwood floor. It was a jarring reminder that I wasn't in my one-room apartment in New York any longer, but in Harvest, Ohio, and sleeping on the floor of my grandmother's guest room.

After our chat in the candy shop, I had given up my bed to Charlotte, hoping the tortured girl would get a good night's sleep. I knew she needed the rest much more than I did, but I was regretting that decision now as my muscles groaned in discomfort.

I waved my hand in the air to fight the stinging of my hand, which for the moment was worse than the soreness in my back. I knew that would shift as the day went on.

Slowly, I sat up, and a wave of vertigo washed over me. I'd had one too many pieces of fudge yesterday to compensate for the stress of the day.

I wished that I had my cell phone in hand so that I could check my messages, but I'd left the phone downstairs charging in the kitchen, as I did every night since I'd moved in with my grandmother. In my grandmother's Amish district, the Amish were allowed to use electricity for their businesses only, not for their homes,

If I was going to stay in Harvest permanently, I knew I needed to find my own place in town, preferably with electricity, but I'd worry about that later.

I sat up and tucked that worry away to ponder at another time. I had enough to be concerned about now with the ACC, a runaway Amish girl who was bunking with me, and possibly being framed for murder.

I chewed on my lip. No matter how much I liked her or how much my grandmother wanted to help her, I couldn't rule out the possibility that the person who'd framed me was Charlotte. The licorice extract had disappeared after she was at Swissmen Sweets visiting my grandmother. And now she was back in the candy shop.

I propped myself up on my elbows and peered at the bed, expecting to see Charlotte there, sleeping on her back like an Amish princess waiting for Prince Charming to come and kiss her awake. There was no Prince Charming. Just me and the empty bed.

Forgetting my aches and pains, I jumped up off the floor. Where could she have gone? I had told her to lie low until I had a chance to talk to my grandmother about her staying at Swissmen Sweets.

There was a small clock on the nightstand—battery-operated, of course. It read eight-thirty. I groaned. I was supposed to wake up at four to help my grandmother make the fresh candies for the day.

Still in my pajamas, I ran down the stairs that led from my grandmother's living quarters to the front room of the shop. I couldn't imagine what my hair looked like after I'd spent most of the night tossing and turning on the floor.

I heard voices in the kitchen. Without breaking my stride, I pushed through the swinging door that led into the kitchen. My grandmother and Charlotte froze as I burst in on them. *Maami* had been cutting fudge into pieces that measured one inch by one inch. She held her knife suspended in the air, while Charlotte held a mixing bowl of melted chocolate and was pouring the hot liquid into waiting candy molds in the shape of Amish buggies. Our buggy chocolates were one of our bestsellers because they were both a candy and a souvenir, and with so many visitors in Harvest for the ACC, the chocolate buggies sold out fast.

Nutmeg was perched on one of three metal stools in the kitchen, licking his paws like he didn't have a care in the world. He was the only one in the kitchen who seemed undisturbed by my dramatic entrance.

Maami set her knife on the cutting board next to her. "Bailey, you are as white as a sheet. What is wrong?"

I glanced at Charlotte.

The girl ducked her head and resumed pouring the remainder of the chocolate in her bowl into the last mold.

"I-I didn't know that Charlotte had come downstairs," I stammered.

My grandmother smiled. "Charlotte has been working with me since four this morning. She is quite good at making candies."

Charlotte blushed. "I used to make candies with my mother at Christmas. I have always liked it."

"I'm so sorry. I was the one who was supposed to be up making the candies for the day. Why didn't you wake me?" I asked my grandmother.

She shook her head. "You needed your rest to compete in the last day of the ACC."

"I know, but . . . ," I trailed off. I was going to say that I hadn't gotten a chance to speak to her before she saw Charlotte.

My grandmother must have sensed my hesitation because she said, "Charlotte, can you peek in the storage space under the stairs and pull out another jar of molasses? I think I will need that for one of the hard candies I'm going to try my hand at today while Bailey is at the competition."

Charlotte set the now empty bowl of chocolate in one of the deep sinks. "Of course."

"Do you know where it is?" *Maami* asked. "The storage space is right under the stairs that go up to the second floor. You can't miss it."

Charlotte nodded, "I know where it is."

"*Gut.* Take your time looking," my grandmother advised.

I suspected that the "take your time looking" was a hint that my grandmother wanted to talk some things over with me. That was good. I wanted to talk some things over too.

The Amish girl gave a single nod and went

through the swinging door that led into the main part of the shop.

After the door came to a stop in its back-and-forth swing, I opened my mouth, ready to speak, but my grandmother beat me to it. "I know why Charlotte is here. She's left her family, and if my suspicions are right, she is getting ready to leave the Amish way altogether. It is what I predicted."

I walked over to the outlet behind one of the industrial mixers and unplugged my phone. The green indicator light blinked incessantly, telling me that I had several messages. I guessed that half of them were from my best friend, Cass. I had tried to call her late last night after Charlotte had fallen asleep, but she didn't answer. Instead, I had left a vague message about making a discovery. As I had learned from experience, it wasn't a good idea to leave Cass a text that said I had found a dead body if I didn't want to be chewed out by my fiery Italian friend.

Normally, I would slip the phone into the back pocket of my jeans, but since I was still in my unicorn pajamas, I just held it. I was certain that I was the only person to wear unicorn PJs in the kitchen of Swissmen Sweets. Ever. "Did you say that she planned to leave the Amish? She told me she was here because she needed to think about what she wanted."

Maami gave me a sad smile. "Don't you think I would recognize the signs of one who is about to leave?"

I swallowed, knowing again that she meant my father. Even though a lifetime had passed, there were still hurt feelings on both sides, but now that I knew my grandmother's history of leaving her own district to marry my grandfather, I wondered if she wasn't thinking of herself as well. As she'd said, at some point everyone had to make a choice about how he or she would live their life.

"I'm sorry. I didn't wake up in time to warn you Charlotte was here. She showed up late last night and needed a place to stay. I knew you wouldn't mind."

She shook head. "I don't mind. There is no need to apologize. The girl needed a place to sleep, and you gave her shelter. It was the right thing to do." She picked up her knife and resumed cutting fudge.

"Maybe. But I don't think her family, her district, or the police will like that she's here."

"Aiden won't mind. He will understand."

"Aiden isn't the only member of the Sheriff's Department," I said.

She stopped cutting and looked up at me. "It is best that we not make it common knowledge around the village that Charlotte is here. It will be better for Charlotte if fewer people know where she is staying."

"You want to hide her from the district?" I asked, surprised. As far as I knew, my grandparents never hid anything.

"We aren't hiding her. If someone sees her or asks if she's here, we will answer honestly. I would never ask you to lie."

"I know that," I said with a smile. "Sounds like a plan."

"*Gut.*" She moved the fudge that she'd cut onto a silver serving tray to be placed in the glass-domed counter in the front room of the shop. There was the hint of a smile on her lips, and a pink tint to her cheeks. It was the best she had looked since my grandfather's funeral. She was happy. She was happy Charlotte was there in Swissmen Sweets, her home. Then it hit me. She could take care of Charlotte, just like she had taken care of my grandfather.

Charlotte needed her when I did not. I frowned. I had tried to fill that void for her, but I was too independent and too stubborn to ask for help, even when I really might need it. Being needed was what *Maami* needed, and I couldn't give her that.

"*Maami*, there's something I have been meaning to ask you."

"Hmm?" she asked.

"I've been seeing an old Amish woman wandering around the village."

"Does she have a hunched back?" *Maami* asked. I nodded.

"You must mean Ruby."

"Ruby?"

Maami nodded. "She lives in a little apartment over a yarn shop on Apple Street. When she feels up to it, she likes to walk around the village."

"I've lived here over a month, and this is the first I've ever seen her."

She shrugged. "Maybe you haven't noticed her before. People like Ruby tend to go unnoticed."

"What does that mean?"

Maami sighed. "She's not right in the head anymore. Most blame old age."

"Do you think it could be something else?"

She shrugged. "I don't know. Talking to Ruby is difficult."

"Where's her family?"

"They own the yarn shop and let Ruby live there."

I ran a hand through my hair, and my fingers got trapped in a nest of tangles, which I knew had been created from my tossing and turning the night before.

"Why don't you go get ready for the competition?" she said. "While you dress, I will make you breakfast."

"Pancakes?" I asked in the same hopeful voice I had used as a child. My grandmother's pancakes were the very best. They were almost as good as my grandfather's fudge.

She nodded. "Pancakes. We could all use pancakes this morning."

I couldn't have agreed more.

Chapter 22

Maami had been right. The pancakes were just what I needed. As Emily and I set up the booth for the day, I could have gone for a couple more even after devouring four.

"The first round of competition today is peanut brittle," I told Emily as I pulled a large jar of peanuts out of the supply crate.

"I hope no one is allergic to peanuts," she said.

I grimaced. "Me too. I think one allergy-induced death is enough for the ACC, don't you?"

Emily wrinkled her nose. "Can I ask you something, Bailey?"

I glanced at her, surprised by her serious tone. "Of course, you can."

She picked up the jar of peanuts and hugged it to her chest. "My sister saw something this morning and told me about it. It's been bothering me some."

I set the bag of sugar I'd been holding on the table and touched her arm. "What is it? What's wrong?"

She put the jar back on the table. "She said that she was in the alley this morning putting some trash in the Dumpster behind our shop."

I nodded encouragement.

"Well, Esther said that she saw Charlotte Weaver leave Swissmen Sweets by the back door."

I frowned.

"It's all over the district that Charlotte didn't sleep in her bed last night. Her family and the church leaders are very upset. Esther said that Charlotte must have spent the night with you. Esther believes that you hid her in Swissmen Sweets and that you may have orchestrated her disappearance from home last night."

I folded my arms. "I orchestrated nothing. Is Esther going to tell the district and Charlotte's family where she is?"

"I—I don't know. Esther doesn't like to get involved in things. She would much rather pretend that she never saw it."

"Then why did she say anything to you?" I asked.

"I think she was making some type of point." She stared at the tops of her plain black sneakers.

"And that point was?" I asked when she didn't answer.

"That I shouldn't be working for you during the ACC and I shouldn't be around you at all. She thinks that your *Englisch* ways will make me turn my back on my family and church too. Both she and Abel think so."

"I had nothing to do with Charlotte's decision to leave her family home last night. I only gave her a place to stay for a night. That's it."

Emily wrinkled her brow as if she remained unconvinced.

"Do me a favor," I said. "If this does come up in gossip, put all the blame on me. Keep my grandmother out of it. Tell them that she didn't know

Charlotte was there. I was the one who let Charlotte stay. *Maami* had nothing to do with it."

"Did Clara know?" she asked.

"She wasn't the one who let Charlotte stay at Swissmen Sweets. That was me."

Emily nodded and returned to emptying the supply crate.

I felt a knot form in my stomach. This was just what I had feared when I'd let Charlotte spend the night at Swissmen Sweets. I didn't want the Amish to think badly of my grandmother or believe that she was defiant in some way for welcoming Charlotte into her home.

I was debating about saying more to Emily when Haddie Smucker walked across the square toward her old table with a crate of supplies in her hands. She set the crate on the table next to ours. The table had been hers before she'd been eliminated from the competition.

Emily and I stood there watching her with our mouths hanging open.

Haddie glared at us. "Can I help you with something?"

"Are you back in the competition?" I asked.

She smiled. "I am."

"How?" Emily asked and then winced. I doubted that she had meant to ask the question out loud.

Haddie narrowed her eyes. "It seems that one of the contestants cheated in the last round yesterday, and they had a brief competition in the church kitchen this morning between the candy makers who'd already left the competition. I came out the victor, so yes, I'm back."

I raised my eyebrows, surprised that I hadn't heard anything about this sudden-death Amish candy maker match. I would have liked to have seen it. I was also surprised to hear that the standoff had occurred in the church kitchen. This meant the church was open today, even though Josephine had died there.

"Who did you replace?" Emily asked.

Haddie glared at her.

I stepped in front of Emily to block Haddie's death glare. "You said someone had cheated yesterday. Who was it?"

She gave me a sideways smile and glanced over her shoulder. I followed her line of sight. Across the square, an Amish woman cried as she packed up her candy-making supplies. The female Amish judge, Beatrice, stood in front of her with her arms crossed. If she was going for nineteenth-century disapproving schoolmarm, she had nailed it.

"That's Susan Klink from Lancaster. Wow," Emily whispered. "I can't believe she cheated. She has one of the largest Amish candy shops in the country."

Haddie sniffed, somehow making it sound triumphant. "Just because you have the biggest of something doesn't mean you came by it fairly."

"How did she cheat?" I asked.

"She went into the church to use the *electric* microwave to heat up her molasses for her licorice recipe. Can you imagine? She used electricity. Of course, that is absolutely off-limits. She, of all people, should know better. Then again, she is Beachy Amish—you know how they are."

I raised my eyebrows. "How are they?"

"They do not always follow the Amish way," Haddie said indignantly.

I frowned and glanced over at Susan again. In

her plain lavender dress, black tennis shoes, and white prayer cap, she seemed to be following the Amish way, as far as I could tell.

"Why did she do that?" Emily asked.

Haddie removed a white tablecloth from her supply basket and tossed it over the top of the table. After she smoothed every wrinkle out of the cloth, she said, "She claims her gas-powered burner wasn't working yesterday morning. She must have panicked and run to the church. Big mistake."

"Why didn't she ask another one of the candy makers for help?" Emily asked.

Haddie shrugged with that smug smile still on her face.

"What happened to her burner to make it stop working?" I asked.

Haddie sniffed. "I didn't hear the reason. In any case, if she was having an issue with her burner, she should have told the judges. Maybe they could have made arrangements for her to continue on, or as Emily suggested, she could have asked another contestant to borrow their burner to heat up her molasses. But to go into the church and do that is just unforgivable."

Unforgivable? That sounded a little harsh to me. My head started spinning. There might be no connection between Josephine's murder and the malfunctioning stove, but I didn't believe it. Two strong contenders had been removed from the ACC. The two incidents had to be related. I bit my lip. They could be related, I amended, downgrading my assumption. I couldn't let my mind jump three steps ahead before I had a chance to speak to Susan

Klink, and if I wanted to do that, I needed to move. Susan was all but packed up to leave.

I turned to Emily. "Can you start the brittle?"

Emily gave me a sideways glance. "You are going to talk to Susan, aren't you?"

"I have to before she leaves."

Emily shook her head. "Go."

Haddie must have overheard us because she said as I was leaving the booth, "Don't meddle where you don't belong, Bailey King. This is Amish business, and you have no right to get involved in any of it."

I didn't even bother to turn around. To me that sounded like a threat, but I'd received more than my fair share of threats. Haddie's comment wasn't even in the top ten.

Chapter 23

A lone tear slid down Susan Klink's red cheek as she tucked a bag of white sugar into her supply cart. She was a pretty woman close to my mother's age, with an upturned nose and large hazel eyes. Those eyes brimmed with tears.

I hesitated, knowing I was intruding on this woman's raw emotion. I almost turned around and returned to my own booth. That would have been the compassionate thing to do.

She wiped a tear from the corner of her eye with her index finger. "I'm very sorry, but I don't have any samples today. I'm sure one of the other candy makers can give you some." She squinted at me. "Oh."

I wrinkled my brow. "Oh?"

"You're the *Englisch* candy maker," she said. "I know Clara and knew your late grandfather very well. All the Amish candy makers who have been in this business for any length of time know each other." She frowned. "I'm sorry I'm not able to chat. I . . ." she trailed off.

There was a cool breeze in the air, and I tucked my hands into the pockets of my down vest. "I heard that you're leaving the competition."

She nodded, and another tear slid down her cheek. She swiped it away. "I'm so glad that my husband decided to stay home in Lancaster with the children during this competition. He would not like to see me cry. It's just my way. When I'm happy, I cry. When I'm sad, I cry. It drives him a little crazy." She gave me a wobbly smile. "It's a long ride back to Lancaster, so I pray that I will be all cried out by the time I arrive home."

I smiled. "I don't see anything wrong with your tears."

"That is kind of you to say."

"I heard what happened, and I'm so sorry. Is there anything I can do to help?"

"*Nee, danki.*"

She rubbed her nose with a handkerchief. "It's just so awful. If I could go back and undo what has been done, I would. Believe me, I would. This can't be happening. I have been running my shop in Lancaster for more than twenty years. I have never had such an issue. This was the first time I've been accepted in the ACC in all that time, and I so wanted to do well. When my stove stopped working, I just panicked. All I could think of was that I needed to heat up the molasses. The church was right there. It was early. I thought I could get there and back with no one noticing. I know it was the wrong thing to do. I got what I deserved."

"What happened exactly? How did your stove stop working?"

She pointed behind the small stove, which was just like the one at my station.

I walked around the stove and took a closer look at the connection between the stove and the gas. The fixture where the propane tank was connected was bent. It was as if someone had taken a pair of pliers and had purposely crimped the fixture so that the hose wouldn't connect properly. I shivered. If Susan had struck a match near the propane tank when the poor connection was on, she could have been killed. Many people at the ACC that day could have been killed.

I straightened up. "Someone did this. This was no accident."

She folded the navy cloth that had been draped over her table and hugged it to her chest. "What do you mean?"

"Someone tampered with your stove on purpose."

She blinked at me through her tears. "Why would anyone do that?"

"Did you show this to the judges? Did you see that bend in the connection between the stove and the propane tank?" I asked.

She shook her head. "*Nee.* I was just so upset when the stove wouldn't come on, and time was running out to make the licorice, I panicked."

"We need to tell Margot and the other judges about this. Whether it was done on purpose— which I think it was—or happened by accident, the malfunction was not your fault."

"But I was the one who went into the church and used the microwave. That was inexcusable." She gripped the handle of her cart with both hands until her knuckles turned white.

"It's not as bad as tampering with the equipment. That's truly inexcusable. We need to tell the police."

Her eyes went wide, and she gripped the cart handle a little more tightly. "The police? Can't I just leave? I have already been shamed by all of this. I have no desire to talk to the police."

I pursed my lips together. Even if Susan didn't want to tell the police, I knew that I had to tell Aiden on the off chance that this could be connected to Josephine's death. "Yesterday morning, you went over to the church to heat your molasses to make licorice?"

She bowed her head. "I did."

"What time was that?"

She lifted her head. "I don't know why that matters."

"Do you know what happened in the church yesterday?"

She placed a hand against her cheek. "Do you think I was there at the same time as whoever killed Josephine?"

"It's possible."

She trembled. "I was there close to ten in the morning, a little past actually. I remember because I needed to be quick to get back to my table in time for the judging."

"How long were you inside the church?" I asked.

"Forty-five minutes. I had just enough time to mix the licorice and pour it into molds. I decided that the molds could cool at my table."

"You took all your ingredients over to the church?"

She nodded.

"Did you have licorice extract with you?" I asked.

She picked up a tea towel from her table and

folded it before dropping it into her supply crate. "Well, yes, I needed it for the recipe."

"What's going on here?" Beatrice asked behind me.

I jumped. I hadn't even known she was there. I wondered how much she had heard. I turned around to find both Beatrice and Jeremiah standing behind me. Jeremiah held his clipboard in his large hands.

Beatrice narrowed her eyes at me. "Bailey, shouldn't you be at your own table preparing for the peanut brittle round?"

"I'm glad you're both here. I don't think you should make Susan leave the competition."

"What you think, Bailey King, is of no consequence."

"But—"

Beatrice narrowed her eyes. "Please don't argue with me, Bailey, or you will put your own place in the competition in jeopardy."

I dropped my arms to my sides. "The competition needs to be fair, and how can it be when someone has tampered with Susan's stove?"

"That is a serious accusation," Jeremiah said.

I nodded. "I know, and that's why I wouldn't say anything unless I was sure."

Beatrice pursed her lips. "And you are sure?"

"I am." I pointed behind the stove. "If you look there, you will see that someone has crimped the fixture where the hose is supposed to attach to the propane tank."

"No one in the ACC would do that." Beatrice sniffed.

"You would have said that no one here could

have committed murder," I said. "But Josephine is dead."

Beatrice's face flushed. "Whatever may have happened to Susan's stove has nothing to do with Josephine Weaver's death. You should remember that she did not die at the ACC."

"That may be, but—"

"There is no 'but,'" Beatrice snapped. "I have known every one of these competitors for years," she argued. "You are the only one who is new. If I were to worry about anyone causing trouble at the ACC, it would be you."

"Now, Beatrice," Jeremiah took a step forward. Even considering that he was three times the size of Beatrice, she remained the more formidable of the pair. "Bailey is Jebidiah and Clara's granddaughter. I think we can agree that she wouldn't do such a thing."

"She's *Englisch,*" Beatrice countered.

Susan ducked her head. "Please, please. This is all my fault. I thank you, Bailey, for trying to come to my aid, but what I did was wrong, and I should be removed from the ACC. I would like to leave quietly."

"But—" I began to argue.

Beatrice took a step toward me. "The decision has been made. What's done is done. I suggest that you return to your table and stop sticking your nose in where it doesn't belong."

This was the second time I had received such a warning today, and it wasn't even lunchtime yet.

Susan lifted her heavy crate of supplies, nodded at the judges, and shuffled away toward the line of buggies parked on Main Street.

"But—" I said again.

Beatrice stepped in my path. "Go back to your booth, Bailey King, before you are removed from the competition as well."

I jabbed my fists into my hips. "On what grounds?"

"I'll think of something."

I wanted to argue with her more, but I saw Jeremiah's face over her shoulder. He mouthed "no" at me. I frowned and decided to let it go for the moment. In any case, I wouldn't be able to investigate what was going on at the ACC if I was kicked out of it.

Beatrice stomped away with Jeremiah on her heels.

As I walked back to my table on the other side of the square, I made the mistake of glancing toward Haddie. The smug expression on her face when she'd told me about Susan's troubles was still firmly in place. If I had to guess who'd tampered with Susan's stove, my money was on Haddie all the way.

Chapter 24

Emily had the sugar in a double boiler for the peanut brittle and stirred it in a slow figure-eight motion, as I had taught her to do. "I was just about to add the other ingredients to the peanut brittle."

"*Danki*, Emily," I said, winking at her when I used the Amish word. "Let's finish up that peanut brittle, so it has time to cool before the judging."

She grinned back. Had it been Cass who was helping make my candies at the ACC, she would have peppered me with a thousand questions about my conversation with Susan and would be dying of curiosity over my confrontation with Beatrice, which clearly had not gone well. But Emily was not Cass. She didn't mention it or ask a single question. I was grateful for that because I was still processing what I had learned. There was a saboteur in the ACC. But would the person have gone so far as to kill one of her fellow competitors in order to permanently remove them from the competition, and if that was true and he or she had committed the ultimate crime, where would the killer stop?

I loved candy making as much as the next candy maker. It was my life's work, but it certainly was not a life or death occupation. It was not worth killing over. I would argue that no occupation, and certainly no contest that gives you little more than bragging rights and extra publicity in the Amish world, ever was.

A few minutes later, the peanut brittle was cooling on cookie sheets lined with parchment paper. The amber-colored candy was molten hot and smelled divine. It took all my willpower not to pluck one of those sugar-covered peanuts from the tray. In any case, that was a bad idea, one that could result in a third-degree burn.

Emily dried her hands on a dish towel. "You have a good chance of winning this round too, Bailey. Swissmen Sweets' peanut brittle is my favorite. I can't believe that any of the other candy makers here could make anything better."

"I appreciate the vote of confidence." I glanced at the time readout on my cell phone. I still had twenty minutes before peanut brittle judging began. That would give me enough time to run over and peek inside the church.

I must have had a look on my face because Emily shook her head. "Wherever you need to go, go. But promise me you will be back before the judging. I don't want it to be like last time when I had to go find you."

I frowned. "Last time, Charlotte found Josephine's body."

She wrinkled her nose.

"All right. I . . ." I trailed off because I noticed Haddie's posture. She wasn't watching me exactly, but her body was too still, as if she was putting all her focus into listening to what I was saying. "I'll be back in time for the judging. I promise."

Before I could change my mind, I ran across the square and the street that separated the green from the church lawn. I ran around the back of the church to the door that led into the utility room.

"Do you see the smudges?" One of the two painters in coveralls asked the other. "We're going to have to repaint this entire part of the fence. This isn't the only job we have today. I don't have time for repainting. Why did that moron touch the fence? And if that pastor thinks I'm paying for that man's dry cleaning, he's got another think coming. I don't have to pay people for their idiotic behavior. He should have seen the sign that said 'wet paint.' How dumb can you be?"

"But where is the sign?" his companion said.

"What? You put it on the fence before we left last night."

"Well, do you see it?" his friend asked.

The larger of the two men walked up to the fence. "What did that nimrod do, tear the sign off and throw it away? Oh, that steams me right through."

The smaller man rolled his eyes. "I don't think he purposely removed the sign. It wasn't like he wanted to get paint on his coat."

"He could have," the first man said in a sulky voice. "You hung the sign up, didn't you?"

His friend threw up his hands. "Yes! You saw me do it. You just said that."

"Then what happened to it?"

The smaller man shrugged. "I don't know. Maybe someone moved it."

"Who moved the sign?" the first painter asked. "Check the rest of the fence. Make sure it's really gone. I thought when we took this church job, it would be easy. Aren't church people supposed to be nice and all?"

The second painter walked the length of the fence. "It's gone."

Painter number one grunted. "I wish I knew who moved the sign. I'd tell them where they could put it."

"Doesn't seem to matter," the second painter said. "We can fix this smudge in the paint and leave. It's not really that bad. Reverend Brook made it sound like the entire fence was ruined."

"That is a small blessing. We have two more jobs to get to today. You knew it would be on us to re-paint and cover the cost. Reverend Brook is a penny pincher. Even if he is a pastor."

"In my experience," the second painter said, "most pastors are."

His friend grunted in agreement.

"Hey!" the second painter yelled. "There's the sign." He pointed into the cemetery.

I looked in the direction he pointed. In the middle of the cemetery, a good thirty feet away from the fence that surrounded it, there was a small stone mausoleum. On the round wooden door, a white piece of paper hung. The smaller of the two men jumped the fence and ran to the tiny building. He ripped the piece of paper from the mausoleum door and waved it in the air. "This is our sign, all right." He hurried back to the fence to show his friend.

"Darn kids," the first painter grumbled as he took

the piece of paper from the other man's hand. "They don't care about anything but having a laugh. They must have been the ones who moved this sign. They don't take the time to think about how much time we have to waste cleaning up their little pranks."

"Well, at least we know how it happened. Let's touch up the fence and leave."

The first painter grumbled in agreement.

I stared at the small mausoleum. It was no bigger than a shed. Why would someone move the WET PAINT sign to the front of the mausoleum? Was it kids pulling some kind of prank, like the painters thought? Had the sign simply blown off the fence and landed on the building? That seemed unlikely, especially since it was secured in place with two bright blue pieces of painter's tape. And on closer inspection, it was clear the small building hadn't been painted in years, if not decades. Who would ever believe that the mausoleum had a layer of wet paint on it?

However, that didn't change the fact that these were the two men I had seen painting the fence yesterday morning, not long before Charlotte found her dead aunt inside the church's organ. They might have seen something.

I stepped out of the shadow of the church. "Hello?"

The first painter jumped back and grabbed his chest. "You again? No, we haven't seen the pig."

I narrowed my eyes. "I wasn't going to ask you about Jethro."

"Jethro?" his friend asked.

I glanced at him. "That's the pig's name."

"Of course it is," muttered the first man.

I pressed on. "Do you know what happened inside the church while you were painting?"

The first painter sniffed. "If you're talking about that Amish lady who got killed, then yeah, we know, but don't think we had anything to do with it, because we didn't."

"Did you see anyone around when you were painting?" I asked.

The first painter raised his eyebrows at his friend. "No. Nobody was around. We were to paint the fence, and we wanted to finish up the job and get in and out of here as fast as possible."

I took a deep breath. "You didn't see anything at all? All morning?"

"There was that raccoon," the second painter mused.

His friend rolled his eyes. "The woods are full of raccoons. Why did you bother to tell her that?"

The younger painter shrugged. "What if I was wrong and it wasn't a raccoon at all but that pig?"

I latched onto that. "It just might have been," I said eagerly. "What can you tell me about it?"

He pulled on his narrow goatee. "'Coons can get big, but I thought it was too big for a raccoon."

"I don't know. 'Coons can be huge," the first painter said. "There was one that lived under my uncle's shed out in Knox County. He just left it alone because, I swear, it was the size of a bear cub. He figured a 'coon that size could have the shed."

His friend shook his paint brush at him. "There is no way that you saw a raccoon the size of a bear cub."

"You can ask my uncle if you don't believe me," the other man said, sounding a little miffed.

His friend snorted. "Your uncle is ninety if he's a day. He's not a reliable source."

"He is. The man is as sharp as a tack. He can recite the capitals of all fifty states."

"What does that prove?"

"Did you see something?" I interrupted the men's argument. "Other than the giant raccoon."

"Looked more like a groundhog to me," the first painter said.

"It was too fast for a groundhog," the second replied.

"How do you know how fast a groundhog can move?"

Raccoon or groundhog, their description gave me hope that they had actually seen Jethro on the lam. I had to get this conversation back on track. It was very close to going off the rails completely. "Where did the animal go?"

"Don't know. It ran into the cemetery. Could be there now, as far as we know."

"It would be if it was a groundhog. My uncle says they're really partial to graveyards." He shook his head, as if groundhog behavior was more than he could fathom. "Let's go get the paint we need to finish this job. Didn't I tell you that these church people are crazy?"

I watched the two men lumber away. I wanted to follow them, but I had too much to do. I had also promised Emily that I wouldn't miss the peanut brittle round. I couldn't afford to if I wanted to stay in the competition. Beatrice would be more than happy to remove me.

I glanced at my phone again. It was seven minutes until judging. If I wanted another peek at the church's organ, this was my chance. I hurried to the back entrance that led into the kitchen, hoping the door was unlocked. I placed my hand on the handle and stumbled back when it flew toward me. Deputy Aiden Brody stepped out of the church with a bemused expression on his face.

I groaned.

Aiden cocked his head. "Not exactly the reaction I want to hear when I run into you. You might make me think that you didn't want to see me."

I felt a blush creep across my cheeks and the bridge of my nose.

"Aren't you supposed to be making candy?" Aiden asked.

"Technically," I said, happy that he made no comment about my blush.

"What on earth are you doing back here, Bailey King?" I heard just the slightest hint of a southern drawl in his words. His accent wasn't nearly as pronounced as his mother's, but if I listened closely enough, I could catch a hint of it from time to time.

"I—I," I stammered. I had to think fast. "I was looking for Charlotte." The Amish girl's name popped out of my mouth, and I wished that I could shove it back in again. The less attention I brought to Charlotte, the better, especially since I knew she was at Swissmen Sweets, helping my grandmother while staying out of sight.

"She's not here," he said. "Funny you should be looking for her. I am too. She and I need to talk. I went out to her family's farm this morning but was told that she wasn't there."

"Oh?" I said as innocently as possible.

He removed his department ball cap and bent the brim, a nervous habit. "It's hard to know if she really wasn't there or if her family just said that to me. Most Amish don't like to talk to law enforcement and will protect their own."

"They have a good reason not to trust the law," I said.

Aiden slapped his hat lightly on the side of his leg. "I can understand that. The sheriff hasn't done much in the county to build a relationship with the Amish districts. If anything, he's done the opposite. I'm working to change that, but it's not easy when my supervisor fights me every step of the way."

I snapped my mouth shut to withhold any comment. I was surprised that he was being so candid with me.

He smiled. "When was the last time you saw Charlotte?"

I bit the inside of my cheek, thinking how I could get out of the direct question without a bold-faced lie. Using Charlotte as my excuse to be creeping around the church had backfired big-time. I couldn't tell him I'd just eaten pancakes with her that morning. I had promised my grandmother that I wouldn't make it common knowledge that Charlotte was staying with us.

I smiled brightly at him, and he scowled in returned. It seemed that the wattage of my smile was losing its impact. Maybe it was time to go to the dentist for a tune-up.

"Are you going to answer the question?" Aiden asked.

"I haven't seen her for hours," I said.

"Bailey," a frantic voice called from around the side of the church.

Before I even saw her, I knew it was Emily and that I hadn't kept my promise of getting back to the table before judging. I was late. Again.

Emily rushed toward me and grabbed my arm. "Bailey, you have to come. Now. The judges are almost at our table."

"Sorry," I said to Aiden with a shrug. "Candy waits for no one."

I turned to follow Emily back to our table, and as I did, Aiden grabbed my wrist. His grip wasn't painful but firm. "Bailey, if you're hiding something from me, I will find out what it is. That's a promise."

I had no doubt that he would, and he was still holding my hand. I stared at the fingers that encircled my wrist and raised my eyebrows.

"I'm sorry." He let go of me. His cheeks were flushed.

I ran after Emily without looking back.

Chapter 25

If Margot Rawlings spent any more time chewing the piece of peanut brittle I had given her for judging, she would grind her molars to the gums. Beatrice and Jeremiah had already eaten their samples and made notes on their clipboards. They judged each piece on texture, flavor, and presentation. I felt peanut brittle was one of my best entries. My very best would be my fudge offering, which would be in the final round. As a chocolatier, I would be devastated if I didn't at least take home the best-in-fudge prize. That was a matter of pride.

Finally, after what seemed like an eternity, Margot swallowed and made a note on her clipboard.

I smiled brightly at all the judges, hoping that they would give me a hint as to how I'd done. Jeremiah and Beatrice were calm and quiet as ever, though Beatrice glared at me over her glasses.

Margot frowned as she made another note. I was going to have to go to the dentist and have my smile checked out. It wasn't having its usual impact.

Jeremiah and Beatrice moved on to the next

table, but Margot remained and pointed at me with the end of her pen. "We expect great things from you in this next round, Bailey. It is chocolate, after all, that is supposed to be your specialty."

"No pressure," I said to Emily when they were out of earshot.

She played with the edge of her apron. "I know chocolate is really your favorite, Bailey. Have you ever thought about making more fruit-flavored fudges for the shop? I know you have blueberry, but what about strawberry?"

I raised my eyebrows. "Actually, that's not a bad idea. The blueberry fudge sells well, and there is nothing to indicate that other fruit flavors wouldn't also do well. As much as it pains me to say this, not everyone likes chocolate. Mango might be fun."

"Mango?" she asked, wrinkling her nose.

I laughed. "Okay, maybe not mango. I know it's not a fruit that is used often in Amish kitchens."

"What is a mango?" Emily asked. "I'd try mango fudge."

I smiled. "Let's get started on the fudge. It's going to take some time to set up." I handed Emily a list of ingredients to gather from our supply crate. Then I started a double boiler on our propane-powered burner to melt the chocolate.

I didn't want to take any chance of not winning the fudge round, so I would be making Swissmen Sweets' top seller: chocolate peanut butter fudge.

Emily set cocoa, evaporated milk, peanut butter, butter, and white sugar on the table. I dropped the butter and poured cocoa and sugar into the double boiler, and then I slowly added the evaporated milk as I stirred the mixture. A calm settled over me as I watched the chocolate come together. It was a calm that I needed after everything that had gone wrong since the beginning of the ACC, but even stirring chocolate, I couldn't put Josephine out of my mind. Why on earth would she drink licorice extract? And if she didn't drink it voluntarily, how on earth did someone else get her to drink it? It didn't make the least bit of sense.

Emily stood beside me. "That smells so good. How do you make it smell so good right from the start?"

"Chocolatiers never give up their secrets." I winked at her. "Can you start a second double boiler for the peanut butter? Just mix it with a little evaporated milk so that it is thin enough to pour into the fudge

She nodded and set to work on the second burner on the stove.

After a few minutes of stirring, the melted fudge was at the consistency I was looking for. "I'm ready to pour," I said.

Emily had already set a baking pan lined with waxed paper in the middle of the table. Using a tea towel to protect my hands from the boiling-hot glass bowl, I lifted it from the pan of boiling water and poured the molten chocolate into the pan.

A small group of tourists watched in wonder as the chocolate slowly flowed out of the glass bowl into the pan. I never tired of watching chocolate myself, so I could understand their fascination.

I shook the last of the chocolate from the bowl, and then I added the peanut butter, making a zigzag pattern over the top of the chocolate fudge. I set down my empty bowl and ran a toothpick through the top of the fudge, swirling the chocolate and peanut butter together. "Done," I said with a smile.

The small group of tourists clapped, and I winked at them. "You will all have to come back when it's ready to eat."

Emily grinned and covered the pan with aluminum foil. "Do you want me to take it to the church to cool?"

The one modern convenience allowed the ACC contestants was the use of the church's freezer to cool our candies, including the fudge. There was no way the fudge would set in time without a freezer, and it would have been far too difficult to have a propane-powered freezer sitting in the middle of the square.

I shook my head. "Let me do it."

She rolled her eyes as if she knew that I was motivated to go to the church by more than fudge. I didn't set her straight because she was right. "I'll be back in a jiffy."

"Sure, you will," she said.

I'd turned the Amish girl into a cynic. I picked up a dish towel and carefully lifted the pan.

I wasn't the only ACC contestant taking my fudge over to the freezer. Lindy, Josephine's assistant, was a few yards in front of me as I made my way across the square. Taking care not to drop my pan of hot fudge, I increased my pace and fell into step beside her. "That looks great," I said, nodding at her pan.

She looked down at her maple fudge. "This was Josephine's favorite flavor. I decided to make it in her honor."

"That was kind of you. I'm sure she would be proud of you for continuing."

She shrugged. "She would be happy that I'm going on, but I don't know that she would be proud. I don't know if Josephine was proud of anyone, not even herself."

I studied her as we walked. "What do you mean?"

She shook her head. "It's a terrible loss."

I bit my lip in disappointment. I knew she had been on the cusp of telling me something about Josephine's character. If I understood who Josephine was, I knew that I would be better able to understand why someone had murdered her. Her church deacon had called her a meddler, but there had to be more to her character than just that. People had many parts to them, and those various parts played many roles in their lives.

Lindy picked up her pace as we reached the church parking lot and walked around to the back side. I increased my pace to keep up with her.

She smiled. "We should hurry to get our fudge chilling as fast as possible."

She was right. When we came around the side of the church, I saw that the fence was freshly painted and the WET PAINT sign firmly in place on it. My eyes traveled over the fence and into the cemetery, and fell onto the mausoleum.

"Bailey?" Lindy held the back door to the church for me.

I shook off the odd feeling that hung over me and slipped through the door.

The church's large white kitchen was crowded as candy makers jostled to make room for their fudge in the large freezer.

Jeremiah stood beside the freezer, presiding over the whole thing. "Looks like we will have just enough room for all our entries. It's going to be snug, but I can make it work." He chuckled.

Lindy handed him her pan of fudge, and he slid it into one the few spaces left. She murmured her thanks.

"Bailey," Jeremiah said in his booming voice. "It's so nice to see you here delivering your fudge yourself. You know, I expected that you would have Emily make the delivery. I've noticed that you have been absent from your table a time or two over the last two days."

I winced. "I'm sorry about that. It's just . . ." I trailed off. I couldn't very well say, "It's just that I'm trying to solve a murder, and it's taking up a great deal of my time."

"Don't worry. I won't let Margot or Beatrice know about your little trips away from the table." His slid my tray of fudge into the last open place in the freezer.

"Thanks, Jeremiah. At least I know one of the judges is being understanding."

He grinned. "Margot and Beatrice are understanding in their own way."

I wrinkled my nose.

He laughed. "You have been at the table during the judging, and that's when it really counts. Are you looking forward to the big announcement of the overall winner? Many of the other candy makers are on the edge of their seats, waiting for the news. It's a great honor to win. It could be a real boon to any candy shop."

I nodded. It would be great for Swissmen Sweets

if I came home with the win in the ACC, but I didn't know how that would happen with Beatrice as one of the judges. "I don't think I stand much of chance of winning the whole thing."

He shook his head. "Don't sell yourself short. I've been very impressed with each one of your entries. All the candies you've made taste like they were made by Amish hands."

I smiled. "If my fudge does well, I'll be happy. Since I am a chocolatier, my fudge is a matter of pride."

He chuckled again and closed the freezer door. "May the best fudge win!"

Across the room, the candy makers filed out the back door of the kitchen. Lindy was at the end of the line. There were still a few questions I wanted to ask Josephine's assistant, but first, I asked Jeremiah, "Is there any way to put Susan back in the competition? You have to agree with me that someone tampered with her stove."

He held onto his overalls as if doing so helped him stand upright. "I understand your concern, but to let anyone back into the ACC after being dismissed, there must be a unanimous agreement among the judges. I believe you're right that someone tampered with Susan's stove, and she has a right to participate, but the judges must agree to let someone back in. I was the only one who wanted Susan to rejoin the competition. My hands are tied." He raised his hands as if to illustrate the point.

"And you were unanimous on bringing Haddie Smucker back?" I asked.

He sighed. "Not at first, but eventually, yes."

I wanted to ask him what that meant, but out of

the corner of my eye, I saw Lindy slip out the kitchen door. I thanked Jeremiah, told him I would see him at the judging, and hurried after her.

Lindy sighed as I caught up to her just outside the back door. "I feel better now that I know my fudge is cooling. All we can do now is wait. It will be what it will be." She smiled. "My grandmother used to say that all the time."

"Are you close to your grandmother?"

"I was. She died when I was a teenager."

"I'm so sorry," I murmured.

"*Danki.* We should go back to our tables. I know Margot wants us to be there as much as possible so that we can talk to the tourtists. The ACC has been a boon for the town."

I followed around the side of the church. "It has. Except . . ."

She nodded. "Except."

She sighed. "I don't know what is going to happen to her shop or me now that Josephine is gone. It will belong to her family."

"What family did she have?"

"She never spoke of any siblings. The only family I know of is the Weavers, her husband's family." Lindy twisted the end of her apron and then let it fall. "I suppose it will be Sol Weaver's decision."

It was interesting to know that her brother-in-law would be the one making the decision about her shop. "Was Sol an owner in her shop?"

She shook her head. "*Nee,* but Josephine's husband is dead, and she didn't have any children. Her brother-in-law is the head of the family, so it will be up to him."

I knew that Berlin Candies was a successful shop.

Would Sol Weaver kill his sister-in-law to take over her business?

"Have you heard from Sol at all about the matter? Does he know what he would like to do?"

She picked up the end of her apron again. "*Nee*, I'm sure he's waiting until things settle down, and I know he will want to consult with the district leaders. It might be some time before I know whether I'll be staying on permanently at the candy shop."

"Are you afraid you will lose your job?"

She nodded. "If they decide to hire someone else or decide to close the shop altogether, I'm gone. I need this work. Josephine knew that. In fact . . ." She stopped herself from finishing that thought.

"In fact, what?" I asked.

"Nothing." She smiled. "I know that your grandfather would be proud of you for winning the taffy round, and everyone expects you to take fudge too. You might win the entire thing, Bailey. Josephine worried about that because she knew how talented you are."

And there was my motive for murder laid out on a silver platter. I was Josephine's greatest rival, at least as far as she was concerned.

We had reached the church's parking lot by this point, and I knew I wouldn't have much more time to talk to her. "I heard that Josephine didn't get along with the owner of the hardware store next to her shop."

She dropped her apron and smoothed it over her legs. "You must mean Jeffrey Galwin. He and Josephine didn't get along. They were always at odds."

"About what?" I asked.

"About everything. Where he parked his car, that her buggy horse blocked his view of the street, that her trash can was turned over in the middle of the night—she insisted he did it out of spite. The two of them were always at each other's throats. I can't tell you the number of times that I was working in the shop and Jeffrey would come stomping in yelling about something else Josephine had done. He would scare off our customers. Josephine would be so upset about it."

"That would have upset me too," I said.

She nodded. "Anyone would be, but Josephine did just the same to him. She would stomp into his store and scare his customers away." She chuckled. "They may be from two different worlds, but they are very much alike. Maybe that's why they didn't get along. At least that's what I always thought." She lowered her voice. "I would never have told Josephine. She wouldn't have liked in the least to be told that she was like Jeffrey."

It seemed that I needed to speak with Jeffrey Galwin, but that would have to wait until the ACC ended.

"Do you think Jeffrey could have gotten angry enough to hurt her?" I asked Lindy.

She wrinkled her nose. "He didn't like her, that is certain, but he had been her neighbor in Berlin for over ten years. Why would he wait so long and put up with so much, only to do something now? He is a hothead, but so was Josephine."

I had witnessed Josephine's anger firsthand. Had Jeffrey's been worse? Had his been violent enough for him to kill someone?

Chapter 26

When we reached the front of the church, Lindy waved at an Amish man. "That's my husband. I should go see what he might need." She smiled shyly at me. "You've been very kind."

I could go back to my table and wait for the fudge to set for judging, or I could finally peek at the scene of the crime. Of course, I chose option two. I glanced back and forth to make sure neither Aiden nor any other sheriff's deputies were around before I ran up the church steps to the main entrance. I placed my hand on the door and opened it easily.

I stepped into the wide entry in front of the sanctuary doors. Faintly, I could hear voices floating down the hallway from where I knew the fellowship hall and kitchen were. I wondered if any last-minute candy makers were bringing fudge over to the church to chill. The judging of the fudge was in ninety minutes. The fudge would need all that time to set up even in the deep freezer.

The oak doors between the entry and the sanctuary

opened inward. I pushed one, and the fall wreath hanging in the middle of it rocked back and forth on its nail.

The large overhead lights were off, but enough light poured in through the windows for me to see every corner of the expansive room. As always, the organ dominated the middle of the sanctuary. The only indication that anything sinister had occurred in what should have been a hallowed place was a band of crime scene tape across the small door that led into the inner workings of the organ.

A small figure with unmistakable strawberry-blond hair and a white prayer cap sat in the front pew with her head bent.

The heavy church door that I had been holding opened slipped from my fingers. Before I could catch it, it slammed with a resounding thud, and Charlotte jumped out of her seat and spun around.

"It's just me." I waved.

She had a hand over her chest. "You scared me, Bailey."

I walked down the center aisle toward her. "I'm so sorry about that."

She leaned back in her seat and stared forward again. "It's all right."

"What are you doing here?" I asked.

"I wanted to play the organ. The playing soothes me when I'm upset. It wasn't until I was here that I remembered that I can't do that. I have a lot of big decisions to make, and I thought playing would help. I was praying for guidance."

I eyed her. "And did you find that guidance?"

She dropped her eyes to the hands folded on her lap. "I don't know."

"Aiden is looking for you," I said.

She licked her lips. "The deputy is the least of my problems."

I wasn't so sure of that.

"I wish I could play," she said barely above a whisper. "Maybe through playing, I would know what I have to do. Whether I have to give it up or the music is what *Gott* wants for me."

"I thought you had already decided to leave the Amish."

"Almost." She bit her lip. "But if I am leaving, I owe it to my family to tell them. My father will be very angry. He will all but shun me, and I wouldn't be the least bit surprised if the deacon asks him to do that permanently unless I return and do exactly as he says." She looked down at her hands again. "He would, you know, and my father would follow the deacon's lead. My father has always obeyed the leaders of the district. It doesn't matter how wrong they might be. He says that *Gott* tells us to obey, and we must."

"And you don't believe that?" I asked quietly.

She shook her head. "How can we obey someone as cruel as Deacon Clapp? He makes up most of his rules not because of what *Gott* wants, but because he has the power to do so. He knows that the members of the district will do whatever he says. He is the one who said my playing the organ was wrong. The deacon we had before never said a word about it, but as soon as Deacon Clapp was blessed as the next deacon, this"—she pointed at the beautiful instrument—"was a sin."

"He has the power to do that? I thought the bishop oversees the district."

She looked at her hands. "Our bishop is very old, and he's tired. I heard my parents talking about him once. They said they believe the bishop is relieved to let the deacon make most of the decisions." She looked up at me. "I did try to talk to the bishop once about the organ and what Deacon Clapp had said about it, but he fell asleep just when I was asking him to intercede."

"A new deacon can come in and change everything? Even the rules of how to live?"

She nodded. "He can. He was appointed to the job by *Gott*. We should not question *Gotte's* choice, but I can't help questioning. I know that's wrong, but *Gott* gave me this talent. Am I supposed to turn my back on it? Is that what He would really have me do?"

"I'm not the one to ask," I said. "My faith is wobbly at best."

She studied me. "Do you not believe in *Gott*?"

I sat next to her in the pew. I examined the organ, the pulpit, and the altar as I mulled over my answer. It was not a clear yes or no question for me. "I do," I said finally. "But I'm not sure it's your God or the God of my grandparents either."

"It is," she said with more confidence than I would have thought possible for someone so torn by the choices she had to make. "Just sitting here, I know I have to leave the Amish way because it's not allowing me to praise *Gott* as I see fit. Praise can be expressed through music and even through making candy." She smiled at me when she said that.

"Like your aunt did."

She frowned. "*Ya*, I suppose. That was Aunt Josephine's way to praise *Gott*."

"Tell me about your uncle," I said.

She raised her eyebrows. "My aunt's husband?"

I nodded. "What happened to him?

"He died when I was six. It was a buggy accident. He was a big man, and I always thought that he was a little scary. Like my father, he was a stern man, but he seemed more frightening when I was a child because of his size. When I was little, I remember that I liked Aunt Josephine very much; she was kind then. It seemed that she changed after Uncle Hiram's death. She became more like he had been."

"Did she ever remarry?"

She shook her head. "*Nee*, but I overheard my mother once telling a friend that another farmer was interested in my aunt. She was a beautiful woman, especially when she was young. I guess I was nine when I remember my mother telling her friend this. Aunt Josephine wanted nothing to do with the other man. My mother said Josephine told her that she would never marry again. By that time, she already had ideas of opening a candy shop in Berlin. She had always been good at baking and making candies."

"Tell me about the buggy accident."

She shook her head. "I don't remember the accident. I wasn't there, and I was very young at the time. I can only tell you what I've heard from my father." She grimaced. "Uncle Hiram is a sore spot with my father. I think most days he likes to pretend that he didn't have a brother. He would have done much better at pretending if my aunt hadn't been around."

"Why's that?" I asked.

She bit her lip as if she realized that she had said too much already. Maybe she had.

"How did the accident happen? Was he hit by a car?"

She shook her head. "The buggy shop that my uncle owned, which is now my father's, is at the top of a hill. The driveway is on a steep incline. My uncle was at the bottom of the hill, standing by himself, waiting for a delivery. One of the buggies at the top of the hill came loose and flew down the hill, hitting him. It killed him instantly. It was such a tragedy. I was very young, but I remember the crying. Aunt Josephine was never the same after that."

"How did she change?" I turned in my seat so that I could see her better.

"She became very strict. She thought that the Amish way was the only way to live. I heard my mother once say that Aunt Josephine had *Englisch* friends when she was young, but not after her husband died. She pulled away from the *Englisch* world. She took the money she had from my uncle and opened Berlin Candies, and her whole life became her candy shop. Well"—she paused—"that and correcting people. She loved to correct people."

"She must have been happy that someone like Deacon Clapp took over the district." I shifted my position on the hard pew.

She frowned. "Maybe. I don't think the deacon cared for her opinions. Even if he might have agreed with them. She was a woman, and he didn't want to hear ideas from her."

I tried not to bristle at that comment. I was only moderately successful. I replayed the scene that Charlotte had described in my head. In my mind's eye, I saw the buggy at the top of the hill and Hiram standing at the bottom, waiting for a delivery he would never receive. He was looking down the road, turned away from the shop. He might have been impatient, tapping his foot and eager to get back to work in his shop. Then he hears a buggy flying down the hillside. He doesn't have enough time to jump out of the way. He's hit, and everything goes dark.

"I'm confused," Charlotte said. "I don't know what I want. For the first time in my life, I don't have a plan." She lowered her voice to a whisper. "And that scares me."

I patted her arm, feeling like the older woman giving advice to the young when in reality I was only a few years older than Charlotte. "Well, right now, you are going to go over to Swissmen Sweets and help out my grandmother. She always says to me that you can find your purpose in the work yet to be done."

She smiled. "That's very Amish of her."

"I wouldn't expect anything less."

"I think you are right. I think helping Clara will clear my head." She squeezed my hand briefly. "Both you and Clara have been so very nice to me. Believe me when I say that I won't forget it. I will repay my debt to you someday."

I shook my head. "There is no debt to repay. We're family. That's what family does."

"I'm glad you moved here, Bailey." Her face fell. "I'm going to need all the family I can find very soon."

I wished I could tell her that wasn't true, but I was afraid she just might be right.

Chapter 27

Charlotte stood up and headed out of the church, presumably to go to Swissmen Sweets and think over all the choices she would have to make sooner rather than later.

After she left, I stood and walked over to the organ. As tempted as I was to remove the crime scene tape and take another peek inside the instrument, I stopped myself. There was nothing else I would be able to find there.

Nonetheless, I was just reaching out for the door when a loud bang startled me. I turned around and saw the old hunched-over Amish woman I'd seen around the village over the last several days. My grandmother had said her name was Ruby.

She stood at the doors to the church and stared at me. I wondered for a moment if she was mute.

I walked down the steps from the platform at the front of the church. "Ruby?"

She looked up at me, but there was no expression on her face.

"My grandmother said you were Ruby." I started

down the aisle at a slow pace. I didn't want to scare her away.

Behind me to the right of the pulpit, a door opened. I glanced over my shoulder to see Reverend Brook coming through the narrow doorway.

"Bailey," Reverend Brook began. "I thought I heard voices. What are you doing in here? Are you still looking for Jethro?"

I turned to face him. "Jethro?" I asked.

"Juliet's pig," he said with a frown.

I blinked. "Yes, of course. I'm sorry. I was just talking to—"

He frowned. "You were talking to whom? There is no one else here."

When I looked back, Ruby was gone.

"But she was here just a second ago," I protested.

"Who was?" he asked.

I shook my head and hurried down the sanctuary's center aisle. "I have to go, Reverend Brook. I haven't see Jethro, but I'm still looking. I won't give up until we find him."

"Thank you," he called after me. "That little pig is very important to Juliet."

I burst out of the church doors and scanned the parking lot and the square from where I stood on the top step of the church. There was no sign of Ruby. That woman was eighty if she was a day. How could she move so fast? I hoped that I could move half as quickly when I was half her age. Had I really seen her? I was beginning to wonder if the old woman was just a figment of my imagination. Had the stress of my grandfather's death and turning my life upside down by moving to Ohio caused me to see things that weren't there? I shook my head. I might have believed that if my grandmother hadn't told me the old woman's name. Knowing she had a name and that that name was Ruby saved me from going absolutely crazy.

Whether I was crazy or not, I knew I wouldn't be satisfied until I spoke to Ruby. My curiosity about the woman could not be pushed down any longer. I had to find her and talk to her, and I had to know if she knew anything about Josephine's death. She continued to pop up rather frequently around the church and the square. Had she seen something related to the murder? Was she wandering around the area because she was trying to tell me something? Of course, if she was trying to tell me something, it would be helpful if she didn't disappear so often.

I ran down the steps of the church and headed in the direction of the square. My grandmother had said that she lived over a yarn shop on Apple Street. I pulled my cell phone from the back pocket of my jeans and checked the time. There was still an hour before the fudge judging began. I told myself that I could get to the yarn shop and back in the time allowed. If Ruby wasn't at the shop, then I would give up, for now at least.

I cut across the square on my way to Apple Street. As I did, I waved at Emily and held up two fingers to indicate that I would be back in two minutes. There was no way that I would be gone for only two minutes, but I had to tell her something.

The tourists, both English and Amish, seemed to be having a wonderful time sampling the free candies that each shop was offering to the crowd. I saw that my own table was quite busy. Laughter and excited voices filled the air, and I had to remind myself that a woman had been murdered just a few yards away from where everyone was having such a good time. My mind could not reconcile this terrible act and the gaiety of the crowd.

I ducked my head to keep from making eye contact with anyone as I dodged a buggy and ran across Main Street to the corner of Apple and Main. When I made it to the corner, I was shocked to look down Apple Street and see Ruby standing in front of the yarn shop. She nodded at me as if she had been waiting for me all this time. Maybe she had. Maybe that had been the reason she kept popping up, because she wanted me to follow her back to her home.

I hurried down the sidewalk just as she disappeared around the side of the building. I threw up my hands. *Here we go again.*

I went around the side of the yarn shop and found there was a set of wooden stairs that led to a second-floor apartment; it had to be Ruby's apartment. The door was ajar as if inviting me in.

There was no point in turning back now, so I hurried up the creaky stairs and through the open door. When I crossed the threshold, I blinked as my eyes adjusted to the dim light. All the shades over the windows were closed tight. A lantern glowed on a small end table next to a rocking chair. It offered the only light in the sparsely furnished room other than the sunlight pouring in through the open door.

Ruby sat in the rocking chair. "There you are. I was wondering when you would come."

I stepped farther into the room but left the door open behind me, not just for the much-needed light but for easy getaway. I didn't think a woman of

Ruby's age could hurt me, but the situation was so surreal, I wasn't taking any chances.

"Ruby?" I asked.

She nodded.

"I'm—"

"Bailey," she said, interrupting me. "I know, dear. I've been longing to talk to you."

I squinted in the dim light. "If you have been wanting to talk to me, why do you keep disappearing?"

She smiled. "One must be patient and ready for the right time."

"Why did you want to talk to me?"

Light from the lantern cast an orange glow on the right side of her face. "You are trying to find out what happened to Josephine Weaver, am I right?"

"Yes, but how do you know that?"

She smiled. "You should be careful, Bailey. Many people know that you are looking for the truth. Not all of them want you to find it."

"You mean the killer," I said.

She nodded.

My heart rate quickened. "Does that mean you know who the killer is? Please tell me or tell the police. Aiden Brody is very kind. He would be a good person to talk to."

Her dry lips thinned as they stretched into a smile. "I know that you believe he is kind. I have seen how you look at him." She paused. "And I have seen how he looks at you in return. It will be a good match in time."

I found myself blushing. Just what I needed: another person in Holmes County who believed Aiden and I were destined to be together. "So, you will talk to him?" I asked.

She shook her head. "It is not the Amish way to get caught up with the police."

"Not even in the case of murder?" I asked.

She shook her head again. "It is not the Amish way."

"Will you tell me then? Did you see something?"

She closed her eyes for a moment as if trying to remember something, and I recalled that my grandmother had said Ruby wasn't all there. Why was I even asking this woman questions about the murder? She was far from a reliable witness. Was I so lost when it came to Josephine's murder that I had to rely on the ramblings of an old Amish woman who spent the majority of her time wandering around the village? But then again, if she spent the majority of her time wandering around the village, she might have seen something. The trick would be deciding how much of what she said was fact and how much the vague thoughts of a tired mind.

"I see many things because not many people notice me." She looked me in the eye for the first time. "You noticed me, though."

I shifted from foot to foot. Her penetrating gaze made me nervous. I much preferred when she didn't look at me. "I did."

She dropped her eyes to her lap. "Josephine wasn't like you. She didn't notice me."

My pulse quickened. This was it. I was about to learn who the killer was. "Did you see the murder?"

She shook her head. "*Nee.* I only saw the pig and Josephine outside the church."

"Josephine had Jethro?" I asked. This certainly was surprising news. Could it be that Jethro's disappearance and the murder were related after all?

She nodded. "She shooed the animal away from her. Josephine never had any patience."

"Where is Jethro now?" I asked excitedly. I couldn't wait to reunite the pig with Juliet. She was sick with worry over him.

"I don't know," Ruby answered simply.

My shoulders sagged. "Oh. Then what did you see?"

"Ever since her husband's death, Josephine has been angry. She's wanted to know what really happened that day her husband died."

"He died in a buggy accident. Charlotte told me that a buggy broke loose and struck him at the bottom of the hill."

"An accident that someone else caused," she said firmly.

"Are you saying Hiram Weaver was murdered?" I couldn't keep the surprise out of my voice.

She shook her head. "I'm saying that someone else is responsible for his death. That is different but does not make the guilt the person feels any less. Love and hate are two sides of the same coin." She rocked in her chair.

I shook my head. I felt like she was speaking to me in riddles.

"Now you should return to your candies. It won't be long until this is all over. It will be over very soon."

The way she said that made me wonder if some Amish believed in premonitions and second sight, but that didn't seem to me to be a very Amish belief. Then again, I wouldn't say that Ruby was a typical Amish woman.

"But you didn't tell me anything. You have to know more than that."

She shook head. "I did. I told you the *why* of your question. It is up to you to answer the *who* and the *how.*"

"But—"

She closed her eyes and leaned back in her chair as if she were settling in for a nap. Maybe she was, because only a few moments passed before I heard her softly snoring. Part of me wanted to shake her awake and make her answer my questions, but I knew there was no point in doing that. I suspected that Ruby only ever said as much as she wanted to and not a word more.

Shaking my head, I went back out of the apartment, closing the door behind me.

Chapter 28

An hour later, Emily and I stood behind my table anxiously watching Jeremiah, Beatrice, and Margot taste my fudge. Beatrice took the smallest of bites and held it in her mouth before chewing and swallowing it. Jeremiah bit his hunk of chocolate peanut butter fudge in half and chewed away. Margot stared at the piece, turning it in her hand before taking a small bite.

I wasn't worried that the fudge wasn't good. I knew it was. Even in the limited time allowed, it had set up beautifully in the church's deep freezer.

I scanned the judges' expressions for any sign that they liked the fudge, but they had their game faces on. They made notes on their clipboards and moved on to the next table.

"Is that *gut* or bad?" Emily whispered in my ear when they had left.

"I have no idea," I whispered back.

"I would not think it was *gut*," Haddie Smucker said smugly. She stood at the edge of her table closest to us. "When the judges tasted my fudge, they complimented it."

I scowled at her. "I'm sure everyone's fudge is good. They wouldn't be in the ACC otherwise."

She nodded as if I had given her the reaction she wanted. Maybe I had.

"Perhaps your fudge would have been even better if you hadn't been running all over the square today meddling in Amish business."

I folded my arms. "What do you know about Josephine's death?"

She snorted. "Nothing. I know when it's not my place to become involved, unlike you."

"But you might know something about Susan's stove being tampered with, am I right?"

She flushed ever so slightly, and I knew I was right to think she was the one who'd sabotaged the candy maker from Pennsylvania.

She lifted her chin. "No matter how the stove was broken, Susan Klink made the choice to use the church's microwave."

"But the broken stove made her panic."

She shrugged as if that was simply a minor detail.

"How many other candy makers did you try to sabotage just to improve your own chances? You must have thought you were awfully clever when it turned out that your tampering coincidentally led to a way for you to get back in the competition."

There were so many things I wanted to say to Haddie, and most of them were not repeatable, especially to an Amish woman, but Emily pulled on my sleeve before I could get any more of them out.

"Bailey," Emily said breathlessly, "the judges are

at the gazebo now. They must be ready to announce the winners."

"Go back to New York, Bailey King," Haddie said as she walked by my booth. "You don't belong here and never will."

Her words stung because they echoed my own thoughts. Emily tugged on my sleeve. I followed her to the foot of the gazebo, the same place where everyone had gathered the night before in search of Jethro. I was losing hope that the little pig would ever turn up. I debated looking for Juliet so I could tell her that Ruby had seen Jethro with Josephine the morning Josephine died, but I was afraid, given the circumstances, that would only make Juliet worry more. I promised myself that I would search for him again that night after the ACC had ended.

Jeremiah held the bullhorn to his mouth. "We're so proud and grateful to have the Amish Confectionery Competition in Harvest this year. It's a true honor. Before we announce the winners, I would be remiss if I didn't mention yesterday's tragedy." He cleared his throat. "Josephine Weaver was one of the finest candy makers in Ohio, if not the whole country. Her talent will be greatly missed." He nodded at Lindy. "We are pleased that Lindy Beiler has been able to carry on in Berlin Candies' name. Thank you, Lindy."

Lindy blushed. Her husband wrapped his arm around her shoulders.

A murmur ran through the crowd of candy makers and visitors who were in Harvest that day for the competition.

I glanced at Haddie, who glared at Lindy for all she was worth. I suspected that it was good the ACC

was all but over or Lindy's stove would be the next
to be tampered with. But could Haddie want to win
so badly that she would have killed Josephine to
remove the competition? Up to this point, it would
have been hard for me to believe that, but the glare
she gave Lindy made me reconsider.

Jeremiah adjusted his grip on the bullhorn. "Let's
take a moment to bow our heads and remember
candy maker Josephine Weaver."

Beside me, Emily dutifully bowed her head, as
did the rest of the crowd. I did so for half a second,
but then I lifted my eyes. My gaze fell on Lindy. She
leaned into her husband's shoulder for support. A
tear rolled down her cheek. Maybe she really did
care about Josephine and miss her, or maybe she
was just fearful about what would become of her
now that Josephine was gone.

I searched the crowd for Haddie again. She
scowled at me, so I looked away and made eye contact with Aiden, who stood across the semicircle
from me. Heat rushed up my cheeks. When did he
get there? I knew he wasn't there a moment ago. I
would have noticed him. He was doing the same
thing I was, scanning the crowd for reactions. I
dropped my head as if in prayer. In truth, I couldn't
withstand his appraising gaze.

"*Danki*, thank you," Jeremiah said. "Now Margot
will announce our peanut brittle, fudge, and overall
winners."

Margot took the bullhorn from Jeremiah's hand.
"Thank you, Jeremiah. Jeremiah, Beatrice, and I
were commissioned to do the difficult job judging
this competition over the last two days." She went

on to announce the winner of the peanut brittle round. Smiling brightly, she said, "Berlin Candies."

Lindy stumbled to the stage with tears in her eyes.

If I won the fudge round, Swissmen Sweets and Berlin Candies would be tied. One of us had to be the overall winner, but I cared about the fudge more than the overall title.

"Of the four candy rounds we've judged," Margot went on, "fudge was by far the most challenging. Everyone had excellent entries. However, as much as we would like to pick each of your selections for one reason or another, there can only be one winner." She paused for maximum effect. "Congratulations to Bailey King from Swissmen Sweets! Please come up and accept your certificate."

Emily cheered and clutched my arm. I smiled and waved at the visitors who turned to look at us. I pried myself away from Emily and wove my way up to the gazebo. As if against my will, my eyes traveled to where I had seen Aiden standing. He was there, clapping for me. He grinned, and the dimple in his right cheek appeared. I looked away.

"Congratulations, Bailey!" Jeremiah clapped me on the shoulder as I reached the top of the gazebo steps.

"Everyone in Harvest is so proud of you." Margot held out a certificate to me.

I murmured my thanks, accepted my certificate, my second of the competition, and quickly returned to my spot next to Emily.

Emily gripped my arm. "Bailey, you're going to win the entire thing," she whispered. "You won two of the four rounds. They have to give it to you!"

I shook my head, unable to speak.

"Now," Margot said. "The moment that you have been waiting for. The overall winner of this year's Amish Confectionary Competition!"

The crowd clapped and cheered. I clutched my certificate in my hand.

Margot took in a big breath. "The grand prize winner is Berlin Candies."

Lindy's mouth fell open. Her husband gave her a little shove toward the gazebo. She stumbled forward.

"How is that possible?" Emily asked in a harsh whisper. "You should have won."

I squeezed Emily's hand. "Don't be upset. I'm happy for Lindy. She deserves it."

"But . . ."

"Emily, it's fine." I held up my certificate. "My chocolate-making street cred has been certified. That's all I care about."

"Street cred?" she asked in confusion.

I laughed. "I'm happy."

"You should be. Winning two rounds of the competition is impressive," a male voice said behind me.

I swallowed and turned to find Aiden standing just a foot away from me. "Do you have some kind of teleporting system that the rest of the world doesn't know about?"

He raised his brows. "Come again?"

"You were over there just a second ago." I pointed to the other side of the gazebo.

He smiled, and the dimple reappeared. "You noticed where I was?"

"Umm." I thought it was wise to ignore that

comment. "You should talk to Haddie Smucker. Another contestant, Susan Klink, was removed from the competition this morning after someone tampered with her stove. I think Haddie was behind it."

Emily gasped.

"Can you prove that?" he asked.

"Well, no." I held my certificate loosely in my hands.

Emily looked back and forth between us. "I'm going to start packing up the table, Bailey."

I nodded, but most of my attention was focused on the deputy.

"Neither can I," he said.

I blinked. "Wait, what? You knew about it?"

He nodded. "Beatrice told me about it this morning."

"Beatrice?" She was the last of the three judges I would have guessed would go to Aiden with a problem. Perhaps I had misjudged the critical woman.

"She thinks it was Haddie too, but there is no proof." He brushed his hair out of his eyes. "I spoke to Susan before she left Harvest, and she doesn't want the Sheriff's Department to pursue it."

"So, you are just going to let it go?" The accusation was heavy in my voice.

"My hands are tied, but if the tampering is related to Josephine's death, no, I won't let it go."

Behind Aiden, tourists both Amish and English were heading to their buggies and cars parked on the street and in the church parking lot. It was hard to believe that, after all the time that it took to prepare for it, the ACC was finally over. Emily might have been disappointed that Lindy had won, but I wasn't.

A group of Amish and English children ran around the playground next to the church. An Amish boy leapt from one of the swings when it was at its highest point on the upswing, just as I had when I was a child. Soon there would be new equipment there thanks to the ACC and all the money it had raised for the village.

"I found Charlotte, by the way," Aiden said. "You might have told me that she's staying at Swissmen Sweets."

"Yeah, sorry about that. *Maami* and I thought it would be best that we not make it public knowledge. Charlotte's family is not particularly happy with her right now."

"I know, and I know that being rejected by one's family is a very hard thing. I do sympathize with her," he said.

I knew he was thinking of his father, who had walked away from his mom and himself, but I couldn't bring myself to say anything about it.

Aiden looked as if he wanted to say something more, but his cell phone rang.

He unclipped it from his duty belt and looked at the screen. "It's the sheriff."

I smiled, not sure whether I was relieved or disappointed by the interruption. "You'd better take it then."

He nodded. "Sheriff?" Aiden held the phone to his ear.

I was dying to hear Aiden's side of the conversation, but he must have seen the eagerness in my eyes, because after a small shake of the head, he turned and walked away, speaking softly into the phone so that I couldn't hear what they discussed. I knew their conversation had to be about Josephine.

I returned to Swissmen Sweets' table, where Emily was handing out pieces of our winning fudge to tourists. "You can buy more of this and lots of other flavors at Swissmen Sweets, just across the street there."

I smiled. Maybe I should put Emily in charge of marketing for the shop.

"Are you happy that your fudge won?" Emily asked when the last piece of fudge was taken.

"Of course I am." I set the dirty pans and dishes that we'd used to make our candies in a dishpan to wash when I got back to the shop. "It was the award that I wanted the most."

"You're not upset that Lindy won the contest?" She scraped chocolate off the silver platter.

I picked up and folded a tea towel that hung from the corner of the table. "I would have wanted to win, yes, but she deserved it. Her candies were great. Josephine taught her well."

She set the scraped tray in our cart. "It's a shame that Josephine couldn't be part of her own shop's success. She wasn't the nicest person in the world, but everyone knew she loved that shop. She should have been here to see how well it did."

I nodded. "Yes, she should have." I looked down at the hand-lettered certificate. "I think I will have this framed and hang it in the front room of the shop. The taffy one too."

"It's not very Amish to boast and show off your accomplishments," Emily observed.

"I'm not Amish." I grinned.

"I noticed," she said with a laugh. "No one will ever confuse you with an Amish person, Bailey King. I can promise you that."

Chapter 29

I gave Emily a hug in front of Swissmen Sweets. "Thanks for your help. You should get back to the pretzel shop before Esther sends out a search party."

Emily sighed. "All right. Tell Nutmeg I'll be over tomorrow with a treat."

I smiled. "You spoil him." I started to push open the door with one hand. The other was on the handle of my cart when she stopped me.

She blushed. "Bailey?"

I dropped my hand from the door and let it close. "Something wrong?"

She licked her lips. "I was wondering if you needed any help around Swissmen Sweets? I can pitch in whenever you like."

"You're asking for a job?"

She wrinkled her forehead. "I guess I am."

"What about the pretzel shop?" I asked. Behind her, I thought I saw a curtain move in the window of Esh Family Pretzels.

"They don't really need me." She stared at the

tops of her black sneakers. "In fact, there is very little that Esther will let me do. You've given me more to do in the last couple of days than Esther ever has. My sister doesn't trust my judgment . . . ," she trailed off.

I knew Emily was thinking of the mistakes she'd made when she was a teenager. I'd learned a few weeks ago that she'd had a baby out of wedlock and given it up for adoption. She had the baby in secret, but her siblings had never forgiven her for it. Even though she was now twenty, they still treated her like a child.

"I know you would have to talk it over with Clara," she added quickly.

"I don't know that we have enough to do at the shop to hire another person," I said honestly. "Can I think about it? And I will talk it over with my grandmother. I promise."

She smiled. "*Ya*, of course."

"Emily!" Abel's sharp voice came from the front of the pretzel shop.

The large Amish man glared at his sister and me in turn.

"I should go." She bit her lower lip. "But you will think about it?"

I nodded. "I will."

"*Danki*, Bailey."

I smiled.

"Emily," Abel repeated.

She ran over to her brother. He opened the door to pretzel shop for her. She ducked her head and ran inside. He gave me one final scowl before he disappeared inside the pretzel shop after her.

I shook my head and opened the door to

Swissmen Sweets again. This time I opened it wide enough to push the cart inside. Nutmeg met me in the front of the shop, but there was no sign of my grandmother or Charlotte. The little orange cat wove around my ankles.

I tried my best not to trip over him as I made my way through the front room to the swinging kitchen door. Inside, Charlotte and my grandmother chatted while they cleaned the kitchen. They laughed together and spoke their language while they worked. A little green-eyed monster in the back of my mind whispered to me that Charlotte looked more like *Maami*'s granddaughter than I ever would. She naturally fit in an Amish candy shop. I was forcing myself to fit. That was the difference.

Maami beamed at me. "I knew your *daadi*'s fudge would win the day." She dropped the rag she held into the dishwater and walked over to me with her arms open.

I accepted her hug. "But I didn't win the whole thing."

She stepped back and returned to the soapy water. "It's no matter. It's the fudge that's important."

I laughed, because she sounded so much like my grandfather when she said that.

"Your win is all Clara has been talking about since we heard the news," Charlotte said, and the little bit of jealousy I felt flew away.

I grinned from ear to ear. "I wanted to win that round too. It really was the only one I cared about."

"We are all sold out of every kind of fudge because of it," *Maami* said. "We will be busy tonight making more."

"You have Emily to thank for that," I said. "She

was directing everyone who would listen to come over here and buy fudge." I didn't add that Emily had asked me for a job. I would wait until my grandmother and I were alone to have that conversation. "Do you need any help cleaning up?" I asked.

Maami plunged her hands back into the soapy water. "*Nee*, Charlotte and I have it well in hand. You should rest after your long day."

"Not just yet. I'm going to go back over to the square," I said.

My grandmother looked up from the pot she was scrubbing. "Why?"

I sighed. "Jethro is still missing. I want to take another look around for him."

Maami frowned. "That is *gut* of you. Juliet is so heartbroken over Jethro. She and Reverend Brook were in here just an hour ago looking for him. I haven't seen her so upset since the first day she came to Harvest."

I frowned. "He couldn't have disappeared into thin air."

Charlotte ran a towel over the white plate she was holding. "Do you think another animal got him?"

I couldn't stand to even consider that. "One more walk around the square won't hurt," I said, thinking about what I'd learned from Ruby. I was reluctant to talk about that conversation, even to my grandmother and Charlotte, because I wasn't sure how reliable Ruby was as a source of information.

I told my grandmother and Charlotte good-bye and headed back outside the shop. When I reached the square, Abel and a couple other Amish men were pulling down the tents and folding up the long tables from the competition. I noticed that

Swissmen Sweets' competition place had already been completely dismantled.

Next to the gazebo, I spotted Ruby. I studied the hunched-over woman and felt a rush of sympathy for her. Abruptly, she turned and walked toward me.

I smiled. "Hello."

"You are looking for the little pig," she said.

My eyes went wide. "I am."

"You should look in the little house. That's where she put him."

"What little house?" I asked. "Josephine, you mean? She put Jethro in a little house?"

"She didn't like him following her, so she put him in the little house. She said he needed to learn a lesson. She didn't know she was the one who would learn a lesson."

"What lesson?"

Ruby shuffled away without another word. I was fairly certain that she didn't remember the conversation I'd had with her in her apartment just a few hours ago. So how could she possibly know where Jethro was?

I watched her walk back in the direction of Apple Street but decided against following her and asking her more questions. Whatever I learned from Ruby might be just the sad ramblings of a woman with dementia.

On the opposite side of the square from where my table had been, Lindy stood in front of her table, looking at all her boxed-up supplies waiting to be toted away.

I walked over to her, trying to shake off the odd feeling that Ruby gave me. "Everything okay?"

"I just realized that I have no way to get this all

back to Berlin Candies. My husband took our children home in our buggy. We'd brought everything in Josephine's buggy, but after she died, her family took the buggy and the horse back to their home." She chewed on her lip.

"I have a car. I can give you a lift to Berlin Candies."

She frowned. "I would hate to be a bother. I was going to find a phone and call my husband. He should be home in a half hour."

I shook my head, "And then he will have to drive a half hour back. You won't make it to Berlin Candies until after dark. After I take you to the candy shop, I can take you home. It's not a problem."

She stared at the stack of supplies. "That would be very helpful. It's been a long couple of days. Are you sure?"

I waved my hand. "Yes, just let me pull my car around to the square, and we will pack up these supplies and be off."

She knit her brow together. "All right."

Chapter 30

Berlin Candies was on Main Street in Berlin, easily the busiest street in Holmes County. Even this late in the afternoon, the street was congested with buggies, cars, and buses. A long line of tourists walked along the street perusing the small shops that sold everything from fabric for quilts to mystic stones. Berlin, unlike Harvest, was a true tourist town, and even though the businesses there were mostly related to Amish culture, other businesses had moved in too. The precious stone shop and a trendy clothing boutique were taking advantage of the tourists that came to Holmes County.

Berlin Candies was in a flat-faced storefront that had been painted dark blue with a large white awning running its length. Right next to it was the hardware store, Holmes County Tools. I assumed I was looking at Jeffrey Galwin's store. It was a little after four, and all the shops in Berlin closed at five.

By some miracle, I got the parking space right in front of the candy shop. It was tight, but my compact fit in the spot with only a moderate amount of scraping along the curb.

As I shifted the car into park, I noticed a CLOSED sign on Berlin Candies' door. "The shop is closed?" I asked.

Lindy opened the car door. "Josephine closed it for the ACC. It was just the two of us working there, and she thought it was more important that we were both at the competition."

"It seems like a gamble to be closed on such a busy weekend. There was no one else who could watch the store? Perhaps a family member or a friend from the district?"

She frowned. "Josephine didn't trust many people, especially with her shop."

"But she trusted you?" I asked.

"As much as she trusted anyone." She climbed out of the car.

I got out of the car too, grabbed one of her crates of supplies from the back seat of my car, and followed her to the glass front door of Berlin Candies. I balanced the heavy crate in my arms, waiting for Lindy to unlock the door. She was turning the key to the shop in the lock when a thin man with long arms stomped out of the hardware store next door. His glasses sat at the tip of his nose. "Finally, one of you is here!"

Lindy pushed open the door to the shop and turned to face the man. "I—"

"I can't have this going on," the man bellowed for anyone on the street to hear. "All the comings and goings from this shop have to stop. I'm trying to run a business next door. I don't know what all you are doing with this candy shop, but it is most certainly not selling candy."

Comings and goings? I wondered. Hadn't Lindy just said the shop had been closed for at least two days? And she was at the ACC all of that time. Who else had been visiting Berlin Candies?

I stepped forward. "Can we help you?"

He glared at me. "Who are you?"

"Bailey," I said, looking him in the eye. "I'm a friend of Lindy's."

"I've never seen you here before." He glared over my shoulder at Lindy. "Now you are bringing your friends around because Josephine is dead? Is that it? You finally got the shop all to yourself, have you? Are you the one who's sending people here to size the place up? Are you already making changes before Josephine is even buried in the ground?"

Lindy stepped back as if his words were blows. "I—I—"

"Wait a second. What are you implying?" I wanted to know.

"Just what everyone on the street knows. That Lindy has been waiting for this day for a long time. I have too. I can't say I'm sorry that that horrible woman is dead. I have nothing good to say about her." He pointed at Lindy. "She didn't like her either. I won't let her deny that. Josephine was awful to her. Maybe," he said, looking at Lindy, "you finally snapped. Was that what happened?"

I glanced over my shoulder. Lindy was staring at her feet. "The same could be said for you, because you obviously didn't care for Josephine," I said. "I've only known you for two minutes, and you have made that abundantly clear."

"Make no mistake about it. I hated the woman." He swung his long arms, causing me to step back. He didn't seem to notice as he went on. "She was nothing but a thorn in my side."

"And where were you yesterday morning?" I asked, keeping my distance.

A slow smile curled his lips. "I see what you're getting at, but it's no use. I didn't do anything to that Amish woman. If I had wanted to hurt her, I would have long ago."

It was close to what Lindy had said earlier when she'd mentioned that if Jeffrey had wanted to kill Josephine, he would have done it much earlier.

"And how do we know that you just didn't snap?" I straightened up so I could look him in the eye.

He laughed. "I wasn't anywhere near Harvest when she died."

"Where you were you?" I persisted.

"I was right here in my store. If you don't believe me, you can ask my two employees who were in the store yesterday morning and two customers, one of whom was Amish. That should be enough proof for you. It was enough for the Sheriff's Department."

I inwardly sighed. Of course, Aiden would have already spoken to Jeffrey. He would have done so at his first opportunity. It seemed that I was always two steps behind him. I reminded myself that finding out who'd killed Josephine wasn't a competition.

Jeffrey went on. "The vultures are already circling now that she's dead. The candy shop, like my store, has a prime location. I wouldn't be surprised if someone makes an offer to buy it before her body is in the ground."

I could understand that. When I'd first arrived in

Harvest in September, my grandfather had been dealing with a greedy developer who wanted to buy his shop because of its prime location across from Harvest's town square. My grandfather had refused to sell, but the developer wouldn't give up without a fight.

Berlin, because it was on Route 39, a main state road that traveled east and west, bisecting Holmes County, was an even better location. I wasn't surprised that developers and others had already come to look at the property.

I glanced at the candy shop. Through the window, I could see that the shop was twice the size of my own and had a beautiful collection of displays. Jars of hard candy shone in the fading sunlight streaming through the window, and colorful boxes of chocolate and caramels were on display. Even though Berlin Candies was in competition with my own store, it would be a shame if the shop was bought out and turned into something else, but maybe that had been the plan all along and the reason Josephine had been murdered.

I felt like something was about to click. Maybe Josephine's murder was about her shop. If the men of her district seemed too eager to examine her shop, what else could it be? What else did she have that someone would want? She was a widowed Amish woman with no children. That wasn't to be envied. However, she was a successful businesswoman and one of the best candy makers around. That was certainly something to envy and want, but was it something to kill for? That was the part I wasn't so sure about.

"Who have you seen here?" I asked Jeffrey. "Who in particular?"

He scowled. "There were a couple of developers who were nosing around this morning. I don't know their names, but I know their type. They wore suits and sunglasses. No one in Holmes County dresses like that, not even the *Englischers.*"

I frowned. It would have been a lot more helpful if he could have gotten the names of the men.

"And her brother-in-law was here," he added. "He had a key, so he was able to get inside."

"Sol Weaver?" I asked.

"That's right. Sol came once by himself, and then he came back a second time with another Amish man, a younger one."

I was willing to bet that the other Amish man had been Deacon Clapp.

"Did they meet with the developers?" I asked.

"Not that I saw," he said.

It sounded as if the hardware store owner had been watching the entire time. There was no doubt in my mind that Jeffrey Galwin had kept a close eye on Berlin Candies when Josephine was alive and was keeping an even closer eye on it now that she was dead.

"While the two Amish men were in the shop, I dropped in." Jeffrey folded his arms. "I wanted to know what was going on. If they are going to sell the place, I want to know about it. I mean, I'm the one who is going to have to live with the new owners as neighbors, not them."

"What did they say?" I asked.

He curled his hands into fists at his sides. "They said that it wasn't any of my business, and they would do with the candy shop what they saw fit." His face turned a dark shade of red. "It *is* my business. My store is right next door. What they plan to do with this building and who moves into it has an impact on me, whether they believe that or not."

That's where he was wrong. It wasn't really his business to know what Josephine's family planned to do with the candy shop, but I wasn't going to tell him that. Even so, I wished that they had told him their plans. Jeffrey was angry enough to blurt out what they were if he'd known them.

He pointed at me. "If you find out that they are selling this place, you tell me." He pointed at Lindy too. "That goes for you too."

Neither of us promised him anything.

He stomped back to his store, stopped at his front door, and said, "Tell those Amish bishops or whatever they are to stay away from my property or I'm calling the police." He slammed the door so hard after himself, I thought the glass would break.

Chapter 31

I drove Lindy home, but try as I might to convince her to talk about the encounter with Jeffrey, she wouldn't say anything. When she got out of the car in her driveway, she thanked me for the ride and helping her get the supplies back to the shop. I watched as her husband met her at the door and pulled her into a hug. I smiled, happy that Lindy had a supportive family to go home to after the ACC, but I drove back to Harvest with a knot in my stomach. I was no closer to figuring out who'd killed Josephine or what had become of Jethro than I had been that morning.

My cell phone rang, and I answered it on speaker. Cass's excited voice filled the car. "So did you win? Tell me you won!"

"I won the fudge round," I said.

"You had better have won the fudge round." She sniffed as if personally offended by the very idea I might not have won the fudge category of the ACC. "If you didn't, Jean Pierre and I would personally fly to Harvest in his jet and knock some Amish heads together."

That'd be a sight. Amish Country would never be the same after their invasion. It had barely survived Cass's solo arrival in September.

I laughed. It was good to hear her voice. "I also won taffy, but not the overall prize. Another Amish candy shop won that."

"What? You were robbed! I might have to fly in and knock some Amish heads together after all," she cried. "There is no way that another candy shop can make candy better than you. You were trained by the very best. You practically trained me, and I'm the best."

I found some of my anxiety fall away as I listened to her outburst. There was no lack of self-confidence in my best friend. I never had to worry about that. After I'd decided to leave JP Chocolates to move to Ohio to be with my grandmother, my old boss Jean Pierre and the search committee had decided to give Cass the head chocolatier job at Jean Pierre's flagship store in New York. They'd made the perfect choice. Cass had just the right kind of talent, smarts, and self-confidence to get the job done and get it done well.

"There's something else." I paused.

"Whaaaat?" she asked, drawing out the word as if she already knew that she wouldn't like the answer.

"During the competition, I found a dead body," I said quickly, just to get it over with. I saw telling this bit of news to Cass as akin to jumping off the high dive at the local swimming pool. It's best to just march to the end of the board and leap. It would be much worse to draw it out. That only led to fear of jumping the next time or, worse, not jumping at all.

Silence. I couldn't even hear her breathing.

"Cass? Are you there?" I asked.

"Bai," she began slowly as if measuring her every word. Since Cass typically spoke at a mile a minute, I found this slightly alarming. "Did you just say that you found a dead body?"

"Yep," I said, faking nonchalance about it.

"Am I getting this right—this is your second body in less than two months?"

I winced when she put it like that. Clearly, Cass wasn't buying my relaxed attitude about it. I shouldn't have expected her to. She had known me a long time. She knew me better than just about anyone. She knew when I was faking calm. Unfortunately. "I haven't really put together the time frame, but yes. And technically I didn't find it. My cousin did."

"Wait! Back up!" she cried. "You have a cousin? Did I know about this?"

"I didn't even know about it until this week. She's the granddaughter of my grandmother's first cousin," I said, hoping that would ease her upset over not knowing I had cousins. I had kept secrets from Cass in the past, and that had not gone well. I didn't want my best friend to think I was hiding things from her again.

"What does that make her to you?" Cass asked, sounding somewhat appeased.

"My second or third cousin."

"Interesting," she said. "Now let's get back to the dead body. I assume Hot County Deputy is looking into the crime. Have you gotten to spend some time with him because of it?"

It was my turn to be silent.

"I'll take that as a yes," she said. "When is your first date?'

"Cass, a woman is dead. I'm not using someone's death as leverage to get a date."

She sighed as if I had learned nothing from her over the last six years of our friendship. "Tell me about the dead person."

I told her what I had learned about Josephine.

"Suspects?" she asked.

"There's Charlotte, but I'm certain she didn't do it. She's just not capable of it, and she was completely shocked when she discovered the dead body. Technically, she was the first person to see Josephine dead."

"It's always the quiet ones," Cass murmured.

"She didn't do it," I said firmly.

"Fine, fine. Don't be so touchy. I can understand that you want to protect your cousin, now that you have one."

I rolled my eyes.

"I know you're rolling your eyes," she said.

"How?" I wanted to know.

"I heard it."

"Whatever," I muttered.

"What else do you have?" she asked.

If I didn't know better, I would have thought that Cass was enjoying this.

"Not much. That's the problem. There is her shop assistant, Lindy, and another Amish candy maker who looks a little bit shady named Haddie. I'm convinced Haddie tampered with another candy maker's equipment to boot her out of the competition, but I have no way to prove it. Aiden believes the same thing, but he can't prove it either."

"Oh, I like her for the crime. A sneaky Amish woman is trouble, if you ask me, and I am glad you and Aiden are consulting each other on the case."

I sighed. "For a minute there, I thought it could have been the owner of a hardware store in Berlin, but it turns out that he has an alibi, which Aiden already checked into."

"I wouldn't expect anything less from Hot Deputy," she said confidently.

"You really shouldn't call him that," I said.

"What, are you going to tell him that's his nickname?"

"Definitely not," I said.

"Then we're good. What else do you have?"

"The last suspect I have is her brother-in-law, Sol, but that is Charlotte's father. I would hate, for her sake, for him to have done it. Her relationship with her family is already strained because she's decided to leave the district, or at least she's almost decided to leave the Amish. She's torn over it."

"Oh, will she be shunned? The Amish are big into that, aren't they? I've been watching those Amish Gone Wild shows to learn more about your culture."

I sighed. "I wouldn't call those shows a fair representation of Amish culture, and I don't know if Charlotte will be shunned. I don't think she has been baptized into the church, so she shouldn't be, but the new church deacon is very strict. I wouldn't be surprised if he changed the rules about that. He's changed so many already. *Maami* asked me to help Charlotte. I'm doing the best I can, but I'm afraid I'm just spinning my wheels."

"Do you need me to come out there?" Cass asked after a beat. "Because I will. I can get someone to mind the place back here. Caden would be happy to do it. He is still trying to prove himself."

Caden had been the third assistant who was in the running earlier that fall to be head chocolatier at JP Chocolates. I was certain he would be thrilled if Cass left so soon after she was given the position, so that he could prove that it should have been given to him.

"No. Aiden is here. He can be my backup."

She laughed. "I knew you liked him."

"I was joking." I paused.

"You shouldn't be. The guy is perfect for you. Unlike He Who Shall Not Be Named."

"Eric is not Voldemort."

"Says who?" she asked.

"I'm not over Eric yet. I want to be, but I'm not." My voice trailed off.

"Even more reason for you to spend time with Deputy Aiden. He's twice the guy that Eric ever could be. Eric was never right for you, and had I known about your secret romance, I would have told you that at the beginning, made you dump him, and saved you a lot of tears and grief over that pond scum."

I couldn't help but smile at Cass's choice of words. I would never call Eric pond scum, but as my best friend, Cass reserved and used the right to call him that, among other much more colorful names.

"Which is why I didn't tell you. I should have. I'm

sorry. You would have saved me a lot of grief," I admitted grudgingly.

"That's over and done with. We are moving forward now, but no more secrets, okay?"

"No more secrets," I agreed as I parked the compact in front of Swissmen Sweets.

"Call me whenever. Day or night," she said. "I know I'm far away, but I'm always here for you. I'll even listen to you talk about Eric if it will help."

I laughed, knowing how much she hated my ex-boyfriend. "I know. And I'm always here for you too."

She laughed. "I'm counting on that."

Chapter 32

My cell phone rang again just as I hung up with Cass. I sighed. It would be just like Cass to call me right back, probably to tell me a creative new way to dispose of my ex-boyfriend that she'd thought up.

"Cass—" I started without looking at the screen to see who the call was from.

There was mumbling on the other end of the line that was most certainly not my best friend. I couldn't make out what the person was saying.

"Hello?"

Nothing.

I was about to hang up when I heard a voice whisper in my ear, "It's Charlotte."

"Charlotte, where are you? Are you at Swissmen Sweets? I'm right outside the shop. I will be inside in just a minute." I pressed my ear against the phone, hoping to be able to hear her better.

"*Nee*, I am at my father's buggy shop," Charlotte said in a breathy voice.

"You are?" I asked, surprised. "What are you doing there?"

"Can you come and get me?" She sounded desperate. "Please."

I sighed. "I'll be there as soon as I can. Where is it located?"

She rattled off the location of the shop while I shifted my car into reverse.

Weaver Buggy Company was at the top of one of the rolling hills Holmes County was famous for. The buggy shop was a large, aluminum-sided barn overlooking the countryside. My small car chugged its way slowly up the hill. The car was a new addition to my life. I had had no need for one in New York, but I had learned, after just a week in Holmes County, that I couldn't get many places without some mode of transportation, and my grandfather's old buggy wasn't a practical option. *Daadi*'s buggy sat in the alley behind Swissmen Sweets. My grandfather had long ago sold his horse to another church member when he became too ill to care for the animal himself. He, like so many Amish, depended on Amish drivers, *Englischers* who drove an unofficial Amish taxi service, to take him and my grandmother around the county.

The small hatchback sputtered halfway up the steep hill, and I was beginning to regret choosing the cheapest option for my first car since high school. The car was made when I was still in high school, so that should have been my first clue that it wasn't a great investment. I patted the top of the dashboard. "You can do it!" I thought it was best to be encouraging when dealing with cars, computers, and any gadget that was threatening to fall apart on me.

Finally, after what seemed to be an eternity, I crested the hill. I gave the dashboard a final grateful pat. "I never lost faith in you. I promise to wash you and get your oil changed on a regular basis. Just keep it together for me, okay?"

Gravel crunched under my car's tires as I parked beside the enormous building. There were five buggies in the gravel lot, but only one of them had a horse tethered to it. The black horse shook his head as if trying to shift his bridle into a more comfortable position, and then he dug his nose back into the feed trough that was attached to a pole just in front of him.

Weaver Buggy Company stirred a memory in the very back of my mind, and it wasn't until I was sitting in my car in the parking lot that I realized I had been there before. I had visited the buggy shop nearly twenty years ago when I was staying with my grandparents for the summer. On that warm summer day, my *daadi* had taken me with him to have an axle repaired. He jumped out of the buggy; I remembered it so well. He was so lithe and athletic back then, so different from the crippled man using the walker who'd finally succumbed to heart disease earlier that fall.

A bear of a man had come out of the aluminum barn to meet my grandfather. The man had even growled when speaking to my grandfather. I'd tried to make myself as small as possible inside the buggy.

The man peered inside the carriage, and there I sat in my frayed jean shorts and teddy bear T-shirt. "That's your *Englisch* granddaughter, is it?" He said

"English" as if it was some kind of disease. It was the first time I realized I was different from my grandparents. Yes, I knew that they dressed differently and didn't have a television, but they were my *maami* and *daadi*. It wasn't until that large Amish man brought it to my attention that I knew I was very different from them, and in that moment, being different felt bad.

"That is my girl Bailey," my grandfather said. "She is my greatest joy."

I remember looking at my grandfather, and he smiled at me with so much love in his eyes that the man's comment about my Englishness stung a little bit less.

There was a knock on the driver's-side window. I jumped and would have hit my head on the roof of my car had I not been restrained by my seat belt.

There was another Amish man at my window, but not the big bear of a man that I remembered. Sol Weaver, Charlotte's father, peered through the window at me.

I unclipped my seat belt and exited the car. He stepped back out of my way.

He grimaced. "Why are you here?"

As subtly as possible, I glanced around for any sign of Charlotte.

"If you are looking for my daughter Charlotte, you're too late. I sent her away. She's not welcome here any longer." His voice was bitter.

I wondered if Charlotte had finally told her father that she planned to leave the Amish life. It certainly sounded like she had.

"Charlotte was here?" I asked, playing dumb. "I just happened to be driving by and remembered this place from my childhood. I drove up the hill for a closer look to see if it was what I remembered."

"You have been here before?" His tone clearly said that he didn't believe me.

"Only once, when I was a little girl with my grand-father. I remember visiting this shop with him when he needed his buggy repaired. There was a different man who met my father at the buggy that day. He was a big bear of a man."

"My brother Hiram," he said, leaving no room for argument on that point.

I opened my mouth to reply, but he was faster. "You can't talk to him. He's dead."

"I'm so sorry," I said quickly, even though I al-ready knew from Charlotte that Hiram had died. I thought it was best not to let Sol know that Char-lotte had already told me this. Also, my mind spun as I remembered my conversation with Ruby in her tiny apartment over the yarn shop. She'd implied that Josephine's death was somehow related to her husband Hiram's death, even though Hiram had died so long ago. I just wished that that little tidbit of information had come from a more reliable source than Ruby. No one would consider Ruby a reliable witness. The Sheriff's Department certainly wouldn't, if it came to that.

"It's no matter any longer. He's been gone close to fifteen years," he said, speaking of his brother's death.

"I'm still sorry."

"It was *Gotte's* will. May His will be done." His face clouded over. "My daughter doesn't look for *Gotte's* will in her life. She forces His hand. I know what she has chosen is not the will of *Gott* for her. How can it be? I had no choice but to send her away from me."

I shifted from foot to foot. Maybe I should go now that I knew Charlotte was no longer there. "You and your brother shared his shop?"

"Amish sons do not share." He said this as if I should have already known it. "The shop was my brother's until he died. He was the oldest." He looked back at the large barnlike building. "This is my shop now, and when I die it will go to my oldest son."

"Could I look inside?" I took a step forward.

He frowned. "Why?"

"It might remind me of my visit here with my grandfather." I knew it was a lame suggestion, but it was the best that I could come up with. I thought if I got a look at the inside of the shop, maybe I would understand a little bit better what Ruby had been implying about the connection between Hiram's and Josephine's deaths.

He frowned.

"I promise I won't stay long," I said.

"Very well. Jebidiah was a friend." He turned toward the barn. "Follow me."

I fell into step behind Sol. The yellow late-fall sunlight reflected off the tin roof. I held a hand up to shield my eyes when a sunbeam hit me squarely in the eye as it lowered in the west.

Once upon a time, the old building had been a horse barn and had been converted into a buggy shop. From the shop's location on the hillside, I could see the entire valley. Black-and-white milk cows spotted the hillside. There was no sign of a black-and-white pig though. I was constantly on the lookout for Jethro. Not that I expected to see him this far from the square.

My boots crunched on the gravel as I kept an eye out for Charlotte. On the phone, she had seemed so eager to leave the buggy shop that I had thought she would be waiting for me outside, but she was nowhere to be seen.

Sol held the door open for me. As I stepped inside, the overpowering scent of wood shavings and grease hit me. There was a faint layer of sawdust on the floor that was noticeable only because of the bright sunlight coming in through the westward-facing windows.

At first glance, I counted five buggies in the cavernous room. Behind one of the buggies, a door led deeper into the building. Three of the black buggies were jacked up onto platforms to access the undercarriage. The other two buggies sat in pristine condition.

"You sell buggies here?" I asked.

"Used buggies," he said. "A buggy isn't made all in one shop. Most Amish men own only three buggies in their lifetime. We, the Amish, take great pride in our buggies and care for them. It is our way. The *Englisch* are the ones who discard possessions when they are still useful."

My grandfather had cared for his buggy like it was a beloved pet. On hot summer nights, he would wash and polish his buggy until it shone.

"Just like a car, there are many pieces and parts," Sol went on. "The bulk of my business is buggy repair. Most Amish in Harvest bring their buggies to me for repair." He puffed out his chest. "I have the best shop in the county."

I raised my eyebrows. Typically, the Amish weren't ones to boast about their achievements. "It must have been hard to take the business over when Hiram died. How did it happen? He must have been relatively young." I knew the story from Charlotte, but I wanted to hear his version.

He picked up a flathead screwdriver from the workbench and smacked the handle end in his hand a couple of times. Perhaps that was my signal to leave, but I ignored it.

"It was a long time ago," Sol said. "He died right at the bottom of the hill here. He was at the bottom of the hill. A buggy got loose, rolled down the hill, and hit him. At the point when he might have realized what was happening, there was no time to get out of way, and it hit him. Hit him and killed him on the spot."

A shadow moved across one of the windows to my right. "Did you see it happen?"

He glanced at me. "*Nee.* I wasn't here that day. One of our young workers was and told me what happened. I should return to my work." Sol turned back to the workbench. When his back was turned, I glanced at the window again. Charlotte waved to me from the other side of the glass. Her eyes were the size of dinner plates as she saw me inside the shop with her father.

I made a shooing gesture at her. That was a bad move because I caught Sol's attention, and he too looked at the window. His face flushed red when he saw his daughter's face peering through the dusty glass. He dropped the screwdriver onto the workbench and stormed to the door.

Charlotte saw him coming and jumped back from the window.

I hurried after Sol. He was yelling even before I reached the door. I couldn't understand what he was yelling at his daughter because it was in their language, but his anger was unmistakable.

Charlotte stood a few feet away. She was hunched over slightly as if his words were putting some type of weight on the back of her neck, causing her to bow to her father. "*Daed*," she said and then switched to English, "I'm not coming home. I have already told you what I think. I have made my choice." She straightened up slowly as if it took much effort and stared her father in the eye.

His face deepened into another shade of red. "No child of mine is going to leave the Amish way. No Weaver has ever left the Amish way."

"*Daed*, this is my choice, not your choice." Her voice was calm and even. She had come to a decision finally, and she was going to see it through.

"You choose to turn your back on *Gott*?" Her father spat on the ground near her feet.

Tears gathered in Charlotte's eyes. "*Nee*. I would never choose such a thing, but I can worship *Gott* in my way. The Amish way is not the only way. I can praise Him with the organ."

"Get out of my sight." Sol turned his back to her.

I shuddered and walked to Charlotte's side. "Let's go," I whispered to her.

"You!" He spun around on the heels of his work boots. "You are helping her? I should have known. You come to our county to pull our children away from the Amish."

"I came to the county to be with my grandmother

and make candy. I don't have any Machiavellian plan," I said.

His brow knit together at my mention of Machiavelli. Apparently, *The Prince* wasn't on the Amish reading list.

He turned back to Charlotte. "If you have made your choice, leave my sight. You are no daughter of mine." He spun around and went back into the buggy shop, slamming the door after him.

The resolve that had appeared to be holding Charlotte's spine erect dissolved, and if I had not been there to catch her, she would have crumpled to the ground.

Her father's reaction came as a blow. It was rejection in the most devastating form. Charlotte, like me, must have known this. Rejection of this kind was like a death, but a death when you know that the other person still lives but chooses not to love you. That loss seemed so much worse.

Chapter 33

On the drive back to the center of Harvest, Charlotte was quiet. She stared out the window with her face slightly turned away from me.

I chewed on my lower lip. There were so many things I wanted to ask her. I wanted to know why she had gone to her father's buggy shop in the first place, how she got there, and how her uncle's death was related to her aunt's death. But I couldn't speak. It felt wrong to invade her grief at that moment, and I knew she was grieving the loss of not only her father's love, but possibly her entire family. Amish families were close-knit. That was one of their best qualities. Family was always first to them. However, the closeness could come at a cost as well. When the head of the family chose to turn his back on another family member, it was likely the rest of the family would too.

Traffic slowed as we drew closer to town, and I was happy to see the remaining tourists in the village carrying brown paper bags of Amish goods from many of the shops. It had been one of the busiest Saturdays I had seen in Harvest. Margot Rawlings was right. The ACC was good for the town.

I squeezed the ancient compact into a semi-legal spot in front of Swissmen Sweets.

Even before I had shifted the car into park, Charlotte had her seat belt off and the door open. "*Danki* for coming to get me, Bailey. I'm going to see if Clara could use some help at the candy shop. She said we have to make a lot of fudge tonight to restock."

I shook my head. "You don't have to . . ."

She shook her head. "I do. The work will do me well."

Charlotte might not consider herself Amish anymore, but her strong Amish work ethic remained safely intact.

Before I could respond, she slammed the car door shut. A knot twisted in my stomach. I didn't know how to help this girl. Perhaps my grandmother would. She'd been in the same place as Charlotte once upon a time, when she'd followed her heart and risked being cut off from her family to marry my grandfather. The difference was that my grandmother had *Daadi* to lean on when she made the choice. Who did Charlotte have? She wasn't leaving for the love of a man. She was leaving for the love of music. And then I realized that she had us, *Maami* and me. She could lean on us.

Charlotte knocked on Swissmen Sweets' front door, and I watched through the windshield of my car as my grandmother opened it, letting the girl in. *Maami* wrapped her arm around Charlotte's shoulders, and the younger woman rested her head on *Maami*'s shoulder as they made their way inside.

Yes, Charlotte had *Maami* and me to lean on during this difficult time in her young life.

I climbed out of the car and was amazed to see how empty the square was. The last few tourists with their brown bags of Amish goodies had climbed into their cars and headed back to the city. It was as if the ACC had never been there. It was after five o'clock, and the village was closed for the night. It would not open again until Monday morning since tomorrow was Sunday and no Amish shopkeeper would dare open on a Sunday, no matter what Amish district they might belong to.

As I stepped through the door to Swissmen Sweets, the bell jangled. Nutmeg greeted me the moment I stepped inside, as he always did. Other than the cat, the shop was empty.

I locked the door behind me.

Nutmeg meowed.

"Where did *Maami* and Charlotte go?" I asked the cat.

He turned and walked to the bottom of the stairs that led to my grandmother's apartment above the shop. Then he ran up the stairs. The kitten was more reliable than Lassie.

At the top of the stairs, I heard voices coming from my grandmother's sitting room at the back of the apartment. The old floorboards under my feet creaked and moaned as I walked to the room. The door was open. My grandmother and Charlotte sat on the sofa together. They had their heads bowed, and my grandmother murmured words I couldn't understand. She was praying. I hesitated in the doorway. I didn't want to disturb them. I stepped back, and the floorboards groaned under the weight of my foot.

Maami and Charlotte looked up. My grandmother smiled at me and patted the girl's hand.

Charlotte stood up and brushed tears from her eyes. "I think I will go read for a little while until dinner. Would that be okay with you, Clara?"

My grandmother nodded.

Charlotte gave me a shy smile and ducked her head before walking around me and through the doorway.

I entered the sitting room and perched on the rocking chair in the corner of the room. "Is she all right?"

My grandmother picked up her knitting, which lay across the arm of the sofa. The Amish work ethic was alive and well in my grandmother. I supposed, if I was honest, I had inherited a lot of it too. It was almost impossible for me not to do something every minute of the day. Sometimes I wished that I could be like some of my friends back in New York, who could unplug during the weekends. When I lived in New York, most weekends I experimented with new recipes or found new ways to manage the kitchen at JP Chocolates or poured over vendor accounts looking for ways to save Jean Pierre money, money that he could then reinvest in the business. I had done that, at least, until I'd met Eric Sharp.

I had thought Eric was the one who would help me have a more balanced life. I had been so very wrong. Eric's life as a jet-setting chef with all the money and women he could want was anything but balanced. It wasn't until I was sitting there with my grandmother quietly knitting that I realized what a lucky escape I had made, and the tiny part of me that had been holding onto some slim hope that Eric would fly to Amish Country to try to win me back let go.

"Are you all right, my dear?" my grandmother asked. Her knitting needles were poised in front of her as she paused mid-stitch to study me.

I shook my head. "I'm fine. I'm worried about Charlotte though."

"I am too." She resumed knitting. "Deacon Clapp paid me a call while you girls were gone. He said if Charlotte doesn't return home tonight, he is going to ask the community to shun her."

I leaned back in the rocking chair. "Can he do that?"

"He is the deacon, and if the district bishop goes along with it, he will."

"Will the bishop agree?" I asked.

She frowned at her knitting and undid the stitch she'd just added. From where I sat, the stitch appeared fine to me, but my grandmother was a perfectionist when it came to her knitting. I couldn't argue against it. I was the same about my chocolates. "I'm afraid he will. The bishop of Charlotte's district is very tired, and he is happy that Abram Clapp is young and willing to take over most of the work of running the district."

"What is Charlotte going to do? Will she go back?" I asked.

Maami shook her head. "She hasn't decided yet. We prayed that the Lord would give her clarity."

"Will you get in trouble for helping her?" I couldn't keep the worry from my voice.

She pushed the yarn farther down her needles

with her fingertips, which were calloused from a lifetime of washing dishes by hand and making candy. "I do not belong to that district of Amish any longer. They have no hold over me. I am grateful that my church leaders are more understanding."

I smiled at her, hoping to lighten the mood. "Even Deacon Yoder's wife?" I asked.

She rolled her eyes over her knitting. "Even Ruth Yoder is better than Deacon Clapp."

Since I knew how much my grandmother disliked Ruth Yoder, that was saying a lot.

"*Maami*," I said tentatively, "you seem happier."

She looked up. "Do I?"

I nodded.

"I am happy to help my cousin," she said and set her knitting in her lap. "The girl needs me right now."

I stared at my hands for a moment. "Is that what you miss most about *Daadi*, helping him?"

"There is so much I miss about your grandfather, it would be impossible to recount it all, but yes, I miss helping him, working with him, and being at his side. Your grandfather and I were partners—helpmates, as it says in the Bible. I took care of him, and he took care of me. There was never any decision that we didn't consult with each other about. I miss that. I suppose I miss caring for someone as much as I miss being cared for."

"You take care of me," I said. "And I can take care of you."

She shook her head sadly. "Bailey, dear, no one takes care of you but you. It's all that you allow. I know this. You have been this way since you were a child."

I opened my mouth to protest, but she was faster.

"This is not a criticism, my child. It is the way *Gott* made you, but I need to care for someone. Charlotte needs me now. *Gott* has brought us together to comfort each other. *Gott* willed it that my Jebidiah would venture onto his great reward before me. His will be done, not mine. *Gott* has let me remain here, but my *gut* work for Him on this earth is not yet complete. With Charlotte, *Gott* is reminding me there is more to be done."

"I wish I could be so sure of God's will," I murmured.

She studied me over her glasses. "You could."

I didn't know if that was true, and that uncertainty was at the heart of my problem.

Chapter 34

I told my grandmother that I was going to go for a walk and asked her not to wait dinner for me. I needed to leave Swissmen Sweets and clear my head. Confusion about the murder and about my place in Holmes County plagued my mind. I wondered if giving up my life in New York had been the right choice after all. It seemed that I wasn't able to help my grandmother the way I had wanted to. Charlotte, in her vulnerability, could help her where I, in my strength, could not. Ironically, that made me feel vulnerable.

I walked down Main Street to the corner of Apple and turned right so that I was walking away from Ruby's apartment and around the outside of the square. I passed the dark windows of the cheese shop, a quilt shop, and a woodworker as I circumnavigated the square. I walked past the church then, and I gravitated to the small, now abandoned playground next to the it. One of the swings gently rocked back and forth in the cold breeze. I wrapped my scarf more tightly around my neck and tucked it into my coat.

The money that the ACC had raised would make the dilapidated playground a showpiece of the village. It was past due for a makeover, but a little part of me would be sad when the swing set that I had played on as a child was replaced by something that was newer and safer and much more colorful than that plain metal contraption.

I sat on the swing that had been my favorite as a little girl and kicked off the ground with my boots. My toes dug trenches into the mulch as I pushed off, just as they had when I was child. I almost expected to see my footprints from two decades ago imprinted in the earth. I knew that they had to be there somewhere. I had spent so much time on that swing set as a young girl.

As my swing rocked back and forth, I felt the tension begin to leave my body. I tried to remember the last time I had been on a swing set. Had I ever taken the time to do such a thing when I lived in New York? It wasn't something I would have had the time for or made the time for.

A laugh escaped my lips. I couldn't help it. I had never felt this light and free in New York. Despite the challenges of living in Harvest and the dead bodies, it was where I belonged. Finally, I was in the right spot. The only thing that could make the moment better was to look down and see my grandfather below me—to see him there and to be able to tell him that I was staying in Harvest for good to fulfill his legacy.

I looked down then, half expecting to find him standing there, even though I knew that was impossible. Instead, another man approached the swing in the twilight, but it was not my grandfather. I let my toes catch at the mulch under my feet to slow my pace. Back and forth, back and forth, I slowed. Finally, I planted my feet firmly in the mulch and brought myself to a jerky halt. By that time, Sheriff Deputy Aiden Body was standing directly in front of me.

"That looks like fun," Aiden said.

My heart thundered in my chest. I told myself it was because of the exertion from the swing. I told myself that it had nothing to do with the handsome man standing a few feet from me.

The swing twisted as I shifted my feet for a better grasp on the slippery mulch, and I yelped, nearly falling off it.

Aiden grabbed the swing's chains on either side of me to straighten me out. Even when the swing was perfectly still, he kept a firm grip on the chains.

"Where did you come from?" I asked in a more accusatory tone than I intended. As happy as I was to see him, I didn't want him to know he had any effect on me. At a time like this, when I felt trapped, the cagey New Yorker I had been for most of my adult life came out.

He smiled a slow smile but still did not release my swing's chains. I thought about climbing off the back of the swing, but quickly dismissed that idea. Knowing my luck, I would fall into the mulch in an unattractive heap, and my foot would become entangled in the swing in the process.

"I could ask you the same thing," he said.

I took a breath. "I was out for a walk, trying to work out the case in my head, and I've been looking for Jethro."

"I was doing the same." He flashed his dimple. "It seems you and I have a lot in common, Bailey King."

I wasn't going anywhere near that comment. "How's your mom?" I asked. "I'm so sorry that Jethro's still missing."

The dimple disappeared. "She's hanging in there."

"He'll turn up."

He frowned as if he wasn't so sure about that. I wasn't so sure about it either. Neither of us voiced that concern though.

"Charlotte is staying at Swissmen Sweets at least for the foreseeable future." He said this as a statement, not a question.

"Umm," I said.

"You don't need to hide it. I was just at the candy shop, and your grandmother told me. I know that Charlotte's left her Amish district, and you and Clara gave her a place to stay as she finds a new way to live. That's very kind of both of you," he said.

"You went to the shop looking for Charlotte again, or you had a sudden need for fudge?" I asked, wishing that he would let go of the chain and back up. He was too close.

He shook his head. "I needed to talk to you. Clara told me you were out looking for Jethro."

"Ahh," I said because saying anything cleverer was next to impossible, considering his proximity.

"I wanted to be the one to tell you that your candy didn't kill Josephine," he said, distracting me for a moment because of how close he was to me.

I pressed the soles of my boots into the mulch. "You were right about it not being something she ate?"

He nodded. "But it was something she ingested.

The coroner finished the toxicology report just a little while ago and gave me a call. From what he can tell, she drank licorice extract. She must have died quickly. Her body didn't even have to digest it before she had an allergic reaction."

I shivered, but I couldn't bring myself to tell him about the bottle of licorice extract that was missing from Swissmen Sweets. That missing bottle would make Charlotte a more likely suspect than ever, since she could have taken it while visiting my grandmother before the competition. I had promised my grandmother that I would help Charlotte. Handing her over to Aiden didn't seem to fall into the helping category.

"From what I can gather, every person at the candy contest had licorice extract, and it was all the same brand made by the same Amish company, located in Pennsylvania. I don't know how I'm supposed to find out which candy maker, if any, gave it to her."

"Does the coroner know how much of the licorice extract she drank?" I asked.

Aiden shook his head. "No. With such a severe allergy, it wouldn't take much to kill her. The confusing thing—well, one of them, as there are many with this case—is why she drank it. There was no sign of a struggle, and the coroner believes someone put her inside the organ after she died. Why would she drink it? She knew she was allergic."

"Maybe she was physically forced to drink it," I suggested.

"There were no signs of a struggle to indicate that." He pulled lightly on the swing's chains, moving

me closer to him by a centimeter, but it felt like
a mile.

I swallowed. "There are other methods of coer-
cion."

He studied me. "That's what I was thinking. If
something or someone she loved was threatened,
maybe she thought she had no choice."

"I didn't get the impression that she was very
close to her family," I said. "However, it looks like
Sol Weaver is planning to sell Josephine's candy
shop."

He raised his eyebrows. "And how would you
know that?"

"I gave Lindy a ride back to Berlin Candies after
the ACC ended and ran into Jeffrey Galwin. He said
Sol was sniffing around the shop today. He's the
one who had the idea that Sol was planning to sell.
The shop does have the best location in the county,
right there in the middle of Berlin. Sol could make
a lot of money."

"Ahh, Jeffrey." He sighed. "He would have been
a good suspect."

"I know," I said.

"You know?"

I shifted on the swing, trying to get a little bit
more comfortable. I wished that he would let go of
the chains, so that I could stand up and step a safe
distance away from him. "He has a lot of anger, especially toward Josephine and her shop. She loved
her business. From what I can tell, it was the most
important aspect of her life, but even if he didn't
have an alibi, I don't see how he could get her to
drink licorice extract. I got the sense that Josephine

didn't care a whit what Jeffrey thought and the feeling was mutual."

Aiden sighed. "And she was nowhere close to her shop or Jeffrey when she died. Everyone has someone or something that he or she is willing to die for. I just have to find out who or what that was for Josephine. If I do, I'll find her killer."

I shivered. He was right. I would die for my grandmother, my parents, and Cass. They weren't the only ones, but those were the names that came immediately to mind. "No sign of Jethro?"

He shook his head. "He appears to have vanished into thin air. My worst fear is another animal got him, but please don't tell my mother that. She would never recover." Finally, he let go of the chains and settled into the next swing over. I felt like I could breathe again.

"What are you going to do now?" I asked as my lungs filled with welcome oxygen.

"Think," he said, kicking the ground and rocking back in his swing. "There are a lot of clues that were planted in this case. Whoever was responsible for Josephine's death was doing her best to confuse us."

"Her?" I asked.

He smiled. "Poisoning is typically a woman's weapon of choice when committing murder. Maybe because it seems kinder and gentler, but my theory is it's because it takes more thought. It's been my experience that when a woman decides to kill, she spends much more time plotting and planning it out than a man does."

"Have you known many murderers?" I asked.

He sighed. "More than I care to think about,

and it only seems to be getting worse." He ran his hand through his dark hair. "At times, it feels like police work is truly an uphill battle, and we are losing ground."

"I know that you're giving it your best." I turned my swing to face him. "Everyone in the county knows that too. We're lucky to have you."

He turned his swing to face me, and our knees touched. He studied me. "I know," he said, breaking the tension, "that the Sheriff's Department is not loved by the community, especially not by the Amish. I want to do whatever I can to change that. We aren't the enemy. We're here to serve the community. That includes the Amish."

"The sheriff might not agree with you on that," I said, looking up. "And he's up for reelection."

He grimaced. "And in all likelihood, he will be reelected. No one is opposing him."

"You could run against him. Someone should challenge his power. You could win." I studied his face hopefully.

"As his deputy, that would be the wrong thing to do." He shook his head. "I don't agree with his policies, and believe me when I say, I don't enforce any of his anti-Amish stances, but if I want to be a sheriff, I would do better to move to a different county than run against my boss. Loyalty is a big deal in law enforcement, and if it looks like I don't have loyalty for my superior, it could ruin my career, no matter where I go."

"You'd rather work for a tyrant instead of challenging him?" I asked.

He sighed. "No, but I try to work within the system

to protect those who wouldn't even be considered if I hadn't been there to speak up for them."

"Like Charlotte," I said, well aware that our knees were still touching.

He nodded in the twilight. "Just like Charlotte."

"Well, for whatever it might be worth, I think if you ran against Sheriff Marshall, you would win. You're clearly the best cop the department has, even if you did think I was capable of murder once," I teased. "Er, *twice*."

He laughed. It was a loud sound and echoed through the stillness of the evening.

"I wasn't joking." I stood, no longer able to stand the physical contact with him, and held onto the chains of my swing as if I needed their support.

He stood up too, right in front of me. "I know, and I appreciate the vote of confidence. I want to have your support, Bailey."

I swallowed. "You have it." My knees felt wobbly, so I sat back down on the swing.

He smiled. "Good. That's enough for right now." He grabbed the chains on either side of me and leaned forward. My breath caught as he kissed me in the middle of the forehead. "That will hold until you're ready." Aiden let go of the swing's chains, and I rocked backward away from him, wondering if I had imagined the kiss.

He turned and walked away.

"Ready for what?" I asked, barely above a whisper, to his receding back.

What did I need to be ready for? A thousand possibilities came to mind at that moment. Ready to solve the murder was one of them, but I knew that wasn't what this conversation had been about. I wasn't ready to contemplate the real business at hand. I hoped that I was wrong about his implication. I didn't need this complication, even though I knew that both Juliet and *Maami* would love it. Aiden knew that. But would he wait until I was ready? It might be a long wait for him. A very long wait.

I kicked off the mulch-covered earth again and swung back into the dark open sky that opened wide to greet me.

Chapter 35

I rocked back and forth in the swing for a few minutes after Aiden was gone. Then I stood up and followed him. The least I could do was help him search for his mother's pig.

When I reached the lawn at the edge of the church, the grass and dry leaves crunched under my feet. In my mind, every step I took was on broken glass. I could hear the crack and the shatter, and it seemed to echo through the silent center of town.

I froze and listened. "Aiden?" I called.

There was no answer.

I already knew Aiden could move fast. He could be back in his cruiser by now, driving to the Sheriff's Department.

Then, I heard it. A little ways away. The same broken glass sound that I was making came from the other side of the church. In the still night, the sound traveled easily.

"Aiden?" I called again.

Still there was no response. I told myself I should abandon the pig search for the night and return to

Swissmen Sweets. Maybe I would have a chance to speak to Charlotte and talk to her about her aunt. Maybe Charlotte would know what her aunt cared about so much that she might be willing to drink licorice extract to protect it.

"Get a grip, Bailey," I told myself. "You lived in New York City, for goodness' sake." There had been countless times when Cass and I had been out in the city and I had come home at an ungodly hour. Or even more times when I had lost track of time working at JP Chocolates and left the shop on my own in the wee hours of the morning. I never once got mugged. I never once felt like I was in danger, not the way I did at that moment, which only made me feel that much more ridiculous. I was in the middle of Amish Country. There wasn't a safer place on earth; at least I would have thought that before the murders. Still, I had nothing to fear.

I took a step forward, shattering an acorn with my foot. It sounded like a gunshot in the stillness. I made a noise that was caught between a cry and a scream. I froze again, hoping to hear Aiden's running footsteps, but I heard nothing. If he was around, he would have heard me. People didn't scream in the middle of the night in Harvest, Ohio, and go unnoticed. I stood there a full minute with the sole of my boot still on the pulverized acorn, and again nothing. Aiden had left the area.

I walked around the church. The light that illuminated the back door of the church had a hospital-level intensity to its glow. I squinted at it, turning away to face the cemetery. Ambient light reflected off the newly painted white fence. A new sign declaring that the paint was wet hung in the middle of the fence, even though I knew the paint must have been dry by that late hour.

My eyes traveled across the cemetery to the mausoleum that stood in the middle of it. The WET PAINT sign was no longer on the old building, but I still wondered how it had gotten there in the first place. Could someone have hung it there on purpose, and if they did, why?

I stared at it a little harder. It looked like a little house. That's where Ruby said the pig was. Could he really be inside?

I had to know. I shook off my fear and walked over to the fence line. Taking care not to mar the new paint, I climbed over the fence and landed on my feet on the other side. The dry leaves that covered the ground crackled in protest as I landed.

The cemetery was dark. The light over the church door didn't reach beyond the fence itself. I tried to push thoughts of goblins, zombies, and creatures that went bump in the night to the back of my mind.

I told myself that I would check out the mausoleum to satisfy my curiosity, and then it would be straight back to Swissmen Sweets for the night.

My pace around the gravestones was brisk. Again, the argument that I had overheard between the two painters played in my memory. Each had been adamant that he hadn't left the sign on the mausoleum. I had to find out if someone else had put the sign there for a reason.

I shook off the creepy-crawly feeling the cemetery gave me. It was now or never. I either went into the graveyard to take a closer look at the mausoleum or I turned tail and ran back to the candy shop like a scaredy-cat. I wasn't going to let myself be a coward, even if I was the only one who would know about it.

I removed my cell phone from my pocket and used the flashlight app to guide my way. If I was really going to be searching for a pig in the dark every night, I was going to have to invest in a flashlight.

Most of the names on the markers were German and even Amish-sounding—Yoder, Hostetler, Young— but the Amish weren't buried there. They were laid to rest in their own plain cemeteries, where the departed's final resting place was marked with a wooden cross or a plain stone. I knew this from my grandfather's funeral, which was still fresh in my mind. The Amish certainly would not be buried in an ornate mausoleum.

In this cemetery, the mausoleum was the centerpiece, and I would have been able to find it even if I hadn't had the light from my phone to guide me.

Although not as lavish as the mausoleums I had seen in New York, I could tell that this one had been built by a family of wealth. I looked up at the worn name. It read Marshall. I shivered. Could this be the final resting place of the cantankerous Sheriff Marshall's ancestors? Was his family's stature in the county the reason he was sheriff in the first place?

I shone the light on the mausoleum door. There was a latch above the ironwork door handle. I stared at the latch. I would have thought that the building hadn't been opened in decades, not since the last person had been laid to rest there, but I couldn't help noticing that the grime around the latch appeared to have been disturbed, as if it had been opened recently. Someone had been inside the small building, and it wasn't twenty years ago, as the last death date on the building would lead me to believe.

I knocked on the door. Immediately, there was a bang and a clatter on the other side of the thick wood. I stumbled back off the single step that led into the building, skittering on the heels of my boots. Somehow, despite the stumbling, I kept myself upright.

More banging came from inside the building, and I was about to turn and run when I heard oinking. Yes, that's what I heard. Oinking.

I jumped back onto the step and threw back the latch, or tried to. Even though the door had been opened in the last few days, the latch was stubborn. The rusty metal cut into my fingertips, and I was glad I was up to date on my tetanus shots.

Finally, the latch gave way. I pulled on the door handle and it moved all of an inch, but it was enough to allow me to wrap my fingers around the door itself and pull with all my might. As if it was attached to a rubber band that had just been let loose, the door swung open. I stumbled off the step again.

The oinking grew louder. I stepped back onto the single step. "Jethro?"

There was the snap of another acorn being crushed behind me. Jethro squealed. Before I could turn around, I felt a hand on my back, shoving me inside the dark mausoleum. My cell phone flew from my hand and clattered across the stone floor. The light went out just as the door was slammed behind me.

I groaned as I rolled onto my side. My knees felt

skinned under my jeans, and the flesh on the heels of my hands was raw. I lay there for a moment listening, straining to hear if whoever had pushed me inside the building was standing outside the door waiting for me to appear.

Jethro pressed his warm, damp snout against my cheek, and I jumped. The pig squealed in return.

I reached over and patted the general direction of where I thought the pig's head should be and touched his back. "It's okay," I murmured as I stroked the animal, hoping to calm him, hoping to calm myself. "It's okay, Jethro."

He snuggled up to me, pressing his body as close as he could without being on top of me.

Slowly taking care not to press the raw part of my hands on the dusty stone beneath me, I pushed myself up into a sitting position. I tried not to think of the fact that I was trapped in a tiny building with at least a dozen dead people and a terrified pig. If I let myself dwell on my circumstances, I would panic, and I would be no use to Jethro or myself if that happened.

Other than my skinned hands and knees, I was fine. I gave Jethro a final pat and rose to my feet. I held my hands out in front of me like a zombie, thrashing at the empty space in the hope of hitting a wall or making contact with an object that would help me get my bearings. I froze as my hand hit cool metal. It could have been a vase, or it could have been an urn holding someone's ashes. On second thought, I didn't need to get my bearings.

I stumbled away from the smooth metal, and my shoulder connected with a stone wall. I spun around and let my fingers lead me around the wall. I stubbed my toe on what I assumed was a casket encased in stone, but I didn't let myself dwell on that possibility either.

After what seem like an inordinate amount of time, my fingers finally moved from the cold stone to rough wood. I knew I had found the door. I gave a sigh of relief. Now Jethro and I could escape. I felt the pig press his snout into the back of my lower leg.

Despite the abrasion on the heel of my hand, I ran my palm all over the door. I found the side with the hinges. They were large, at least three inches in length and as wide as my wrist. I ran my hand across the surface of the door in the opposite direction from where the hinges were to the logical place where the door handle should be, but there was no handle.

There was no handle on the inside of the door at all. There was no need for anyone inside the mausoleum to get out. I felt like someone had grabbed me by the throat as fear began to bubble up from my center. If there was no door handle, then I was truly trapped. What was worse, whoever had pushed me inside the mausoleum knew that too and could come back at his or her leisure to finish me off.

I took another deep breath. There had to be another way to escape my prison. My cell phone. That was what I needed. With my phone, I could call for help. When whoever attacked me had shoved me into the small building, my phone had gone flying from my hand. I winced to think what the phone's condition was after it had crashed into the stone floor.

Gingerly, I dropped to the floor. I yelped in pain as all my weight settled on my skinned knees, but there was no other way to find the phone other than scouring the mausoleum's floor inch by inch on my hands and knees. Jethro snorted next to me, and I realized he'd noticed what I was up to and had his snout on the cold stone floor. I doubted he knew what we were looking for, but I appreciated his piggy support.

I ran my hand back and forth over the dusty floor in a sweeping motion, taking care not to miss an inch of the surface. There was nothing there other than small pebbles, dust, and—I was almost certain—the world's largest spider, which thankfully scurried away when I encountered it.

I shook the creepy-crawly feeling from my hand that the spider left behind. Taking a deep breath, I slid my hand across the floor again. This time, it came in contact with a smooth object that went skittering across the floor. I followed the direction it went in by the sound. I moved more slowly. I didn't want to knock it out of the way again. Finally, my thumb grazed it. My hand wrapped around a small smooth object. It felt like a bottle. In the blackness, I touched the top of the bottle, and it was sticky. I held it under my nose, and the overwhelming scent of licorice assaulted my nostrils.

I knew what this bottle was, but I hoped I was wrong. I wouldn't know for certain until I had some light. I stuck the bottle into my jeans pocket and began to search again for my cell phone.

It had to be in there somewhere. In the dark, it could be right next to me and I wouldn't know it.

Then I heard something outside. There was a scarping sound right outside the wooden door.

I made one more frantic sweep across the floor

in search of my phone, and I found it. My fingers curled around the device, and I hugged it to my chest. The screen was cracked, but the phone was operational. I quickly turned on the flashlight app and shone the weak light around the room. There was an overturned stone vase in the corner. The flowers that had been inside it were long dead. I picked up the vase. It weighed a good six pounds. It would make an effective weapon if it came to that. Next to where I had found the vase, there was a crack in the foundation, and water pooled at the spot where the floor and the wall met.

I was about to call the police when Jethro shoved his snout into my face.

He was covered in dust and wide-eyed. It was difficult to say how traumatic his stay in the mausoleum had been. He had been there for almost two full days without food, and it showed. The only water he had had to drink was from this crack in the foundation. In his mouth, he held a note.

I set the vase back down and took the note from him. I studied it under the light of my phone. It was just a plain quarter sheet of paper that had been folded in half.

I glanced at the door, willing it not to open.

I unfolded the note. It was in English. Because the Amish learned English in school, that was what they used when they wrote. Pennsylvania Dutch was more of a spoken language.

Josephine,
Meet me behind the church at 10 am to discuss your suggestion. I will be able to get away then. I'm sure we can come to an agreement.

There was a rattling at the door as someone tried to open it. I skimmed to the end of the letter, which was signed, "JB."

And that's when I knew who was on the other side of the door, waiting for me.

Chapter 36

Clumsily, I tucked the note into the inside pocket of my jacket. The door began to move. I didn't have much time. I dialed 911 on my phone. The operator came on as a crack of light appeared around the door.

The operator asked me what my emergency was. Before I could answer, the door opened. Leaving the phone on, I tucked it in the back waistband of my pants, praying that the operator could hear what we were saying.

"Jeremiah Beiler," I said loudly. "What are you doing here at the church cemetery with a knife?"

If he noticed that I was talking abnormally loud, he didn't show it. He glared at me. "Why couldn't you leave this alone?" In his right hand, he held a knife as long as my arm. The sharp metal weapon caught the moonlight coming in through the open door. I supposed my chances were better with a knife than a gun. Maybe I had a shot at getting away from him and the knife. I would have no chance of escaping if he had a gun. No chance at all. But I was basically trapped in a windowless stone room the size of a walk-in closet. I was a sitting duck.

"Leave what alone? Looking for Jethro?" I asked. "Juliet is my friend. Of course, I had to keep searching for her pig."

"Did you find him?" Jeremiah asked.

"No," I lied. "I'm afraid he might be gone for good. Juliet will be heartbroken."

"We all have our reasons to be heartbroken," Jeremiah said.

"Maybe," I said, trying to sound as conversational as possible. "Maybe it would be easier if we discussed this outside the building. It's too dark in here, don't you think?"

Jethro hid behind me, and I hoped he was doing his best to keep out of sight. I didn't think that Jeremiah would take it well if he knew that I'd lied to him.

"We can talk about it right here," Jeremiah said.

I supposed it was just wishful thinking to expect him to let me go so easily. I wracked my brain for any way to get around him, but nothing came to mind. Jeremiah was a large man, and he almost filled the doorway. The few spare inches on either side of him weren't nearly big enough for me to squeeze by. I had to think of another way out. I removed the note from my pocket.

"What's that?" Jeremiah demanded.

"Maybe you can tell me since you wrote it."

"Give it to me," he said.

"Did she want to talk to you about Hiram?"

He froze in the midst of trying to rip the paper from my hand. "What did you ask?"

"Hiram. This all comes back to Hiram, doesn't it? You worked in the buggy shop for the Weaver family. I remember seeing you there when I was a child. I thought at first it was Hiram that I remembered, but then I knew I was wrong. It was you."

"So what if it was?" he asked.

"Sol said he wasn't there the day that Hiram died, but one of the young men who worked for him was."

"And if it was me, what does that mean?"

I swallowed and glanced down at the knife in his hand. "I think you know how Hiram really died, and maybe so did Josephine."

"It was an accident."

"If it was an accident, why is it still haunting you?"

"It was an accident," he bellowed, and his voice reverberated off the walls of the mausoleum. "A complete accident. I ran into the wheel stop holding the buggy at the top of the hill. I was tired. I had been moving mulch all day. I was careless. I hit the stop with my wheelbarrow just right and sent the buggy flying down the hill directly at Hiram. The buggy was too fast. There was no way I could stop it. I yelled for Hiram to get out of the way, but he must not have heard me. He never moved, and when the buggy hit him, he never moved again." His breath became shallow.

"Do you think Sol knew?" I asked.

"He might have, but since he was the new owner of the buggy shop, he never questioned me. He believed me when I said I didn't know how the buggy broke loose."

I was certain Sol did know what had really happened, but there was no way I could prove that.

"After Hiram's funeral, I was destroyed by what I had done. I couldn't eat or sleep, so I went to Josephine and confessed everything. She said she understood and that I'd suffered enough. She said she wouldn't tell the church leaders or the police. I was so grateful. She kept her word all these years."

"Until now?" I asked.

"Until now. She wanted to win the ACC so badly, and I was her way to do it. You don't know how important this competition was to Josephine. If she won the ACC, it would validate her business and everything she'd done after her husband's death. Everyone expected her to remarry after Hiram died, but instead she opened Berlin Candies and put her heart and soul into that shop."

"She was blackmailing you?" I asked.

"She wanted a guaranteed win. She wanted to win the ACC, and she was blackmailing me to make sure that it would happen. I couldn't let her do that. If she got her way this time, I knew it wouldn't be the last time she asked. I wanted to talk to her in person to reason with her. But there was no reasoning with that woman. I never thought she would do it. For a time after her husband's death, we were *close*."

I weighed the implication of the last word he'd said. "You were lovers then."

He bristled. "Just for a short time when we were both hurting over Hiram's death. We knew it was wrong. It didn't last long, but we loved each other for a time."

Something that Ruby had said came back to me, "Love and hate are two sides of the same coin." In her confused, wandering way, she had been trying to steer me toward the realization that Jeremiah was the killer.

I shook my head. "This doesn't make any sense. There were no signs of struggle on her body. How did you make her drink the extract?"

"She drank it on her own."

"Why?" I asked, confused.

"If an Amish woman doesn't have her reputation, what does she have?" he asked.

My mouth fell open. "You blackmailed her right back and threatened to tell about your affair with her, and she killed herself to avoid being shamed by the community, a particularly strict Amish district."

Aiden had been right. Josephine's death had been at a woman's hand.

"But that would tarnish your reputation too," I said.

"It's different for a man." His tone was matter-of-fact.

I felt sick, knowing that this was true, especially in the Amish community. I had seen how Emily's own family had treated her after her affair that led to an unplanned pregnancy.

"The irony of it all," Jeremiah said, "is that Josephine's shop did win the competition. It was all for naught. All of it."

"You put her body in the organ," I said. "Why?"

His index finger twitched on the handle of the knife. "I had to do something so that people wouldn't connect her death to me, and it seemed fitting."

"How?" I asked.

"Everyone knew she was upset with Charlotte about the organ. Charlotte would have a reason to want her dead."

Jethro, who had been trapped in the mausoleum all this time, wanted to get out. With a squeak, he charged Jeremiah, who wasn't ready for someone to hit him at shin level. He stumbled onto the step outside the mausoleum, but with the knife in his hand, he wasn't able to right himself. He fell back with a scream.

I scooped up the pig and ran out of the building, jumping over the groaning Jeremiah as I went.

"Bailey!" A flashlight bobbed over the gravestones. "Bailey."

It was Aiden.

"Over here," I called and waved, holding Jethro to my side in the other arm.

He caught his breath and pulled up short, taking in the scene. "What is going on here?"

"Jeremiah just tried to kill me, and he's responsible for the death of Hiram Weaver fifteen years ago."

"Hiram Weaver? I'm looking for the murderer of Josephine Weaver."

I glanced back at the groaning deacon. "He's responsible for that too. Trust me." I handed him the note.

He took it from my hand. "I can't believe all this happened, and I was just inside the church."

I hugged Jethro to my chest and glanced down at Jeremiah, who was moaning and clutching his obviously broken leg. "Don't worry. Jethro and I handled it."

Aiden shook his head as he ripped his radio from his belt and called the incident in.

Epilogue

A week later, I sat in a pew in the middle of Juliet's church. My grandmother was at my side with her hands folded on her lap. Juliet, with Jethro sleeping on her lap and Reverend Brook at her side, sat on the other side of my grandmother. The seat to my right was empty.

At the front of the church, Charlotte sat with her back to us as her fingers flew across the organ's keys, and the music she created rose through the pipes and filled the space.

The deacon of her new district, my grandmother's district, had told her that she didn't have to choose between her love of music and her love of God. He thought she could have both. Charlotte planned to continue living at Swissmen Sweets. Even though she remained Amish, she had left her home district. Her family wouldn't welcome her back, and neither would Deacon Clapp. I knew a time would come when Charlotte would have to make that final decision to join the Amish church, whichever church it might be, or leave forever.

Thankfully, it was not on this day, a day to celebrate all her hard work and her talent.

The church was full of Amish and English people who were there just to hear Charlotte play. I had never known an organ to have so much life. It was no wonder she was so torn when Deacon Clapp had said that she had to give it up.

I watched Charlotte's hands move across the keys so closely that I didn't know there was someone standing at my side until he cleared his throat.

I jumped and looked up to find Aiden, still dressed in his Sheriff's Department uniform, looking down at me. His dimple was on full display, which did nothing for my nerves.

He gestured to the small open seat beside me. I nodded that he could have it, scooting over to make room for him and causing everyone down the line in my pew to do the same. Both Juliet and my grandmother looked down the pew in our direction, and the two women shared a secret smile as Aiden took the seat beside me.

His hand dropped onto the pew's seat next to my own. He squeezed my hand. I pulled my hand away and folded my hands in my lap, wishing that I'd had the nerve to hold on to him.

After a moment, I snuck a peek at Aiden, who was looking forward, engrossed in the music, just like everyone else there. He had a secret smile on his face that matched the one his mother and my grandmother had shared just a moment ago. That's when I knew my heart was in all sorts of trouble.

Swissmen Sweets
Black Licorice

Ingredients
- ½ stick of butter, plus extra for greasing the pan
- ½ cup granulated white sugar
- 2 tablespoons molasses
- A dash of salt
- ¼ cup maple syrup
- ¼ cup sweetened condensed milk
- ½ teaspoon black food coloring
- 6 tablespoons cornstarch (can substitute flour)
- ¾ tablespoon licorice extract (can substitute anise extract, which is easier to find)

Directions
1. Line a 9" x 9" pan with parchment paper. For easy removal, the paper should be 2 inches higher than the sides of the pan.
2. Spread butter onto the parchment paper.
3. Clip a candy thermometer onto the side of a heavy saucepan. Don't let the thermometer touch the bottom of the pan.

4. Mix the butter, maple syrup, sugar, condensed milk, salt, and molasses in the saucepan. Bring to a gentle boil, stirring continually to avoid burning the mixture.

5. When the mixture reaches 240°F, remove it from the heat, and stir in the corn starch and black food coloring. When those ingredients are fully mixed, add the licorice extract.

6. Pour the mixture into the 9" x 9" pan, and refrigerate for 30 minutes.

7. Remove the pan from the fridge, remove the candy from the pan, and cut into 1" x 1" squares.

Don't miss the next Amish Candy Shop mystery!

PREMEDITATED PEPPERMINT

Chapter 1

Peppermint is much more than a Christmastime treat. It has a thousand uses. It has been used to freshen breath, flavor beverages, calm nerves, and even grow hair. But as far as I could tell, it did not have the power to repel ex-boyfriends.

This conclusion was confirmed when Eric Sharp walked through the front door of Swissmen Sweets, the Amish candy shop that I ran with my Amish grandmother in the middle of Holmes County, Ohio. No, I wasn't Amish, but my father's family was. Up until a few months ago, I had spent most of my adult life in New York City, working as an assistant chocolatier at JP Chocolates for world-renowned chocolate maker Jean Pierre Ruge. After my grandfather's death in September, I left city life behind to take over Swissmen Sweets. I never regretted that decision. My only regret about leaving New York had been created by the New York tabloids, which had revealed where I'd gone, and that meant Eric Sharp knew just where to find me.

At the moment Eric walked into my shop, I was

up to my elbows in peppermint and white chocolate. I was spreading the molten white chocolate mixture on a cookie sheet to cool. After the peppermint bark solidified and cooled, I would break it into pieces, place the pieces in cellophane bags, and tie them closed with bright red ribbon.

Eric smiled when he caught me staring gape-mouthed at him. Even if the shop were full of customers, which it was not on a weekday midafternoon, Eric would still have been able to spot me quickly. I was the only person in the shop wearing jeans. My grandmother and her cousin Charlotte, who both stood behind the glass-domed counter bagging candies, wore plain Amish dresses, black aprons, and white prayer caps.

Eric strode toward me, but before he reached me, my grandmother smiled brightly at him. "May I help you?"

I wanted to blurt out, "No, you may not help him. He's not staying."

But, of course, I didn't.

Eric grinned that smug grin that once upon a time I thought was so confident and attractive. Now I saw it for what it was: condescending. "I see what I need." He made a point of looking at me when he said this. "Hello, Bailey. It's nice to see you again."

"I can't say the same about you." Somehow, despite the fact that my throat seemed to have closed up, I was able to spit out the words.

My grandmother and Charlotte stared at me, clearly shocked at my rudeness. Eric chuckled. "You still say what you think, Bailey. I'm glad living with the Amish hasn't robbed you of your spunk.

I ground my teeth. "What are you doing here, Eric?"

"I'm here to visit you."

My frown deepened. I wasn't buying it. "You flew to Ohio to visit me? A person you haven't spoken to in over three months?"

He nodded, doing his best to appear sincere, but failing. "I know how much you love Christmas."

It was true I loved Christmas. It was my favorite time of the year. I loved the parties, the carols, the food, and more than anything, I loved the sweets, but I knew Eric hadn't flown all the way to Ohio because Christmas was a few days away and I was a big fan. The Eric I knew didn't do anything for anyone unless he also got something out of it.

"I've taken a few days off from my bakeries, and I thought it would be a great idea to have a real country Christmas for once. It would be a nice change of pace from the hustle and bustle of New York."

My brow furrowed. "You took time off of work?" When he made that claim, I knew he was lying. Eric was the biggest workaholic I knew. He was a bigger workaholic than I was, which was saying something. Before moving to Ohio, I easily worked one hundred hours a week at JP Chocolates. Eric didn't take time off from his bakeries. Ever.

I was about to argue that point with him when the glass door to Swissmen Sweets opened again, and two disheveled twenty-something men walked into the shop. One man was carrying a large video camera, and the other carried a boom microphone. Both wore large headphones.

I dropped my spatula into the peppermint bark, most likely condemning the utensil to a chocolatey death, but I didn't care. I had much bigger problems than a lost spatula. I waved my hands in the air. "No no no. Get out!" I came around the counter to the public side of the shop as if I was shot from a cannon.

Charlotte and my grandmother stared at me openmouthed, but I didn't stop to explain my actions. There wasn't time. I had to get Eric and his film crew out of my shop.

Eric shuffled back with his hands raised. "There is no reason to make a scene."

I glared at him. "There is every reason to make a scene. I will not let you turn my family's shop into a sound bite for your show!" Just before we'd broken up, Eric had been given the chance to film a reality baking show. As the bad boy of the NYC pastry world, he was just what a popular cooking network was looking for to boost its ratings and give it an edgier image.

Maami lifted the piece of wood that separated the front of the shop from the back counter and stepped through the opening. "Bailey, what is going on? Do you know these men?"

I winced. One advantage of my grandmother being Amish was she'd been shielded from most of the headlines about my relationship back in New York. She knew that I had been dating someone, and that I had broken up with him just before moving to Ohio. She didn't know who he was or what he did, and she most certainly didn't know he was standing in the middle of her shop with a film crew.

Before I could answer, Eric stepped forward. "You must be Bailey's grandmother. I've heard so much about you." He held out his hand to her.

Maami stared at his hand, and after long pause, she took it for the briefest of handshakes. I knew she didn't want to be rude, but typically Amish women didn't shake hands with people they didn't know, especially strange men, and to *Maami*, Eric must have looked very strange. He had perfectly styled blond hair and was wearing a Rolex watch that had cost more than my car.

"I'm Eric Sharp," he went on to say. "I'm sure you have heard of me from Bailey."

Maami looked to me. "*Nee*, Bailey has never mentioned you."

This only made Eric chuckle again. "Well, I will just tell you that Bailey and I were *very* good friends back in New York, and I have missed her."

It took all my strength not to roll my eyes.

"Since she hasn't told you much about me, I suppose you don't know that I am a pastry chef in New York—the best pastry chef, actually."

I snorted.

Eric went on as if I hadn't made a noise. "I'm doing so well, in fact, that I have my own television show, and that's where you all come in. We are filming a holiday special set in Amish Country. We haven't settled on a title yet, but I know we will soon. As you can imagine, the network is in love with the idea!" He smiled as if that was reason enough to let him keep filming. It wasn't.

"I'm sure they are," I said. "But I'm not. It's time for you to leave." All the time I was talking, I realized that the crew was getting my reaction on film, probably high-definition video and audio too. Eric only allowed the very best technical people to take part in his projects. I turned to them. "Turn those things off. You don't have permission to film in here."

The two young guys looked at Eric, and he nodded. They lowered their equipment and shuffled to the corner of the room beside the large display of jarred candies.

Eric turned to me. "I don't know why you are making such a fuss, Bailey. Don't you realize what a show like this could do for your shop? Don't you want free advertising for Swissmen Sweets?"

I felt a twinge. He had a point. The exposure could be unbelievable for the shop.

He must have noticed my hesitation because the smug grin was back on his face.

Before I could give him an answer, the shop door opened for the third time that afternoon, and the last person on the planet I would have wanted to see at that moment stepped into the candy shop.

Tall and loose-jointed, Sheriff's Deputy Aiden Brody stood just inside the doorway to Swissmen Sweets. His eyes were alert, as if he could feel the tension in the room. As a seasoned law enforcement officer, Aiden was tuned into the mood of his surroundings, and the current mood in Swissmen Sweets was anything but welcoming.

He took in the sound and camera guys in the corner of the room. The sound guy had his boom leaning over his shoulder like a baseball bat ready to be taken out onto the field.

"Anyone want to tell me what's going on in here?" Aiden asked.

And that's when I knew my first Christmas in Amish Country would be anything but peaceful.